The Lure

A Northwoods Mystery, Volume 2

Karen Casebeer

Thank you!
Kar

Published by Karen Casebeer, 2024.

THE LURE

First edition. December 16, 2024.

ISBN: 979-8227454324

Written by Karen Casebeer.

Epigraph

lure

noun: An object usually of leather or feathers attached to a long cord and used by a falconer to recall or exercise a hawk.

Merriam-Webster

verb: To persuade someone to do something or go somewhere by offering them something exciting.

Cambridge Dictionary

Chapter 1: October 2019

Forensic Detective Quinn Macarthy and Sheriff Gilda Hansen were stuck in traffic near the corner of Division and 14th Streets. They were headed to a favorite café which served breakfast all day. As they inched forward, they noticed a familiar sight on two corners of the busy intersection. Three men holding signs. On the northwest side of the junction, a man was dressed in a suit. He was bent down on one knee, a hand splayed across his face. His sign was written on a broken-down cardboard box and read, *Will Work for Food.* The other two stood on the opposite side, closer to 14th. One was dressed in jeans and a hoodie. His sign read *No Job. Will Work for Anything. Thank you!* The third man sat in a wheelchair. A blanket covered his lap, hiding whatever was or wasn't there. On the inside of an open pizza box stained with grease, he'd written. *Homeless and Hungry. Any Help? God Bless.*

As the light changed, Gilda moved her Jeep ahead. "I don't see a single driver looking at them. Everyone averts their eyes to another direction."

"I know," Quinn replied softly. "It's like they're invisible."

They proceeded on Silver Lake Road, pulled into the Copper Ridge Marketplace, and took the left fork up the steep hill to the Hilltop Café. It was a beautiful fall day, so the women opted to sit outside. The server immediately brought them coffee and took their orders. Neither felt like talking, so they took in the vista before them. The hillside trees splendid in fall color. The deep blue of West Bay in the distance. The red spires of the Grand Traverse Commons to their left below. A deep thicket of pine trees near the corner where they'd seen the homeless men. Whorled, green branches hid what was within.

The server set down their meals and left. Gilda had ordered an omelet. Quinn, the breakfast burrito. Both moved the food around on their plates.

"It's hard to eat after seeing those homeless men without money for food," Quinn said.

"I hear you. I've lost my appetite, too. You ever think how close regular people are to being in that situation? Homeless. No job. Can't pay for food and basic needs."

"I do, Gil. But the homeless ARE regular people. During my recent training with the Homeless Alliance, I heard that seven out of ten Americans are one paycheck away from being homeless."

"Sobering."

They finished what they could of their meals and headed back down Silver Lake Road, both immersed in thought about the sign-carrying men and another story that was unfolding in the news. Three nights before, a homeless man had died from injuries after being hit by a light gray 2007 Buick. He'd been crossing Division near the stand of pines they'd seen from the Hilltop Café. The guy, dressed in all black, was intoxicated at the time of the crash. The driver wasn't ticketed.

As Gilda turned her Jeep north onto Division towards the bay, they passed a memorial in the grassy median. Bouquets of artificial flowers, a small cairn of rocks, and a crude cross made of popsicle sticks.

"This was where he died, right?" Quinn asked.

"Yeah. You can still see the skid marks on the pavement. I only wish he'd not been one more homeless drunk. He might've seen the Buick coming."

"What're you saying, Gil?"

"Well, uh, doesn't substance abuse cause homelessness? You know, can't hold down a job because of drinking. Leads to evictions, foreclosures, and eventually the streets."

"In some situations, it might be a factor. But substance abuse doesn't cause homelessness."

Gilda went quiet for a while, continuing to the marina. Quinn had gotten an Audubon text that a pair of loons had landed on the bay, and she wanted to check them out.

As they parked by the rocky north shore, Gilda decided to ask one more question, fearful of showing her ignorance again.

"So, if substance abuse doesn't cause homelessness, what does?"

"Lack of housing. Or maybe I should say lack of affordable housing. In a city where the average home price is over $400,000, a lot of folks don't stand a chance at competing in that kind of market."

"Okay, I get it. And it's not just a problem for people wanting to buy a home. I heard this morning on NPR that housing is also unaffordable for half of all U.S. renters. Those making under $30,000 a year are especially vulnerable."

Chapter 2: February 29, 2020

Quinn loved her work at the Five-County Forensic Center, commonly known as FC2. State-of-the-art laboratories all under one roof made the center unique. Ballistics, toxicology, fingerprinting, DNA testing, and a whole wing devoted to forensic pathology. Their own morgue, autopsy lab, and a full-time forensic pathologist working as medical examiner to determine the cause of death in victims.

But her dream job wasn't the only love in Quinn's life. Playing ice hockey and nature photography were right up there, too. Lake Michigan scenery, wildlife, and birds were her favorite subjects.

Today, she and Patrick Elliott were headed to farmland west of Kingsley to photograph bald eagles. Patrick was a DNR conservation officer who enforced laws related to fish and wildlife, state parks, and outdoor recreation. As a licensed peace officer, his work sometimes crossed paths with Traverse City law enforcement. But Patrick and Quinn had first connected through the local camera club. Having police work and photography in common, they'd become friends.

"So, what've you been up to?" Quinn asked as they drove to their photoshoot.

"Nothing out of the ordinary. Been a quiet winter so far. Cold and snowy, but that's nothing new. What about you?"

"Same here. Been kinda worried, though, about what's going on out west."

"Whaddya mean? Have I missed something?"

"Oh, you know. The new virus that probably came from China and seems to be spreading across the west coast."

"You're worried about that? I'm sure they'll nip it in the bud soon. It'll never make it to Michigan, let alone Traverse City."

"I'm not so sure. I saw a telebriefing from that CDC doc. She said the disruption to everyday life might be severe."

"Pure overreaction," Patrick mumbled.

Dropping the topic, they arrived at their destination and pulled off onto a slight rise in the road. A line of old deciduous trees stood about seven hundred feet in the distance, their bare branches stark against the gray sky. Nearer the car, a field dotted with spent corn dregs brought back memories of last year when Sandhill Cranes had fed there. In between the trees and the cornfield lay the *Roadkill Café*, dubbed that by local birders who knew it was where the county dumped roadkill deer. It was a way to get dead deer off the roads and feed animals trying to survive the seasonal cold at the same time. The cafe also attracted opportunist-feeding bald eagles every winter. Currently, there were two adults perched on empty tree branches and three brown-mottled juveniles feeding on two carcasses on the ground.

"Those young ones are sure active," Quinn said. "Flying in, pulling off a hunk of meat, and then flying away to eat it."

"Yeah, they're very territorial with their food."

"I wouldn't be surprised if a scuffle broke out. How old do you think the juveniles are?"

"I'd guess the one that flew off is the youngest, not yet a year old because there's no white showing in its feathers. The one on the ground is a year and a half to two years old. You can see some white feathering around its neck. The one dominating the deer carcass is the oldest, probably almost three. Significant white is visible around its crown and neck. It's being aggressive with the meat, too."

They watched and took pictures as the bird used its great wings for leverage, lowering itself until it was firmly latched onto the carcass and then pulling until it separated a large chunk with its extended talons and beak. Its head was stained with red like a proud warrior bloodied in battle, daring any of the others to approach.

"Oh, look!" Quinn said. "There goes one of the adults flying off the tree branch."

They watched as the eagle flew just above them and landed on the other side of the road at the edge of a frozen farmland pond. Quinn slowly drove her Subaru Outback forward, turned the car around, and crept up to get a better vantage point. The eagle waddled over to what looked like an iced-over fishing hole. Using its lethal hooked beak, it pecked at the cavity until it opened to water. The bird dipped its head in and out several times, seeking prey. The feathers surrounding its beak became wet and stood on edge, giving it the appearance of a punk rocker with a spiky updo.

When the eagle came up with nothing, Quinn asked, "Are there fish in the pond?"

"Might be, although this pond is pretty small," Patrick replied. "The eagle could also be after turtles or frogs buried in the mud. Ready to head back to town?"

Chapter 3: March 2

Quinn was leaving the ice and raised her stick towards her friends standing at the rail. Besides Gilda and Patrick, newspaperman Ian Doyle and his wife Hannah had become her fan club, attending most of her hockey games at Centre Ice Arena and then celebrating at Kilkenny's Irish Pub afterwards. The fivesome had become friends a couple of years ago when they'd worked to solve two murders. The law enforcement officers had provided the muscle and Ian the research. Since then, Ian had become Traverse City Bureau Chief for the downstate newspaper, *The Chronicle*. He and his wife had recently sold their home in Royal Oak and moved to their newly renovated cottage on Crystal Lake.

"Great win!" Gilda yelled. "One more to clinch the title."

"Shots at the bar," Ian added, turning his thumbs up.

Nodding her head and pushing her stick, she skated towards the locker room, but another voice from across the arena caught her attention.

"Hey, right winger, good game!" an unfamiliar voice shouted.

Quinn turned and saw a man she couldn't identify. He was dressed in jeans, a heavy coat, and a black wool watch cap. He had a scraggly beard and continued yelling at her until she raised her stick in appreciation. As she approached the locker room, she turned a final time and saw security guards moving towards him. Unsure what was going on, Quinn shook her head and went in to take a quick shower and get dressed. She passed through the lobby on the way to her car and saw the same man standing nearby, arguing with the guards. He looked towards her, nodded, and their eyes met. A flash of recognition coursed through her. An old school chum from Detroit? A fellow student from college days? When she couldn't connect it, she continued out the door into the wintry night.

Quinn arrived at Kilkenny's to find it packed. She made her way to a corner round table where her friends were seated. The server quickly brought over a fifth of Bushmills and shot glasses. She took their orders of Gaelic egg rolls, chicken wings and a hearth-baked pizza.

"Slainte!" they all cheered as they raised their glasses of Irish whiskey to Quinn's victory.

"You played well, Quinn," Gilda said.

"Thanks, everyone. It was a fun game. Anyone know why it's so crowded and loud here on a Monday?"

"Trivia night," Ian explained, pouring them all another shot.

Their food came, and they hungrily dug in, moaning with pleasure as they bit into the pizza topped with wild mushrooms, soppressata, and pepperoncini. More shots followed.

"Who was that guy who yelled at you when you were coming off the ice?" Gilda asked.

"I'm not sure. On the way to my car, I got a closer look at him as he argued with security in the arena lobby. He looked somewhat familiar, but I couldn't place him."

"Maybe we'll see him at another game," Gilda added.

"Okay, it's time for us to call it a night," Ian said, noticing that everyone had finished eating. "We've got a long drive home to Crystal Lake."

They donned their heavy parkas, hugged, and headed towards the exit. Just before they reached the parking lot, Gilda turned and said, "Hey, you all take care. Get plenty of rest. They already have four cases of that new virus in Illinois, and it'll be coming across the Lake next. I have a feeling we're gonna be gearing up soon."

Patrick shook his head and looked at her, "Sheriff, I think your whiskey's talking."

Chapter 4: March 5

Gilda and Quinn were on their way to the Pines. It was nearly midnight when they'd both been awakened by a call from Chief Hank Yeager, head of the Traverse City Police Department. He said there'd been a fatal fire and could use some extra help. Unlike some cities and counties where jurisdictions were competitive and fought for case control, the TCPD and the Sheriff's Department had a long history of interdepartmental cooperation. Both agencies had the attitude that the more help they got in preventing and solving crimes, the better it would be for the region.

The Pines, as it was known, was the urban tent city occupied by the homeless community. Located on the northwest corner of Division and 11th Streets, around 85 people experiencing homelessness camped there on any given night. During the winter, the census might drop because the emergency overnight homeless shelter accommodated those who couldn't tolerate the cold. But the shelter wasn't for everyone. Some opted to remain outdoors. Either they didn't want to follow shelter rules, or they couldn't stand bunking next to others broken by trauma, untreated addiction, or mental illness.

As Gilda and Quinn approached the area, they saw red and blue twirling strobes from both the fire and police departments. Together, they cast a purplish glow over the whole site. Both officers were mentally preparing themselves for the squalid conditions they were about to enter. Empty food cans, liquor bottles, and discarded syringes littered the grounds. Burned tin foil, a sign of fentanyl use, was everywhere. But worse were the unsanitary conditions throughout because the porta potties had been removed after inhabitants had vandalized them, and sanitation companies refused to service them anymore. It looked like a war zone, where every day the occupants woke up trying to survive.

Chief Yeager saw them and waved them over to a drooping, half-melted tent.

"Thanks for coming out on such short notice," Yeager said, extending his hand to them both.

"What've we got here?" Gilda asked as they walked closer to the scene. The stench of burnt flesh caused her to gag, and she quickly pulled a tube of Vicks from her pocket and swiped a thick stripe under her nose to control the odor.

"From what we can tell, the victim was sitting on his couch cooking hot dogs on a small grill. We found an open, almost empty bottle of Stroh 160 Rum on the floor. He must've been intoxicated and upended the grill onto himself. A couple guys in adjacent pop-ups saw the fire, pulled him out of the tent, and called 9-1-1. But it was too late," Yeager said.

"You ID the guy?" Gilda asked.

"Nothing firm. Guys who pulled him out said he was known as Riley."

Quinn looked around the tent. At one end of what was left of the couch was a charred Bible with sticky notes protruding. An open backpack stood at the back of the tent. She donned nitrile gloves and rummaged through it, hoping to find a driver's license or some other firm identification. Without that, unless someone came forward from the news reports, he'd probably suffer a fate like other homeless people who'd died in the city last year. Buried at state expense in a local cemetery plot designated for the unclaimed. Only a few sets of clothing and minimal toiletries were in the backpack. Nothing to place a firm identity on Riley or to notify next of kin. Quinn looked up just as Gilda pointed to a folded wheelchair at the back of the tent.

"I wonder if he's the same guy we've seen with signs on the corner," Gilda said. "He had a blanket draped over his lap."

"That's him," Chief Yeager said. "He's out there most days. An amputee."

"A veteran?" Quinn asked.

"From what I've heard."

"Double whammy. Homeless and disabled," Gilda said. "So, what's next, Chief?"

"While first responders get his body loaded up and sent to the morgue, why don't the two of you interview the folks standing around? Maybe you can learn something."

"Will FC2 be doing an autopsy?" Quinn asked.

"I doubt it. As soon as we get out of their way, the fire department experts will do a cursory check of the site to make sure arson isn't involved. It's standard procedure in fires of this type, but it appears to be a clearcut case of accidental death. At least to me."

Chapter 5: March 6

He'd only been here ten days but saw on the morning news that COVID had hit the Metro Detroit area. Who knows how long it will take to reach Traverse City, he wondered. He knew his parents were just trying to protect him when they sent him here to live with his mom versus staying in Santa Monica with his dad. The virus had spread like wildfire out there, freaking out all the adults. He scoffed at the thought.

It wasn't like he'd never been to the area before, but coming for two months in June and July was way different than arriving in March. Jesus, there was still snow on the ground. At least during the summer, he could go over to Empire or Frankfort and fuck around at the beach. He wondered how long they'd make him stay.

So far, his time here had been boring. All he'd been doing since he flew in was walking, walking, and more walking. At least he'd learned his way around his mother's new neighborhood. They called it The Commons. It was supposed to be the rad place to live in Traverse City. He'd read online that some developer bought up the grounds of the old insane asylum for a buck and then was spending millions to renovate it. Go figure.

His mom's condo was in what they called Building 50. It had lots of trendy shops and restaurants. Reminded him of the Third Street Promenade in downtown Santa Monica. Same rich feel. Her new place was a loft with high ceilings, brick walls, and huge windows. He had his own bedroom now and didn't have to share the space with her office.

She was easier on him than dad was. Since she worked from home, she let him drive her Acura MDX almost anytime he wanted. Not that he knew where he was going. She'd even given him his own credit card and told him now that he'd turned nineteen, he was ready for more responsibility. Wonder where she came up with that bullshit, he laughed.

He didn't find The Commons all that beautiful, though. Especially at night when he walked around alone, he was spooked about it being a former insane asylum. He'd read in one of the gift shop books about the place being haunted. A few nights ago, when his mom went long past dinner time on a conference call, he was forced to make do for himself. Work had always come before family for her.

So, he decided to walk over to Pleasanton Bakery for a pizza. It was just across the parking lot if he went out the back entrance and across Cottageview Drive. The bakery was cozy inside, and the pizza was always awesome. But something about the open fire in the brick oven drew him in while he ate. Sent him back in time to another fire. He even felt woozy but, at first, chalked it up to how hungry he was. Or maybe his meds were off. He'd not been regular with them since he'd arrived. He'd even overheard his parents fighting about it over the phone. Dad had personally seen to it that he kept on the regular schedule his psychiatrist prescribed, while mom argued he was old enough to manage them himself. Knowing her, he thought, she didn't want to bother.

He'd finished eating his pizza and was heading back to Building 50. He must've lost his way in the dark, or maybe the strange glow coming from the stand of pine trees at the edge of the neighborhood pulled him in. He drew closer and saw light coming from a group of ten or twelve tents.

"Camping in the middle of winter when it's only ten degrees outdoors? Doesn't make sense," he mumbled.

Then he stepped forward into the trees and stared through the branches. The ground was littered with plastic food bags, a pile of wet mattresses and blankets, drug syringes, and empty liquor bottles. His breathing quickened. Through the blue nylon tent nearest him, he saw a man sitting on a couch cooking something over an open fire on a small tabletop grill. Was the guy stupid or what? Or maybe he was just trying to keep warm, he thought.

He watched a while longer until the stench of the place settled over him. Not just the repugnance of it all but the actual stink. He looked down and saw he'd stepped in a pile of shit. Not dog poop or animal scat, but human shit.

He gasped and backed away as fast as he could without slipping. Realization finally set in what this place was.

"It's a homeless encampment," he growled to himself, his voice sounding disembodied. "Jesus Christ, these people can be dangerous," he rambled on. "What the fuck is wrong with them. Why would they wanna live like this?"

He took another step away and felt himself losing it. It'd been a long time since he'd spiraled out of control, but he could feel it happening. His heart raced as rage filled his body. He felt hot. Weird thoughts flooded his mind. He was confused, disoriented even.

"Do I wanna do this?" he asked himself. "He deserves this, doesn't he? Dirty unemployed scumbag."

His mouth was so dry he couldn't swallow. He tried to stop the craziness by using the deep breathing exercises he'd learned from his therapist. But it was too late.

Chapter 6: March 7

It was rare that Quinn had Saturday hockey practice, but with the playoffs starting soon, coach wanted them to have all the ice time they could get. As she skated off the rink, the voice she'd heard a few days ago yelled, "Another good practice, right winger!" She turned and raised her stick in appreciation, wondering who this guy was. He'd looked familiar when she'd seen him in the lobby that night, but she still hadn't been able to place him. Was he stalking her? Or just a lover of the game. From his scruffy appearance, she wondered if he was a street person. Quinn looked around for security but knew they were scarce except on game nights. She quickly pushed away her fear and entered the locker room. She was a cop, after all. She showered, dressed, and then headed to the Blue Line Bar within the arena for an early lunch.

She found a booth and was fiddling with her phone while waiting for her burger and fries to arrive. The guy who'd yelled at her on the ice suddenly slid into the seat across from her. Up close, she immediately recognized him from his pale blue eyes and lop-sided grin.

"Mind if I join you?" he asked.

"Not at all," Quinn replied. "You're Keegan Cammack, aren't you? Former right winger for the Detroit Red Wings. Stanley Cup winner with the 1990 Edmonton Oilers, if my memory serves me right."

"I used to be," he said. "Now I'm just Mack."

"Okay, Mack. I'm Quinn Macarthy."

"I know who you are, detective. Your bio's in the hockey program."

The server brought Quinn's burger basket and soda and also a cup of black coffee for Mack. She watched him greedily bring the coffee to his mouth, his hand shaking slightly but not spilling a drop. He was so fidgety she wondered if he was using.

"You want something to eat, Mack?" Quinn asked. "I'd be happy to share my fries."

"Nah. I'm good."

"What brings you here?"

"To the rink? I still enjoy watching good hockey players. You're one of the best. Fast. A wicked wrist. And you've got guts. Not afraid of the game."

"Thanks, but I meant to this particular area?"

"Oh. I always thought I'd retire to Traverse City. Fell in love with the place when the Red Wings held their training camps here. Liked the city. The beaches. Good hockey town, too."

"Yeah, I understand. In my rookie years as a cop, I worked a couple hours north of here for the Lakeland County Sheriff's Department. No hockey whatsoever. So, I jumped at the chance to come to TC when the forensic center opened. Not only for the job but for the city and being able to play hockey again."

It appeared Mack had fallen on hard times. His well-worn outerwear and scruffy beard told part of the story. His wet black tennis shoes without socks the rest. Quinn felt the urge to help but didn't want to make him feel like a charity case.

"Mack, tell me what you're up to here in the city."

"Well, uh, I walk a lot. All over the city. Like talking to people. Most of them are good," he said. "I make money canning. You know, returning empty beverage cans to the grocery store for ten cents each. Makes me self-sufficient, along with my pension."

"Are you well?"

"Uh, so-so. Have a lot of concussion symptoms."

"Like, CTE? Chronic Traumatic Encephalopathy?" she asked.

"Yeah, that's it. They call it punch-drunk, too. Ali had it."

"Where are you staying?" Quinn asked. But before he could reply, Quinn's phone rang. "Detective Macarthy," she answered. With that, Mack folded his hand into a goodbye and left the booth.

"It's Gilda. You done with practice?"

"Yeah. Just finished some lunch here at the rink. What's up?"

"I just got a call from Ted Roberts, the new Medical Examiner. He finished the autopsy on Riley and wants to meet with us. You know, the homeless guy who burned in his tent."

"Autopsy. I didn't know they were going to do one. Chief Yeager seemed to think it was an accidental death."

"Turns out, the fire chief found accelerant on Riley's clothes. Decided to do an autopsy to establish a firm cause of death. How soon can you be at FC2?"

"Five minutes. I'm just down the road."

Chapter 7: Later that Day

Dr. Ted Roberts had been Medical Examiner at FC2 for less than a year but was already popular with the forensics unit. He was a good communicator, had a sense of humor, and advocated a team approach. The previous ME had left the same position due to his "my way or the highway" attitude. Robert's positive and collaborative manner was already changing the departmental culture. The sign on the morgue conference room door was an example: *OUR DAY BEGINS WHEN YOURS ENDS*. In work that could be painfully dark and depressing, Roberts knew how to keep his department professional yet upbeat, even if his humor was sometimes corny.

Quinn was the last to arrive for the meeting. TCPD Chief Hank Yeager, his lead detective Captain Buzz Broderick, Gilda, and her two newest hires were already there. Veteran cop Flint Thompson had replaced rookie Noah Fitzgerald after he'd been fired for vigilante behaviors. Flint had spent most of his career with the Minneapolis PD and had come to Traverse City after he and his wife purchased a small vineyard they planned to farm in retirement. Gilda's other new hire was Vernadeane Novak. She'd come to the Sheriff's Department on a grant funded by the U.S. Department of Justice. She was trained in law enforcement and criminal justice but was also a licensed social worker. Vernadeane provided support and wrap-around services to those falling through the cracks, especially people experiencing homelessness, mental health issues, and substance use disorders.

"Okay, let's get started, folks," Dr. Roberts said. "I know it's a Saturday, and I don't want to take more of your weekend, but the results of the fire department's assessment and my autopsy warrant immediate action."

"Bring it on, doc," Gilda said.

"I see you're locked and loaded, sheriff," Roberts said, referring to the gob of Vicks smeared just below Gilda's nose to ward off the nauseating chemical smells of the morgue. "I'll begin with the arson report. When the fire chief arrived at the scene, he immediately noticed a faint odor of accelerant and brought in an ADC to check it out."

"Excuse me, doctor. What's an ADC?" newbie Vernadeane Novak asked.

"Good question. ADCs are Accelerant Detection Canines. They're specially-trained dogs able to sniff traces of accelerant at a fire scene."

"Gotcha."

"When we got a positive response from Sparky, we sent what was left of the decedent's jacket to Trace for further analysis," Roberts said. He looked at Vernadeane and then added, "Trace is the lab where we process small particles of evidence that are transferred between people, objects, and the environment during a crime. Things like hair, fiber, and other minute residue."

"Let me guess, doc. The guy was drunk, spilled booze on his jacket, and accidentally pulled the grill over onto himself," Captain Buzz Broderick interrupted. "The Stroh 160 Rum ignited the fire."

The room went quiet as they pondered the detective's comment.

"You're partially correct, Captain. The 80% alcohol content of the Stroh 160 Rum found on the front of the victim's coat was a factor. But it wasn't the principal accelerant or the cause of Riley's death," Roberts said.

Those around the conference table leaned forward like children at a library story hour waiting for the ending to be revealed.

Roberts continued, "The ignitable liquid that started the fire was hand sanitizer."

"Hand sanitizer?" Chief Yeager asked. "We didn't find any evidence of hand sanitizer at the scene, doc."

"The killer didn't leave it. He poured sanitizer on the vic, upended the grill coals on him, and left the scene, taking the small container with him," Roberts said.

At the word killer, the room erupted with questions. "Killer! You're saying the homeless guy was murdered?" "How could hand sanitizer be an accelerant." "What're you saying, doc? The perp is some kind of clean freak?"

"Hang on, everyone. Let me answer your questions one at a time," Roberts said. "Hand sanitizer is a powerful ignitable liquid, about 60% alcohol in content. It acts almost like napalm in volatility. With the sanitizer sprayed on top of the residual rum, we had a highly explosive combination."

"I've heard of situations where people put sanitizer on their hands but don't properly rub it in until it dries. Then they light a BBQ or a cigarette and ignite themselves in the process," Flint Thompson added.

"I think we're going to hear more stories like this as the COVID-19 virus spreads. People not being clean freaks, necessarily, but wanting to keep themselves safe. I've already heard some stories from places with strong outbreaks of the new virus that there's been a run on hand sanitizer," Roberts said.

"I don't see how this has turned into a murder case, doc," Quinn said. "Just because hand sanitizer was found on his jacket, how does that translate to murder? How do you know the perp took the container with him? Maybe Riley used it himself, and the container burned in the fire. Those folks in the Pines aren't exactly living in sanitary conditions. Couldn't he have been trying to keep himself as clean and healthy as possible while living in such squalor?"

"Good ideas, detective," Roberts said. "But you've all been under the assumption that the fire caused the decedent's death. Riley died because his throat was slit. Exsanguination due to damage to the carotid and jugular vessels was the official cause of death. The perp slit the victim's throat. Then he poured hand sanitizer on his already alcohol-soaked jacket and dumped the hot coals from the grill onto him. The killer used the fire as a cover-up for his actions. We have a homicide here, folks."

Chapter 8: March 14

The police departments had been so tied up investigating Riley's murder that Quinn didn't have any free time for photography. But on Saturday, when she'd heard Sandhill Cranes had returned to farmland west of Kingsley, Quinn and Patrick headed there to take pictures.

"You a believer, yet?" Quinn asked as they drove west on M-113.

"Huh?"

"Oh, don't play dumb, Patrick. You know exactly what I mean," Quinn said as she turned north on Schneider Road towards the spent cornfields where they usually saw cranes. "The World Health Organization declared COVID a global pandemic. The president and the governor proclaimed states of emergency. And the virus has arrived in Michigan. Aren't you watching the news?"

"Look, there they are!" Patrick said, pointing to a pair of cranes munching on corn dregs in a field near the intersection with Clous Road. While most of the snow had melted, a few small piles still dotted the landscape.

Pissed at Patrick's sidestepping her concerns, Quinn let her anger go when she sighted the first cranes of the season. She'd long felt an odd kinship with these ancient-looking birds with their gray plumage stained with iron oxide, long skinny legs, and red foreheads punctuated by piercing yellow eyes. She even had their bugling call as the ringtone on her iPhone, something that irritated her colleagues when she forgot to put her device on silent during meetings. She was still deeply pained when she recalled the number of cranes who'd died from the counterfeit pesticides trafficked illegally by the Russian mob in the last case she and Patrick had worked.

Quinn pulled off the road onto the verge a respectful distance from the cranes. The birds looked up from their eating and watched the intruders. One went back to eating while the other stood tall and alert. Both photographers pulled out their long-lensed cameras, slid down their windows, and began shooting. Suddenly, one crane tossed a short corn stalk into the air and moved closer to its mate.

"Here we go," Patrick said. "They're gonna dance."

They watched as the pair spread their wings and leapt upward, kicking their legs towards each other and ending the dance by bowing at their mate.

"Well, that was short," Quinn said.

"Looks like a practice run before they mate."

They drove on through the intersection that had a pond on each corner. They reached the *Roadkill Café*, but it was empty except for a few deer carcasses being picked to the bone by crows. The bald eagles had left for better hunting grounds. Patrick surveyed the area with his field glasses.

"Hey, Quinn, take a look at this, just beyond the carcass. What's it look like to you?" he asked, handing over the binoculars.

"A big splotch of blood. Could be the site of another deer carcass."

"Yeah, but there aren't any bones. Just a big pool of red atop a blob of snow."

"Let's go take a look."

They packed their camera gear, and Quinn grabbed the portable forensic kit she always kept in her car. As they walked towards the spot, the crows kicked up a ruckus with loud cawing.

"They don't like us encroaching on their meager feeding ground."

"Too bad. We've got to find out what this is."

As they approached the spot, it indeed looked like blood resting on a mound of dirty snow.

"Something was killed here," Quinn said.

"The stain is large enough to be human. Too bad we can't find out if it is."

"Oh, but we can," Quinn said, circling the bloody splotch and taking pictures from every angle. "There will be DNA left on that snow patch. We just need to collect and test it."

Quinn went on to explain that as critters go about their daily lives, they release skin cells, hair, droppings, blood, urine, and other biological materials into the environment. These materials contain trace amounts of the animal's DNA, which then become incorporated into the water, snow, and soil. She said the genetic traces are called environmental DNA or eDNA.

"Duh," Patrick said. "It's like when we collect hair snares from bears to keep track of the problem ones attacking bird feeders in high-population areas. I just didn't understand eDNA could be collected from surface areas, too."

He watched Quinn finish her picture documentation and open her forensic kit. She took out three sealed jars and plastic-wrapped spoons, broke open the seals, and scooped bloody snow samples from different areas into each of the small jars.

"Want to make sure I have enough for good testing," Quinn said as she packed up her gear, and the two of them walked back to the car.

"You think you'll be able to identify the species from these samples?" Patrick asked.

"FC2 will be able to determine whether it's human blood. If it's not human, we'll assume some big critter bit the dust here. Just want to make sure we're not dealing with a crime scene."

Chapter 9: March 25

The TCPD and Sheriff's Department had hit a wall investigating Riley's death. They'd walked the downtown streets speaking with area homeless people, visited the Pines several times hoping someone would talk, and even dropped by the Middle Coast Mission, the city's homeless shelter. But no one they spoke to was willing to give up any information.

Quinn also had gotten back the eDNA report from the bloody spot at the *Roadkill Café*. Results from the FC2 lab indicated the blood wasn't human. They couldn't identify what animal had died at the spot, but at least Quinn knew it wasn't a crime scene, which put her mind at ease.

Truth be told, these investigations weren't foremost in the minds of area law enforcement. A week earlier, COVID-19 had hit northern Michigan, with cases diagnosed in both Traverse City and Gaylord. There were probably more victims, but with the four-day turnaround for test results, it was difficult to pin down how many had been infected. Then yesterday, the governor issued a statewide stay-at-home order limiting all non-essential business services, banning dine-in eating, and closing bars, theaters, gyms, and schools. Hospitals restricted visitors and canceled non-urgent surgeries. Mandatory facemasks and social distancing outside the home were also part of the order.

With concern elevated about how they would handle the pandemic and execute the governor's order, Chief Hank Yeager and Sheriff Gilda Hansen called an emergency meeting of all law enforcement operating within the county: Traverse City Police Department, Grand Traverse Sheriff's Department, Five-County Forensic Center, Department of Natural Resources Conservation Officers, and Michigan State Police troopers from the Traverse City unit. They scheduled the meeting for the auditorium at FC2, the only space large enough to accommodate the gathering.

As officers entered the parking lot, they got a taste of what was ahead. Masked sheriff's deputies were spaced six feet apart in a line leading to the auditorium. They paused each arriving officer to maintain the required social distance. Each officer was handed a plastic bag containing masks, gloves, goggles, disinfecting wipes, and hand sanitizer.

"Mask up, officers," echoed throughout the line as they all dug through their bags, searching for face coverings.

As Patrick Elliot came through the line, he grabbed the bag and moved forward, a scowl radiating across his face.

"Mask up, officer. That means you, Elliott, " Detective Flint Thompson yelled as he blocked Patrick's path until he complied.

When everyone was inside the auditorium, seated in every sixth chair, the room quieted as Chief Yeager and Sheriff Hansen walked on stage. The two had decided beforehand that Gilda would make the initial remarks, and Hank would handle the questions and answers.

Gilda was a legend in law enforcement circles, having been the first female elected sheriff in the State of Michigan. Despite nearing retirement age, she was wiry and spry, dressed in her brown uniform and signature fleece-lined bomber jacket with *GTC Sheriff* stenciled across the back. Chocolate leather western boots hand-tooled with red roses and green foliage completed her ensemble.

As Gilda stepped to the podium, she surveyed her masked audience. Known for her bluntness, she began, "I heard some grumbling as you entered the meeting this morning. I expect it will be the last."

The auditorium had been quiet, but not enough to hide the cocky whisper and chuckle from the back, "Them's fightin' words."

"Damn, straight they are, officer. Cuz we're in a war now. A war against COVID-19," Gilda said. "We're in a global pandemic, and this whole country is in a state of emergency. The only way we're gonna do our sworn job of protecting others is to protect ourselves. And that begins with the little bag of PPE you were given today. PPE stands for Personal Protection Equipment. You're going to hear a lot about it over these next few days and weeks."

She asked the officers to look through their bags, telling them masks were mandatory at all times while on the job. She also advised them to wear goggles and gloves when dealing with the public, especially at crime scenes. Gilda said that hand sanitizer would become their best friend during COVID. She ordered them to use it often and disinfect all frequently touched surfaces with the wipes, including desks in their offices, steering wheels in their squad cars, and handles on doorknobs, cars, and refrigerators in the break rooms.

Gilda next discussed operational changes that would go into effect immediately. "We're closing the public lobbies of all departments, shutting down fingerprinting for things like handgun registration, and taking as many incident reports as possible over the phone or online. If someone has an emergency or crime in progress, we'll respond the same way as always, but armed with PPE and avoiding face-to-face contact when we can. We're also requesting that dispatch ask all callers if anyone at the scene is showing signs of COVID. I'm going to turn the meeting over to Chief Yeager now, who'll try to answer any questions you have. Remember, we're all new at this, and we're feeling our way through this crisis."

Hank Yeager had been the police chief for over twenty years, nearly as long as Gilda. He had a no-nonsense, rugged look to him, craggy face, light gray crewcut, Nixon nose, and light hazel eyes that took in everything. But when he exchanged places with Gilda at the podium, his voice squeaked into the microphone. Talking to large groups was not his favorite part of being police chief.

"Who has the first question?" Yeager asked.

"There seems to be a lot of gray areas about how we're supposed to enforce the stay-at-home order," an officer from the front row asked.

"It's my understanding," Yeager said, "that local chiefs are not going to determine who is and who isn't essential personnel. In the first place, it's not our order. And secondly, it's an executive order, not a court order. We hope that follow-up statements will clarify the specifics."

"What about fines?" the same officer asked.

"That'll be up to the courts, but right now, it appears that infractions are misdemeanors punishable by fines up to $500 and 90 days in jail. Who else has a question?" Yeager asked, pointing to someone on the left side of the room.

"What about traffic stops?"

"If everyone stays at home, like we saw this morning on the drive in, traffic is going to be greatly reduced. I suggest you relax minor traffic offenses, like expired plates. Use your judgment and make decisions on a case-by-case basis."

"What about breathalyzer road tests for impaired driving?"

"Good question, officer. We don't know a lot about that yet, but our first information is that COVID seems to be spread through coughing and sneezing, so you're gonna want to make sure you're masked, gloved, and goggled when asking a potential drunk driver to forcefully exhale into a breathalyzer."

"What about enforcing rules against large gatherings?"

"That's important to contain the pandemic. I just heard the Detroit PD already broke up a party of 24 on the first night of the order. Someone saw the invite on social media, raided the gathering, and broke it up. Keep your eyes and ears open. One more question, and then we need to get back to work. Yes, Vernadeane, whaddya have?"

"What's happening to support the homeless population? They can't exactly stay home if they don't have one."

Chapter 10: March 31

Middle Coast Mission was the local emergency cold-weather homeless shelter. With a capacity of 80 beds, MCM was typically open 6 p.m. to 8 a.m. from November through April. They gave their guests dinner, a place to sleep, breakfast, and respectful treatment. Except for the executive director, the shelter was staffed entirely by volunteers from local churches.

But on this last day of March, with plenty of cold weather left in the winter, the shelter was closing due to COVID. Fears about the spread of the virus in the confined quarters of the bunkroom and dining hall had fueled the decision. In reality, MCM was also closing because its staffing had dried up with the stay-at-home order. Retirees made up much of the volunteer force, and with seniors being especially vulnerable to the virus, they were opting to stay home.

Vernadeane and Quinn, along with two nurses from Street Medicine, were at the shelter as residents were being discharged to the streets. When they heard the mission was closing, the two officers stopped by a thrift store to stock up on items that might help homeless people survive the balance of winter. Dying from hypothermia was real for these folks.

As the homeless departed from MCM, they were given a blanket, sleeping bag, tent, and a tarp. More tent encampments would probably be popping up in addition to the Pines.

"Looks like we're gonna be sleeping rough," one homeless man said, his eyes shining with terror as he took the proffered equipment and planted it in his small luggage cart.

"How about some wool socks and hand warmers?" Vernadeane asked.

"I guess if you think they might help," he replied. "Where should I go? I don't want to go to the Pines. Too dangerous at night, I've heard."

Vernadeane just looked at him, his hopelessness piercing her heart. Not knowing a good answer, she said, "Maybe you could try one of the city parks, like Hull or F and M. Or near one of the Tart trails."

"They'll let us stay there?" he asked.

"We can hope. These are trying times," she answered.

At a nearby table, the nurses were assessing people who were especially vulnerable to living outside. A nineteen-year-old with cerebral palsy who navigated the sidewalk with metal braces. An elderly man they'd been treating for chronic bronchitis. A woman with a young child walked up from the street, hoping to find help for herself and her daughter. They hadn't been staying at MCM because it was an adults-only shelter. With no place for these high-risk folks to go, the outreach team started putting them up at area motels to give them respite from the cold. The relief on their faces when they received a housing voucher was palpable.

As Quinn worked the van to outfit people with cold-weather gear, she caught sight of Mack. He wore the same black tennis shoes she'd seen him in before, and his baggy trousers were held up with a bungee cord. He was pushing a small grocery cart unsteadily up the sidewalk. His whole body was shaking. She wondered again if he was using. Or drunk.

Quinn rushed towards him and asked, "Mack, what's going on?"

"I'm so fucking cold, Quinn. No place to go. Library's closed. Restaurants shut down, so I can't even get a cup of hot coffee or use the bathroom."

Realizing his shakes were due to exposure, she insisted Mack go inside the shelter to warm up. While he hated the close quarters there, he agreed to take a shower and have a hot breakfast. It was past discharge time, but the executive director saw a man in dire straits, so he allowed him inside. As Mack recovered, Quinn emptied his cart and threw all his belongings in the washer. She went to the van and selected new clothing for him: long underwear, jeans, fleece-lined sweatshirt, wool socks, boots, and an insulated winter jacket with a hood. He looked like a new man when he was freshly outfitted.

"Thanks, Quinn. I thought it was all over for me. Even a little meth didn't help."

"I've got something else for you," she said. "We had a few extra motel vouchers meant for vulnerable folks. You're going indoors for a week."

"Oh my god! You're kidding me."

"Hop in the van, and we'll drive you there."

"You know what tomorrow is, don't you?" he asked. "April Fool's Day. I'm gonna wake up and find this has all been a joke."

Chapter 11: April 7

Gilda and Quinn were running the Boardman Lake Loop Trail shortly after sunrise. With the final games of her hockey season postponed due to COVID, Quinn had ramped up her outdoor exercise to stay in shape. They'd just crossed the extended boardwalk at the south end of the lake by Logan's Landing when they heard piercing screams coming across the lake. The shrieking didn't stop like it would if a person had been startled by a snake or wild animal. No, the unending cries were from someone experiencing terror. With the Sheriff's Jeep parked behind the library, the only thing the officers could do was call dispatch and hoof it the remaining two miles of their run.

Panting and out of breath, Gilda and Quinn approached the boat launch near Hull Park. They noted how strange the group appeared with their masks. They had to look twice to identify each other from only their eyes. TCPD detective Buzz Broderick had already arrived. Detective Flint Thompson and social worker Vernadeane Novak from the Sheriff's Department were there, too. Medical Examiner Ted Roberts and the Crime Scene Investigators were just getting out of their vans. State Police Trooper Nick Wagner and his Belgian Malinois sniffer dog, Grit, were also on the scene.

Vernadeane immediately went to comfort the woman who'd been screaming. The rest of the investigators moved towards the object of her fright, a dead body face down near the trail.

"Male victim," the ME said. Kneeling, he pointed a gloved hand towards a large gash at the back of the victim's head. "Blunt force trauma. Maybe the cause of death."

"Looks like he was camping here," Flint said, pointing to the small tent just off the trail.

"Shit. Another homeless person with no place to go after the mission closed," Quinn said.

At the mention of blunt force trauma, three CSIs fanned out, looking for an object that could've caused the wound. A discarded hammer, a nearby rock, maybe a baseball bat. Another CSI stood next to the ME and took pictures of the deceased and the scene from all angles. Grit strained at his leash, begging to work.

The ME turned the body over, and they all gasped in horror. The witness began screeching again at the loud collective exhale, knowing they'd seen something more dreadful than she had.

"Jesus, Mary, and Joseph," Quinn whispered when she saw the blood.

"Damn," the ME said. "A second homeless man with his throat slit."

"Just like Riley but without the fire," Buzz continued.

"Hard to tell if it's the same since Riley was so burned. But there are similarities. Not sure if blunt force trauma or exsanguination from the slit throat was the COD. I'll know more after the autopsy," the ME said.

"Doesn't look like he's been dead long," Gilda commented. "Muscles looked stiff when you rolled him over."

"Rigor mortis has set in, but the skin hasn't purpled yet, and it doesn't blanch when pressed. Probably two to six hours, but I'll pin it down more after I get a body temperature. Lucky for you, sheriff, there are no bugs or putrefaction."

Gilda nodded and smiled weakly as she clutched the tube of Vicks in her jacket pocket. The ME bent down and began dictating into his lapel mic the particulars of the scene. He looked for some identification on the man but came up with nothing.

Quinn walked over to Vernadeane, who'd managed to calm the witness.

"I'm Detective Quinn Macarthy, ma'am. Do you think you can answer a few questions now?"

"I think so. I'm Ruthie Osborne."

"Tell me what you saw this morning, Ruthie."

"I was out for my morning exercise. I usually walk with a friend before work, but she's sick with COVID right now, so I came alone. I've done it before and had no reason to be afraid. I'd just parked my car and was starting the trail when I happened to look down and saw the body. All I could do was back away and scream."

"Did you notice anyone else around or anything suspicious nearby?"

"To be honest, I didn't notice anything. I just closed my eyes, retreated from the body, and screamed. I think I might've gone into shock."

"I'm guessing you still are, Ruthie. Here's my card. I'll contact you in a day or so to see if you've come up with anything else. Do you have a support person you can stay with for at least a few hours?"

"Yeah, my mom lives in town. I'm gonna head there now."

As Quinn walked back to the scene, she noticed the body had been lifted into the van, and the CSIs had gathered around the tent. They'd donned booties and gloves in addition to their masks. They pulled the tent flaps back and shined flashlights inside to highlight the contents, looking for signs of a struggle. But the interior was as neat as a 6 x 5 foot space could be. One CSI immediately spied a wallet and wristwatch on a crate next to a bag chair. She tiptoed inside and brought the wallet out.

"Michael Stafford. Grand Rapids, Michigan," she read from the driver's license. Then she pulled apart the wallet and discovered $117 inside."

"Doesn't look like a robbery," Buzz said.

"At least we have a firm identity on this guy," the ME concurred. "We can try contacting next of kin to find out what Stafford was doing in Traverse City."

At this point, the ME and the other detectives left the scene to the CSIs for further processing, hoping fingerprints would turn up on something. The three CSIs who'd been searching the trail area for a weapon had come back empty-handed. State Trooper Nick Wagner finally let Grit off his lead, but without anything but the victim's scent, the frustrated dog just ran back and forth around the tent.

Chapter 12: That Evening

Quinn was bushed when she walked into her two-bedroom condo off Garfield Road. The early morning run and finding another dead homeless man had done her in. But no one was more ready for relief than Ruby, her five-year-old red mini-Goldendoodle. She grabbed her Chuckit Flying Squirrel, ran to the doors leading to their small, fenced yard, and dropped to the ground to pee. When she'd finished, Ruby brought her favorite toy and released it at Quinn's feet, begging for play and attention. After fifteen minutes of throwing and retrieving, they headed back indoors. The dog's tongue lolled out the side of her mouth.

Quinn had bought her condo in 2014 when she'd moved to Traverse City to take the FC2 job. The location was perfect. Close to work, the ice rink, and restaurants along Airport Road she liked to frequent. While the condo had been in good shape when she purchased it, she'd done several upgrades to suit her taste. Changed out the slider for French doors. Refaced the kitchen cabinets and installed a faux granite countertop. She'd also replaced the beige carpeting with hardwood floors and bright area rugs.

Quinn set down fresh food and water for Ruby, toasted a brioche bun, and filled it with her staple of tuna salad. She carried the meal to her study, sat down at the desk, and powered up her computer. Ruby quickly crawled into the keyhole underneath and rested her head on Quinn's feet. While she ate, Quinn developed pictures in Lightroom she'd recently taken of early bloodroot and liverwort in the woods behind her condo. She was just about finished when her landline rang. She knew right away it was probably her dad, who never called her cell.

"Hi, Pixie," her dad said, calling her the nickname he'd used her whole life. It referred to her short haircut versus her size.

"Hey, dad. What's up?" knowing exactly why he'd called. "You and mom staying safe during this COVID shutdown?"

"Oh, yeah. Home like we've been ordered. Getting a little cabin fever, though. Missing everyone."

Hint, hint, Quinn thought.

"Say, uh. I thought I'd check out the plans for Sunday so we can get food in," he continued.

Here it comes, she mused. "Plans, dad?" Quinn said. "I know Sunday is Easter, but we're under a mandated stay-at-home order. Nobody's going to be traveling this holiday."

"I know, Pix. But I talked to your brothers, and they said they'd make the drive if you would. They're leaving it up to you."

At the mention of her brothers, she thought it was just like them to make her the bad guy. "Chickenshits," she mumbled. They probably didn't want to disappoint their aging parents. There were five kids in her Irish Catholic family, all males except her, the second youngest. All were in law enforcement, including her dad, and all had played ice hockey. Rowan, the oldest, was an FBI agent at the Cleveland office. Colin was a captain in the Highland Park Criminal Investigation Unit, the department her father had retired from. Neil, brother number three, was an Assistant D.A. for the City of Boston's Murder Bureau. He'd been looking for an equivalent position closer to home now that their parents were getting old. But with COVID, he wasn't sure this was the time to be making a change. Tully, the youngest, was a Lieutenant in the Detroit Police Department, working as a K-9 handler.

"You know, dad. I think we should all stay put this year. Everyone but me works and lives in big cities where COVID levels are staggering. I don't think we should put you and mom at risk. Besides, we were all together just three weeks ago for the Corktown parade."

Corktown had once been Detroit's oldest neighborhood and Irish quarter. On St. Patrick's Day, green still reigned supreme. Her parents had started raising their children there when her dad had worked for the DPD. Like many city dwellers, the race riots of the sixties had driven them to the suburbs. Her dad had gotten a new job as a detective for Highland Park PD, and they'd bought a home in Berkley. It's where Quinn and Tully were born. But on St. Patrick's Day, they all returned to Corktown for mass at Most Holy Trinity, rode the parade route in dad's Killarney Green 1960 Lincoln Continental convertible, shared a few pints of Guinness at the Gaelic League, and ended the day with mom's shepherd's pie, soda bread, and moss pudding at home.

"I was afraid that's what you'd say," Dad said. "Better safe than sorry, I guess."

"How's mom doing on her new medicine?" Quinn asked. Her mother had been diagnosed with rheumatoid arthritis, and getting around was difficult, with swollen, inflamed joints crippling her movements. The NSAIDs had stopped working, and steroids could only be used short-term in a crisis. She'd just started on methotrexate.

"Doesn't seem to be doing much. Probably too early to tell," Dad said. "How's your investigation going on the burned homeless guy?"

"Hit a dead end on him, but this morning we found a second homeless man with his throat slit. We found out he has a sister living in Traverse City, and we're talking to her early tomorrow morning to see if we can learn more about him and why he was here."

"Got a lot on your plate, sis. I'll talk to you again Sunday. Love you, Pix."

Chapter 13: April 8

Quinn and Flint Thompson were on their way to Michael Stafford's sister's house over on Bates Street. They'd found a phone among his belongings and found the sister in his contacts.

It was the first time Flint and Quinn had worked together on a case, and she was anxious to get to know the new hire from Minnesota. They were a bit early for their appointment and were just passing a drive-thru coffee shop when Quinn said, "How about a cup of coffee?"

"They have bagels too?" Flint asked. It sounded more like begels.

It took Quinn a second to figure out what he was saying, but she answered, "Only one way to find out."

She pulled her car into the long line, ordered, and then parked in the nearby lot so they could enjoy their food. Takeout had become the only way to savor restaurant fare during the early pandemic, and people were eager to find legitimate ways to get away from their homes.

"How's your bagel?" Quinn asked.

"Not bad," Flint replied. Quinn assumed that was Minnesotan for good.

"You and your wife looking forward to getting started on your vineyard this spring?"

"You betcha, except that our beginning wine grower classes have been postponed because of COVID. We hope we don't miss this whole first season."

They finished eating and headed the few blocks to Bates, where Paula Stafford lived. Quinn had learned she was a single mom with a four-year-old daughter. Their home was a tiny bungalow on a row with several of the same kind. Hers was well kept, painted a pale gray-green with window boxes containing artificial winter berries.

Through the open breezeway connecting the home and one-car garage, Quinn could see a swing set in the backyard.

They went to the front door and rang the bell. A small blond woman with a youngster clinging to her legs opened and invited the officers inside.

"I'm Paula Stafford, Michael's youngest sister. This is Lexie, my daughter. You must be Detective Macarthy."

"I am. This is Detective Flint Thompson. Thanks for giving us some time. We're so sorry for your loss."

"Thank you. To be honest, I half expected this to happen."

As Flint and Quinn sat on the couch Paula had offered, they checked each other out, wondering what the masked noses and mouths looked like. The little girl walked towards Flint.

"Oh, for cute," he said. "You mind if I give her a lollipop?"

"Not at all. You a Yooper?"

"Cripes, no. Minnesota. The Cities."

Steering the discussion back to Michael's death, Quinn asked, "Why were you half expecting Michael to be murdered?"

"There's been a lot in the news about how dangerous living on the streets is. You know, all the violence in the Pines."

"What can you tell us about Michael?"

"He was my oldest brother. A Marine Corps vet. Worked mechanical jobs in the Middle East. While he wasn't a combat soldier, he took his fair share of fire just by being over there. Did four tours. Kept reupping for the money."

"How long had he been in Traverse City?"

"Three weeks or so. Came to visit us, but I soon realized he meant to stay. It was too crowded with him here, though. A complete lack of privacy with him taking over the living room of my small home. I didn't like leaving Lexie alone with him when I had to work. It put a strain on our relationship."

"Good gravy," Flint said. "You think he'd hurt her?"

"Not in the way you're implying," Paula said. "But I knew he was using. I didn't want my daughter around it. He'd had several arrests for heroin and meth in Grand Rapids. His record kept him from finding work or being approved for a home. People didn't want to rent to him either."

"So, what'd you do next?"

"I wanted to get him out of the nomadic lifestyle he'd been living since his discharge. Hoped to get him some help versus just kicking him out. Got him an appointment with the Homeless Alliance. I knew he was missing out on benefits and services that might help him get clean and find housing."

"Did he buy in?"

"He no-showed the appointment."

"Uffda," Flint said as Quinn and Paula looked at him like he was speaking a foreign language.

"Have you made any progress finding his killer?" Paula asked.

"We're working on it," Quinn said. "We just got the report back from the dive team, which combed the north end of Boardman Lake searching for the murder weapon. They came up with nothing."

"We'll learn more this afternoon when we get back Michael's autopsy results. We'll keep you posted anyhoo. Thanks for your time, Ms. Stafford. Your Lexie is a keeper."

Chapter 14: That Afternoon

Quinn and Flint drove straight from Paula Stafford's home to FC2. The meeting hadn't begun yet, and small pockets of law enforcement officers were engaged in private conversations. Gilda sat next to ME, Ted Roberts. A thick line of Vicks drawn across her upper lip stuck to her mask.

"So, tell me, Doc. Did your new SUV arrive yet? You won't want to go through another winter with that little front-wheel-drive Audi of yours," Gilda said.

"I did. Picked up my new Toyota Highlander on Saturday. It's a beauty. Opulent Amber."

"Sounds cool. You buy it locally or build it online?"

"I got it online through Rigor Motors," he said just loud enough to get everyone's attention and a few snickers. "Let me start our meeting by saying I hope you're all masking up, sanitizing often, and generally staying safe. Wouldn't want to lose any of you to the coroner virus."

Groans erupted throughout the room at Robert's second cornball joke. They knew what he was doing, though. Lightening them up before the blood and gore from the autopsy report.

"Michael Stafford died of sharp force injuries to the neck. Severed the carotid artery and jugular vein, causing hypovolemic shock and death by exsanguination."

"Sounds similar to Riley's death."

"In more ways than one, as you'll shortly see. Stafford also had significant trauma to the head. The killer probably knocked him out and then slit his throat."

"Any idea what was used for the head trauma?"

"Not for sure. Maybe a rock. His wound didn't seem to have the properties of a tool, such as a hammer or a crowbar."

"What about the knife? You get a take on that?"

"Some. We used a micro-computed tomography scan of the stab track to virtually cast the striation patterns. Looks like the wound was made with a small, coarsely serrated blade, possibly from a folding pocketknife."

"Like a Grim Reaper or a Black Manta?"

"Maybe. Hard to pin it down more than I have. We did find two fibers in the wound, which we've sent to Trace Evidence to see if they can figure out where they came from. Now for the weird part. When we opened his mouth, we found a small blue oval pill on his tongue."

"What the hell?"

"We don't know what kind of pill it is, but we're working on identifying it. It made me curious whether there was a pill on the first victim's tongue, too."

"Probably wasn't much left of Riley's tongue after he was burned."

"You're right about that, officer. The victim's mouth was mostly destroyed from the arson, but I did find a partial tongue remaining. It had some residue on it also, which we're comparing with what we found on Stafford. My hunch is they'll be a match."

"So right now, it seems like the same person killed both men."

"Appears that way," Doc said.

The room went silent.

Finally, Flint voiced what everyone was thinking, "Looks like we've got a serial killer."

"We could be headed in that direction," Vernadeane said. "But I think it takes three murders taking place over more than a month to qualify as a serial." Despite being hired as a support person for vulnerable, unhoused populations, Vernadeane was a trained mental health professional who recognized pathology when she saw it.

"While it's only been two victims, it's been long enough," TCPD Detective Buzz Broderick said. "Riley died March 5 and Stafford on April 7."

"I'm wondering whether our guy could also be a signature killer," Vernadeane offered. "A murderer who leaves a calling card at the scene of his crime. In this case, a pill on the tongue."

"Is there a meaning to the signature?" Gilda asked.

"Can be part of the killer's psychological deviance, but sometimes it's just done for effect, like posing a body in a certain way."

"So, should we try to find the meaning behind the signature?"

"It can help some. Mostly, a killer's signature ties one case to another. Like Ted Bundy, who always left a double bite mark on his victims. Or the Boston Strangler who tied his garrotes into bows around his victims' necks."

At the mention of serial killer, Quinn took an unwelcome dive back to her past. Specifically, her 1992 rookie year working for the Lakeland County Sheriff's Department when Xander Tobin had targeted bicycle riders as his victims. She'd learned a lot about serial killer pathology from that experience. A mental illness that can't be changed through treatment. The department thought Tobin had died in a fiery truck crash in the mountains between Tennessee and North Carolina. But then he'd secretly returned to Lakeland County. Sheriff Ed Robbins and Quinn had captured him just before he opened fire on hundreds of bicyclists participating in a Ride of Silence meant to honor his victims. She'd ended up tackling Tobin and sending them both through an open barn loft window before he got off a shot. They'd both been seriously injured from the fall. Tobin, paralyzed and wheelchair-bound, was sent to prison for life. Quinn had ended up in the ICU with lacerations, a broken nose requiring surgery, and several broken ribs. Most of her wounds had healed except for a gash below her mandible, which left a jagged keloid scar. Luckily, her prominent jawline kept it mostly invisible to others. While the scar didn't hurt, it prickled and burned when she was nervous. Stupid as it might sound to others, the scar's tingling had become an early warning sign when danger was present, like hair rising on the back of your neck or having goosebumps. Today, sitting in the meeting and learning they might be facing a serial killer, her scar sent shivers through her body.

Chapter 15: April 15

Quinn arrived home and took Ruby for a brisk walk around her neighborhood, blowing off steam. She'd planned to hide some smelly treats on the route beforehand to keep up the scent training Ruby'd gone through as a puppy, but Quinn was too wiped out. When they returned to the condo, she flopped in her easy chair, took out her phone, and ordered a burrito bowl from Qdoba for delivery. She spent the next half hour processing what she'd learned that day about the investigation.

Law enforcement teams had been walking the city streets hoping someone had information on Michael Stafford's death, but no one offered anything. Probably didn't help he'd been in Traverse City less than a month. They'd learned from Trace Evidence the pill found on Michael's tongue was Olanzapine, often sold under the brand name Zyprexa, an antipsychotic used to treat schizophrenia, bipolar disorder, depression, and agitation. The small amount of pill residue in Riley's mouth turned out to be Olanzapine, too, officially linking the two cases. Quinn mulled over why the perp would leave a pill on his victim's tongue but drew a blank.

The doorbell rang, and Ruby raced Quinn to the front door to see who was there. She collected her delivery, gave the dog a bully stick to keep her occupied, and settled back in her chair to enjoy her meal and the evening news. Middle Coast Mission was partially re-opening, but just in the afternoon as a place to use the showers, do laundry, work on computers, and charge phones. They'd erected a large outdoor tent and set up socially distanced chairs and tables to safely accommodate folks with no place else to go. The newscast next switched to Lansing. While the stay-at-home order was less than a month old, people were already protesting against its extension. A reporter showed a scene where several thousand cars were lined up, honking their horns in what they were calling

Operation Gridlock. Another hundred or so protesters occupied the Capitol lawn. Quinn had seen enough of the news and flipped off the television, something she was doing more often these days.

She headed to her study, hoping to work on a series of pictures she'd taken recently. She'd been hiking in the Brown Bridge Quiet Area and had spotted the bushy tail of a red fox. Quinn had watched from a distance and saw a fox kit peeking its head out of a den. She'd returned several times until she was rewarded with photographing five kits romping near their mother. The pictures would make a nice collage to give Patrick for his birthday.

After finishing her photography work, Quinn was going to try something new with her computer. They were calling it Zoom, and it was a way to virtually hold meetings during a time when in-person gatherings were prohibited. Tonight's intergovernmental meeting was between the county, the city, and the townships, and all participants would show up from their homes. The growing homeless population was on the agenda. Quinn'd never been to a meeting of this kind, but tonight's topic was timely, so she decided to attend. She followed the directions for connecting to Zoom, but by the time she arrived and figured out how to manage the various controls, the meeting was already underway.

"Since the mission closed, tent cities have popped up all over. I've heard the number of tents in the Pines has already tripled," one township official said. "With tourist season just around the corner, we can't have people seeing our beautiful area look like this."

A red-faced city commissioner took over the screen and quickly retorted, "I don't believe what I'm hearing from this official after what the townships have done to the homeless population camping in their parks."

"At least we've had the balls to do something." Nobody gasped at the township officer's foul, accusatory language because no one was at the meeting. They were all at home zooming on their computers with their voices muted, as per the instructions.

"We got fed up with homeless campers trashing township property," the official continued.

"Well, just so you know, your actions have displaced at least thirty homeless people. And guess where they've ended up. In the Pines. Doing the right thing isn't rocket science, man."

"We're within our rights shutting down these new homeless encampments. Our township ordinances prohibit camping in our parks."

"I suggest you talk to your attorneys," the red-faced city commissioner said. "The 9th U.S. Circuit Court of Appeals has deemed it cruel and unusual punishment to evict indigent, homeless residents from public property if they have nowhere else to go."

"Gentlemen, gentlemen. This bickering back and forth isn't doing anything to solve these problems," a woman said. "I'm Vernadeane Novak, the support and outreach officer for the Sheriff's Department. I can see we need to do more education on this issue, but the city commissioner is correct. The courts have ruled it's a violation of the First, Fourth, Eighth, and Fourteenth Amendments to kick people off public property under the false premise that they have a choice in the matter."

"Total bullshit, Bernadette. There's no way in hell I'm gonna allow Traverse City to turn into some Hooverville or Shantytown. Over my fucking dead body." And then the Zoom screen suddenly went blank.

Huh, Quinn thought. Meeting adjourned.

Chapter 16: April 17

Quinn had stopped by Centre Ice to clean out her locker after learning the hockey season had gone from postponed to cancelled. The same was likely to happen with baseball, too. She couldn't imagine a summer without the Tigers. As she was leaving the arena, she spotted Mack standing inside a bus shelter and pulled over.

"Hey, you want a ride?" Quinn yelled. His motel vouchers must've run out, and he was back on the streets. "Where you headed?"

"Street Medicine," he said, climbing in and throwing his bag into the back seat.

"You sick?" she asked, hoping she wasn't being exposed to COVID. She pulled open her glove box and handed him a mask.

"No, I'm fine. Mostly. Gotta have my arm looked at," he said, holding it out to show an ugly abscess in the crook. She didn't say anything, but their eyes met. Probably infected from bad needles. Sometimes, it was hard for her to shake the picture she had of Keegan Cammack signing autographs for hockey fans with this Mack living under a bridge and doing drugs.

"So, how's the can collecting business going?"

"Non-existent since the governor declared bottle returns off limits due to the COVID. I'm working on getting into a plasma donation program to supplement my pension."

As Quinn pulled up behind the mobile unit from Street Medicine, she noticed a visible difference to the Pines. Not only were more tents packed in, but the fire department had come in and trimmed up the dead limbs that stuck out at eye level.

"You staying here now?" Quinn asked.

"No way. Gotten too violent since the mission closed."

"Yeah, we're getting lots of calls needing public safety assistance."

"Plus, they're taking away people's privacy. Trimming the trees, adding lighting, and putting in security cameras."

"Some hard choices, Mack."

"There's no peace here either. Some guy drives down 11th Street in the middle of the night yelling, 'Get a job, you fucking slobs.' I also heard that someone's been going through the Pines, hitting and shaking the tents to collapse them on whoever's inside. Don't know whether it's the same guy, but it scares me shitless."

Someone tapped on Quinn's window, and she saw it was Vernadeane. She was heavily involved in Street Medicine, which was connected to the hospital's family practice residency program. Vernadeane had told her that lack of housing has a significant impact on health, sometimes reducing life expectancy by thirty years.

"You got a patient here?" Vernadeane asked.

"Yeah, needs to have his arm looked at."

"Follow me, Mack," Vernadeane said as she led him to the large mobile unit outfitted to treat trauma, burns, and lacerations. It also did blood work, X-rays, and provided folks with someone to talk to when they were lonely and scared.

While Vernadeane got someone to look after Mack, Quinn and a family practice resident moved into the camp. The city manager had recently issued an order not to enter the Pines without a police escort, so she was glad to help with that. As they approached the tents, they yelled out hellos, asked about medication updates, and distributed Naloxone as they went, knowing some residents were vulnerable to opioid overdose.

A guy known only as Moose noticed her uniform and approached. "I don't understand why you cut the trees. Seems like you're trying to expose us. If we're not causing any trouble, why would you harass us? Cops are supposed to serve and protect."

"I hear you, Moose, and I understand where you're coming from. But the Pines has gotten so overcrowded since the pandemic that our calls have tripled here in less than a month. We're just trying to keep the officers safe who come to help."

"Harrumph," Moose replied gruffly. "Why don't it seem that way?" he mumbled as he wandered back to his tent.

Mack tapped Quinn on her shoulder, and she turned and said, "You all fixed up?"

"Good as new."

"Need a ride someplace, Mack?"

"That'd be grand, lassie," he said, slipping into an affected Irish brogue.

Quinn laughed and replied, "Centre Ice or someplace else, bucko?"

"Aye, that'd be good...unless you're looking for a roommate."

"Jaysus, Mack. You think I'm an fecking eejit?"

Chapter 17: April 20

They'd been pounding the pavement, following up on leads, and were meeting to put it all together. Chief Yeager and Detective Broderick from TCPD. Vernadeane, Gilda, Flint, and Quinn from the Sheriff's Department. They felt a sense of urgency, knowing if their killer was a serial, he'd strike again soon.

"So, what've we got today?" Gilda asked, her voice muffled below her mask.

"I've been working the medication angle," Buzz started. "You know, the Olanzapine found on both vics' tongues. The pill's imprint code allowed us to ID the product and follow its distribution. We've learned the pill under Stafford's tongue came from Southern California."

"Hmmm," Quinn said. "You think the killer might be from that part of the country?"

"Yeah. That distribution center serves California, Nevada, Utah, Colorado, Arizona, and New Mexico."

"Huh. Good lead to start with. Maybe a person from one of those states traveled here for some reason."

"Not many people are flying these days. I just heard air travel is down 96% percent from a year ago."

"Uffda," Flint said. "And now that they've tacked on a 14-day self-quarantine after a flight, who'd want to fly?"

"You say that often, Flint. Uffda," Quinn said. "I haven't a clue what it means."

Flint took a swig of the pop he'd brought with him and answered Quinn's question. "Uffda can mean a lot of things in Minnewegian. For many, it means 'I'm surprised or overwhelmed.' When you hear it from me, it almost always means 'shit.' My version of a curse word."

Bringing the conversation back to the topic, Buzz said, "We're wondering if the guy flew in sometime mid-February or early March before the pandemic reached TC."

"That makes a lotta sense. Perhaps he wanted to get away from the West Coast where COVID had been raging since the end of January and early February."

"We thought so, too," Buzz continued. "We've started checking all flights from California to Traverse City from the third week in February through the second week in March. Our computers tell us the largest hub and most common connection goes from LAX through O'Hare to TC. It's painstaking work, but it seems to be the right approach, knowing the Olanzapine came from there."

"Good work, detective. What else have we got?" Gilda asked.

"Maybe we should talk about the killer some. You know, his personality," Quinn said.

While she waited for someone to dive into this new topic, Quinn got up and walked around the room to refresh everyone's coffee. Then she sent the plate of fresh scones from the Third Coast Bakery around again. Everyone was grateful for a break in the discussion and the chance to unmask while they ate and drank. Even though it wasn't hot in the FC2 conference room, they were sponging off the perspiration that masking created.

"What've you been thinking, Quinn?" Vernadeane finally asked.

"When I was a rookie in Lakeland County, we went after a serial killer named Alexander Tobin, who targeted bicyclists. I remember our consulting psychologist said he had a mental illness that couldn't be changed through treatment."

"Right, that kind of illness is a personality disorder, or PDO, for short," Vernadeane said, getting up and moving towards the whiteboard. "There are three main signs of a personality disorder. PERSISTENCE, RIGIDITY, and GLOBALISM," she wrote in all caps. "PERSISTENCE refers to the disorder being long-lasting and part of the individual's personality since at least age thirteen. RIGIDITY involves the maladaptive behaviors exhibited in the individual's interpersonal relationships. They don't learn from their mistakes and are quick to blame others for their problems. And finally, GLOBALISM means that people with a PDO exhibit their symptoms in all settings. For example, a teenager might be defiant at home, but they will also show oppositional behaviors with friends, at school, and playing sports. Any questions?"

Everyone had been furiously taking notes from Vernadeane's impromptu presentation. Flint raised his head and said, "Geez, Louise. You sure know your stuff."

While they were all getting acquainted with Flint and his "Minnewegian" accent, as he called it, they chuckled at his comment to Vernadeane.

"I've always wondered why someone with a PDO would take a drug like Olanzapine if their problem can't be changed," Buzz said.

"Good point, detective. While the behaviors that're part of their personality can't be changed, they can be managed. We don't know enough about our perp yet to formally diagnose him, but let's say he has Anti-Social Personality Disorder, which is common among serial killers," Vernadeane said. "Antipsychotic medications like Olanzapine can help manage patients' anger and reduce their aggressiveness. Keeps them under better control."

"Thanks," Buzz replied. "That clarifies it."

"Cops always gotta talk about motive when investigating murders," Flint said. "I was taught to look at the 'Four Ls' to find a motive. You know, lust, the guy gets a sexual payoff. Love, like maybe in a mercy killing. Loathing, the perp hates the person. And, loot, the killer gets financial gain. Anyone else been thinking about motive?"

"Hard to think how someone could get a hard-on killing homeless people," Buzz said.

"It'd be more like fueling combativeness," Vernadeane replied. "Testosterone can stoke both sexual and aggressive arousal."

"What if someone has a grudge they're trying to settle against homeless people?" Gilda said.

"I've been thinking along those lines too, but wondering if it might be a hate crime," Quinn offered. "I learned at my training with the Homeless Alliance that close to six hundred people in our country have been killed since 1999 solely due to lack of housing. Shot, stabbed, set on fire, or drowned only because they were homeless."

"The homeless population is certainly vulnerable and easy to target," Vernadeane added.

"Hadn't considered a hate crime," Chief Yeager said. "In light of that idea, we need to get a warning to the homeless community to be extra cautious in the face of these two murders. Warn them to stick together and not sleep alone. We'll also step up patrols in areas they frequent, especially the Pines."

"How about an anonymous tip line," Quinn suggested. "We've had no luck getting people on the streets to talk, but perhaps they'd be more willing to call in information anonymously."

They sat around in silence, munching their scones and thinking about their cases. Finally, Gilda asked, "Anyone have anything else?" When no one answered, she said, "Good work. Let's get back at it."

Chapter 18: April 28

The investigators had been working round the clock checking names of people who'd flown into Traverse City from LAX through Chicago. Fifty-nine had arrived between the third week of February and the second week of March. The majority of passengers were on round-trip tickets. They set those aside for now because the detectives figured they were visitors or businesspeople who'd be returning to California in a week or less. Only eleven had one-way tickets to TC, three women, and eight men. They were awaiting further information from the airlines on the eight men. Names, addresses, and photo IDs. It wasn't much to go on, but at least it was a start.

Then, the officers had gotten a second lead, this one from the anonymous tip line. The tipper even left her name. Connie Jordan. Said she worked at a coin laundry on the east side of town. Connie gave its address and said she'd like to talk to an officer about an unusual encounter with a customer that'd made her uncomfortable. Buzz and Quinn headed to the Eighth Street laundromat along with several CSI technicians.

"You must be Connie Jordan," Quinn said as she extended her hand and introduced Buzz. "Tell us what happened."

"A young guy has come in twice. I hadn't thought much about him until I heard about the second homeless guy murdered and the tip line you'd set up. I've been going back and forth for the last couple of weeks, whether it was something or nothing. Just my nerves acting up."

"Ma'am, you're doing the right thing by calling us," Buzz said. "You wouldn't believe how some of the most heinous crimes have been solved by hunches like yours."

"What do you remember about this guy?" Quinn asked. "You said he was young."

"Yeah, probably late teens or early twenties," Connie replied.

"What'd he look like?" Buzz asked.

"Medium height, maybe 5'8" or so. Light brown hair, almost blond. He had a tan, too, not something you see around here this time of year."

"How was he dressed?"

"Jeans, nice ones, not ripped. He had on a cotton tan worker jacket. Lined with fleece, I think."

"So, what set off your alarm bells?" Quinn asked. "You had some interactions with him?

"I did. The kid had stripped down to his t-shirt and boxer shorts and was washing his jacket and jeans. Thought that was kinda strange, but not uncommon these days. I wondered if he was homeless and only had the clothes on his back. Or maybe he'd gotten something on his outerwear."

"There's more?" Buzz prompted.

"There was something in the washer that clanged the whole time. I wondered if it was broken and went over to ask if I could help. He rebuffed me, though, not wanting to talk. Said he'd left his keys in his jacket pocket, and that's what was making the noise. He gave me a nasty look and turned his back. I took it that the conversation was over."

"Which machines did he use," Buzz asked. Connie pointed to a washer and dryer at the far end of the row.

"You mind if we bring in our CSI team to see if they can find any evidence?"

"Not at all, but it's been a while. You're gonna find a gazillion prints, including mine."

"That's okay. We just want to see if anything pops up in our system. We'll also take your prints to rule them out from the others."

"Okay, no problem. Maybe you'll luck out since we're in the off-season and have fewer customers now. Those machines at the end of the line get used less than the others. People prefer doing their laundry out in the open at places like this."

Connie went back to her work washing, folding, and pressing the laundry that wealthy people had dropped off. Sometimes, she felt resentful about doing other people's dirty work. It was a job, though, and the owners were good to her, allowing her to use their private restroom to shower. Do her laundry for free. She even ate her meals while she worked. Since she and her boyfriend had broken up, she'd had no place else to go except here and her car to sleep in.

CSI got to work on the laundromat. One dusted for prints on the end washer, dryer, and folding table. When he found one, he photographed it and then brought out hinged fingerprint lifters, which included a lifting tape and a backing side. The lifting side had a special adhesive that was aggressive enough to lift the powder without ripping. Another tech had the tedious job of swabbing the nooks and crannies inside the washer for blood traces that might give them DNA. He methodically used cotton-tipped applicators to swipe all the recesses where blood might still reside after repeated washings. He collected eleven potential blood samples and placed them in self-contained tubes to ensure safe transport without contamination. The last CSI removed the filters from both the washer and dryer. He dumped the findings onto clean white evidence paper, unwrapped a new trace evidence roller, and rolled it over the filter contents, much like one would use a lint roller to remove dog hair from clothing. It took several tries to pick up all the vent contents. Finally, he placed the roller strips into sterile bags, ready to submit to the experts at FC2. As they gathered their equipment, Quinn thanked Connie and gave her a business card if she thought of anything else.

Chapter 19: April 30

It'd been one of those unexpected spring storms. Temperatures were back in the twenties with six inches of new snow. Just when Quinn thought good weather was here to stay, winter always has one last dig. Her phone bugled, and she looked at her screen and saw it was Mack. She'd given him her number but hadn't expected him to use it. Too much pride.

"Hey, Mack," Quinn said. "What's up?"

"I'm having trouble walking. Could you give me a ride to Street Med?"

"Yeah. Where are you?"

"In the parking lot of the soccer fields on Keystone."

"Be right there."

It took her just ten minutes to reach the complex from FC2. She flipped the switch on the heated passenger seat to high as she drove. Pulling into the entrance nearest Cass Road, she looked around for Mack. The fresh snow covering the fields seemed out of place, with the bleachers and goal nets already set up for the new season. No high schoolers would be practicing today. When she finally spotted Mack leaning against the closed concession stand, she could hardly believe her eyes. She'd seen him just two weeks earlier but could tell he'd lost more weight. He'd traded his bungee cord for a dog leash to hold up his already baggy pants. He waved and limped towards her, wincing each time he set foot on the ground. She threw her car into park mode and went over to the passenger door to help him inside. For a few minutes, he just sat there, soaking in the warmth, much like Ruby did when lying in a patch of sunshine coming through the French doors.

"Where's your bag of belongings, Mack?" Quinn asked.

"Dunno. Must have lost it somewhere."

"Where'd you sleep last night?"

"Under the new bridge."

Holy shit, she thought. What was he doing sleeping under the Robbins Bridge in this kind of weather? Then she chastised herself, knowing it must've been the best shelter Mack could find in the freak snowstorm.

"Let's take a look," Quinn said as she pulled out of the soccer complex. The three-year-old Robbins Bridge carried busy Cass Road over the Boardman-Ottaway River. The driveway down to the river hadn't been serviced yet, but she put her Subaru into X-mode and plowed through the deep snow. She immediately saw Mack's bag leaning against the outhouse. She grabbed it and threw it into her back seat. As she drove out of the park, she looked over at him. His sallow complexion deepened her concerns. She knew skin infections ran rampant among homeless people due to their unhygienic living conditions. She worried that Mack was suffering from more.

She found the Street Medicine mobile unit parked on 11th Street, not far from the Pines. The snow had made it difficult to drive more deeply into the tent settlement. Quinn helped steady Mack enough so he could climb the three steps inside. The nurse and doctor on duty took one look at him and helped him onto a bed. While they began working to undress him, Quinn went back outside, looking for Vernadeane.

"So, tell us what's going on, Mack?" the doctor asked as he worked to pull off his boots and wet clothing. The nurse dressed him in a clean gown and wrapped him in warm blankets.

"I've been having trouble walking. I don't think the wound on my arm is healing either."

The nurse touched his forehead with a thermometer and recorded 103.4 degrees on Mack's digital chart. When the doctor finally wiggled his boots off, he noticed the skin on his feet was blotchy, a mix of white and blue. The tissue felt hard and cold to the doctor's touch. Two toes on Mack's right foot had turned black.

"Looks like you've got a bad infection and a severe case of frostbite, Mack. We're gonna get you fixed up soon, buddy."

The nurse took Mack's arm, applied a tourniquet to help locate a vein, and inserted a needle. She set up an IV bag, gave it a saline flush, and then administered fluids, painkillers, and antibiotics. When she'd finished, she put a second set of warm blankets over Mack's body and feet. Just then, Quinn re-entered the mobile unit with Vernadeane on her heels.

"We gonna transport him to the hospital?" Vernadeane asked.

"Yeah, no sense waiting for an ambulance when he's critical, and we're two blocks away."

"I'll get the paperwork going," Vernadeane said. "Don't want to lose another homeless guy due to red tape."

As the Street Medicine unit rolled slowly towards the hospital, Quinn gently sponged Mack's face with warm water, trying to figure out the bond she felt for this man. Was it their shared love for hockey? Or maybe his Irish charm drew her in, reminding her of her heritage. Maybe she just felt empathy for his homeless situation and wanted to help. While she mulled it over, Mack moaned slightly as the mobile unit pulled into the bay at the emergency room entrance. Vernadeane quickly hopped out and went inside to run interference with the authorities about another indigent hospitalization.

Chapter 20: May 10

Quinn had visited Mack daily for the nearly two weeks he'd been hospitalized. He'd lost two toes on one foot and three on the other due to frostbite. As he'd come off the anesthesia from surgery and the illicit drugs out of his system, they'd been able to have some good conversations. Quinn learned Mack had been using meth both as a painkiller to manage his concussion symptoms as well as a way to stay awake at night so he could protect himself and his belonging from attacks.

"If I go to sleep, I don't hear anything, and that makes me vulnerable to someone sneaking up on me." Mack had said. "I sleep with one eye open and one eye closed."

His comment had stuck with Quinn, helping her understand the complex reasons for drug use among homeless people. Not just using them to self-medicate but to keep themselves alert to the dangers of living on the streets.

Yesterday, Mack had been released from the hospital, and she'd settled him in a room at the Travel Inn near East Bay. Vernadeane had secured vouchers for his stay there, and Quinn hoped the warm weather would continue once his two weeks were up because she knew his feet couldn't stand more frostbite. His unsteady gait from the missing toes already concerned her.

So when Patrick asked if she wanted to take a short road trip Saturday morning, she'd jumped at the chance to immerse herself in something different. Being out in nature was keeping her sane during the pandemic. Patrick hadn't said where they were going, but when he headed north on Garfield from her condo, Quinn had an idea. Old Mission Peninsula.

Finally, Quinn asked, "Are you gonna tell me where we're driving?"

"I read an article in my DNR newsletter that a new peregrine falcon repopulation project is coming to our county."

"Let me guess, to Old Mission Peninsula?"

"Yeah, it's an offshoot of what's been happening in Southeast Michigan."

"What's going on there?"

"The peregrine falcon population became endangered after DDT decimated their numbers. Once the pesticide was banned in the 1970s, there's been a concerted effort to restore them to the upper Midwest. One especially successful project is the Detroit River-Western Lake Erie Basin."

"Interesting. I've heard that the local Audubon Club takes trips there during the spring and fall bird migrations."

"Yeah, it's become quite the hotspot. Peregrines nest there but also in urban areas. I read that one pair even laid eggs on the Ambassador Bridge."

Patrick stopped talking when he turned onto seasonal back roads and began using the Tahoe's GPS. They finally stopped at what appeared to be a construction site. A sign said *The Peregrine Falcon Propagation and Training Center*. Another sign, larger than the first, read *Keep Out. Private Property*.

"What a great surprise," Quinn said. "Thanks. I needed to do something different."

"I thought you'd be interested."

Despite the warnings and it being a Saturday, the area teemed with activity. Two buildings were going up with workers putting on siding and nailing down roof tiles. One was further along than the other. It looked like a pole barn, about 250 feet long and 50 feet wide. The gable roof was slanted from a height of twenty feet, sloping down to fourteen. The roof and end walls were painted white, probably to reflect the summer heat. The side walls were covered with slats to let in light and air. Between the openings, they could see workers sectioning off rooms around the outside of the interior. Perches had already been built throughout.

"Let's go check it out," Quinn said, jumping down from the Tahoe."

"So much for private property," Patrick added.

As soon as they entered the site, they heard an argument going on just around the corner of the building. Three men were going at it. One was dressed in workman's clothing and held a clipboard. Another wore the brown shirt and pants of a DNR uniform. The third was attired in the garb of an Arab. A white flowing robe and a checkered red and white head cloth held in place by a black cord. They stopped their heated discussion and turned to the interlopers.

The DNR guy immediately recognized Patrick's Black Tahoe emblazoned with the gold seal of a Michigan Conservation Officer.

"How may we help you?" he asked. "I'm guessing you saw the no trespass sign."

"We did, but our curiosity got the best of us," Quinn said, grinning with her charming smile. "I'm forensic detective Quinn Macarthy, and this is conservation officer Patrick Elliot."

"We're both avid bird photographers and are interested in this project," Patrick added.

"Ah, very good and welcome. I'm Sheik Badr-Uddin, originally from the Arabian Peninsula. Dubai in the United Arab Emirates. I'm the owner and director of this project," he said with only a slight trace of accent.

"Nice to meet you," Quinn said. "What can you tell us about the center? It's not exactly what we'd expect to find in the middle of the Northwoods."

The sheik laughed. "You're right. Falconry is a very new sport in your country. Less than a hundred years old. Where I come from, the sport dates back to at least the third millennium B.C. During its early beginnings, falconry wasn't even a sport. It was how desert Bedouins hunted prey to feed their families in a time before there were guns."

Patrick and Quinn could tell the sheik liked to talk and let him continue.

"Over time, falconry became an integral part of desert life and a favorite pastime of Bedouin tribal leaders. The ruling sheiks of the UAE still own and fly falcons. Even so, my country has drastically changed over the last fifty years. We've become a modern, oil-exporting country with a highly diversified economy. My home city of Dubai has developed into a global hub for tourism, retail, and finance. We have the world's tallest building and the largest man-made seaport," Sheik Badr-Uddin said. "I'm very proud of my country. But with all the oil money, it'd be easy to forget our local customs. Falconry is a way we keep our history alive."

"How interesting!" Quinn exclaimed. "I'm curious, though, why you're setting up here in Grand Traverse County. It's hardly similar to your Arabian climate."

"Sometimes the desert is too hot for anything during the day. Most of our sport takes place in the hours just before sundown or inside air-conditioned complexes. We've been looking for a more moderate climate to propagate and train our peregrines. We think your county and the surrounding National Lakeshore will be ideal. The birds will feel right at home in your beautiful dunes. We also chose this area because we're looking to introduce our sport to new parts of the world. The U.S. is ripe for those opportunities, being such a great sports nation."

"Huh," Quinn replied, dying to know more.

"I can tell, detective, you're eager for more information. Might I take you to dinner some evening and tell you more about our plans? Right now, my construction foreman is anxious to move this along. COVID has created supply chain issues, and with plans for a grand opening festival next spring, I'm afraid we must get back to work."

Quinn gave the sheik her business card so he could contact her in the future. They shook hands goodbye, and Patrick and Quinn walked back to his Tahoe.

As they got inside, Patrick said, "You amaze me, Quinn Macarthy. You attract an endless list of admirers wherever you go. What is it about you? Your red hair, peaches-and-cream skin, or is it those emerald-green eyes?"

"Oh, Patrick. Nip it. You, of all people, know I'm not interested in that man. But you gotta admit there's interesting stuff going on there."

"I want to learn more, too, but I have the feeling it'll be secondhand through you."

"Man, I have to find a way to get my shaggy hair cut soon, regardless of the COVID rules. Can't go to dinner with a sheik wearing a baseball cap."

Chapter 21: May 12

He came out of the convenience store and walked to the side of the building where he'd parked his mom's Acura. "Thank god for 7-Eleven," he muttered. "I don't think I can get through the night without my Lavender Honey-Bee Buzz coffee and chocolate glazed donut." He'd seen ads on television that said it was a light and calming brew, but it hadn't seemed to help him. At least so far. Maybe he should be drinking it in the morning instead of near midnight. "Oh, well," he mumbled. "Haven't been sleeping anyway. At least the caffeine keeps my headaches at bay."

The ringtone on his phone went off, and he looked down at the screen. "Why's dad calling so late? This is probably the fifth or sixth time today," he grumbled. But he knew. His dad was worried his mother wasn't monitoring his medicine. And he was right. She'd not kept him on a schedule like dad had. He didn't care, though. It was nice not having a dry mouth and constipation. The best part was being able to get hard so he could jerk himself off to sleep at night.

He'd let the ringtone keep playing instead of sending it to voicemail. Leaning against the east wall of the convenience store, he swayed to the death metal song, singing the lyrics as he moved:

Down, pound the ground, with your body crushed beyond dust
Beaten and broken, broken and bleeding, horribly quashed
Cry if you can, scream if you will, die if you must
Crushed beyond dust, crush, crushed beyond dust.

He finally got into the SUV and set his drink in the cupholder. He pulled out the donut and shoved it in his mouth, consuming it in three bites. He felt a little queasy. Maybe he'd eaten it too fast. He was dizzy, too. He wondered if he was spiraling out of control again. He could feel the panic setting in. His chest tightening, too. Angry thoughts raced through his mind. Maybe he should drive straight to mom's loft to stay out of trouble.

He looked into his sideview mirror and saw a large, bright green dumpster directly behind him. He turned the car wheels to avoid it and backed up. Didn't dare put a dent in mom's Acura, he thought. He nudged up against something and looked into the backup camera to see what was stopping him. Nothing was there, so he accelerated in reverse, continuing to rise onto some object. Finally, he stopped and jumped out of the car to take a look. Another wave of dizziness forced him to lean against the car to steady himself.

"Fucking A!" he yelled. "Another homeless guy sleeping here instead of the Pines." He couldn't tell if he was asleep or dead, only that his car tires were on top of the man's body.

"Well, buddy. It ain't no safer here," he said.

He got back in the Acura and pulled ahead of the body. Then he threw the car in reverse and ran over it a second time. He backed up one more time to make sure he'd gotten the lousy scumbag good. Finished with the job, he pulled forward and squealed his tires as he pulled out of the 7-Eleven onto Fourteenth Street.

He felt oddly calm as he drove, even though he was sweating profusely. He buzzed down the car window to get some fresh air as he headed to The Commons. But more than calm, he felt devilish, maybe even godly, as he sang:

Cry if you can, scream if you will, die if you must
Crushed beyond dust, crush, crushed beyond dust.

Chapter 22: May 13

Quinn hadn't slept well, and at 4 a.m., she'd turned to reading to pass the rest of the night. Helen MacDonald's *H Is for Hawk* had been on her bookshelf, and she decided to give it a try after visiting the falcon propagation center. Not fifty pages in, her phone rang.

"Macarthy," she growled.

"We've got another homeless death, Quinn. Meet us at the twenty-four-hour convenience store on Fourteenth Street," Gilda said.

"Shit. The one right around the corner from the Pines?"

"That's the one," Gilda replied, clicking off.

Quinn dressed, took Ruby out, and set down a bowl of kibbles. While the dog ate, she brewed coffee in her Keurig and grabbed some cheese and crackers before she headed out the door. Not that she felt like eating.

Quinn arrived at the scene and found the small parking lot packed with police cars, first responders, the medical examiner's van, and a mobile crime scene lab. She had to park at the strip mall across the driveway from the 7-Eleven.

She jogged over to the store and came upon CSIs working on tire tracks in the parking lot. One was photographing black impressions left on the pavement. A second was putting down a sheet of rubber with a low-adhesive gelatin layer on one side to lift imprints from the surface.

"You get good ones?" she asked.

"Yeah. The killer squealed his tires as he drove away. Laid down some nice rubber for us."

Quinn left the CSIs and walked over to Ted Roberts, who was dictating into his label mic while a photographer took pictures of the dead body. As she approached the ME, she saw the DB and quickly turned away, gulping air so she didn't wretch on the scene.

"Holy, Christ," she said. "What happened here?"

"Multiple runovers by a medium-size vehicle. Crushed the poor bastard."

"Any ID?"

"None that we've found. The face is so disfigured he'll be hard to identify."

"Can you tell if his throat is slit or there's a pill on his tongue?"

"Not yet, but it could still be the same perp. Killers change their methodology in different situations, especially if they've been surprised and don't have time for prior planning."

"Where's everyone else?"

"Gilda's inside interviewing the manager. The others are in there too, going through surveillance tapes."

Quinn walked inside the 7-Eleven and found Gilda talking to a man wearing a black and green work uniform.

"Hey, Quinn, glad you're here," Gilda said. "This is Roger Taft, the night manager. He was just describing the young man who'd come in to buy coffee and a donut. Said he's a regular and almost always orders the same thing. What'd you call it?"

"Lavender Honey-Bee Buzz. One of our specialty coffees. The lavender's supposed to be calming, but with how many the kid consumes daily, I don't see how it could be."

"You say he was a kid?"

"Kid, young man. Hard to tell. Probably late teens to early twenties."

"What'd he look like?"

"Medium height, blondish hair, thin, quite tan."

"How was he dressed?"

"Hmmm. A beige jacket and jeans, I think."

"So, you served him, and he left. What happened next?"

"I went back to stocking shelves. Pretty slow at night. I heard tires squeal and ran outside to see what was going on. I caught sight of a light-colored SUV speeding up Fourteenth Street towards Silver Lake Road. Then I saw the body over by the dumpster and called 9-1-1."

"Were you alone in the store?"

"No, my assistant was in the back room on break. She's probably got the surveillance tape ready to watch. The Yooper is with her along with another cop."

They followed Taft to the back office, where two monitors were set up. He introduced them to his assistant, Lucy Heywood. Flint was seated next to Chief Yeager.

"You ready for us?" Taft asked.

"Yeah, we've already watched it once. The tape's pretty dark, though. I didn't realize our streetlight was burned out in the parking lot."

Heywood rolled the tape for Gilda and Quinn to view. It started with the kid buying a coffee and donut inside the store. They watched him leave and turn to the side of the building, where a light-colored SUV was parked. Without good lighting, he'd become more of a shadow figure. They saw him lean against the building, then enter his vehicle, and carefully back out of the parking space to avoid a dumpster. They watched as the SUV's back end rose as if it were driving onto some kind of platform. The car door opened, and the light inside the car identified the driver as the same kid who'd bought coffee inside the store. He went around to the rear of the car to look at what was there, ran back inside the vehicle, and reversed it back and forth several times. In the dark, it wasn't clear what he was running over. The kid finally left the parking lot at a high rate of speed, squealing his tires as he did.

"Jesus," Gilda said. "I'm glad there wasn't more light to see what was happening. It was graphic enough just watching the car roll back and forth over what was there."

"It's weird knowing we might be seeing our perpetrator for the first time," Quinn added.

"You think it's the same guy?" Flint asked. "Was his throat slit like the others?"

"Doc couldn't tell yet, but he said that sometimes perps change their MO when they don't have sufficient time to plan. Like if they've been caught off guard."

"We'll want to take the tape along for evidence," Gilda said to the store manager.

"I'll also want a copy," Quinn said. "You all weren't there when Buzz and I interviewed Connie Jordan, the one who called the anonymous tipline about the young man who'd washed his clothes at the laundromat where she worked. The guy who ordered coffee tonight is a perfect match to Connie's description. Age, size, hair color, tan. His clothes are also the same as what he wore to the laundromat. If she looks at the tape, she might be able to make a firm identification. I think our multi-media department at FC2 will also be able to lighten the video to get a clearer picture of both the driver and the vehicle," Quinn said.

"Uffda," Flint said. "Maybe we've got him."

Chapter 23: May 18

Quinn had spent the morning writing reports from the leads she'd run down over the past few days. They were slowly putting together the puzzle of the homeless killer but still had too many missing pieces to come up with an identity. With the weather sunny and the temperatures nearing seventy, she decided to take herself out for lunch. Restaurants had begun functioning at half capacity as long as people wore face masks and tables were spaced six feet apart. Many had even added outdoor seating. Quinn hadn't eaten in a restaurant for nearly two months, and it seemed like the perfect day to break out of pandemic mode and head downtown. On the way, she grabbed her Tigers baseball cap. With over eight weeks of growth on her pixie haircut, she was looking pretty shabby.

She found a parking spot a short walk from Mama Lu's Taco Shop and immediately seated herself at one of the new outdoor patio tables. Her spirits lifted as she breathed the fresh air and took in the beautiful flowering pear trees lining Front Street. It'd been a long time since she felt such joy and hope, even amid a triple murder investigation. When the server brought the fish tacos she'd ordered, she savored eating something different from her cooking and worked hard not to moan in delight at this small return to normalcy. Now, if only the governor would re-open the hair salons.

She finished her lunch and decided to walk down Front Street to take in the still-closed retail shops. She stopped at Horizon Books and looked at the window displays. During COVID, she'd downloaded books to her iPad, but she longed to hold a real book in her hands again. She knew it wouldn't be long.

And then she heard it. Someone playing an outdoor piano. She moseyed over to the Chase building, where one of the street pianos was located. It'd been painted with bright colors and designs by Interlochen students who frequently provided entertainment with their musical talents. Sometimes, a bass or saxophone player joined in. Often, an instrument case was left open near the piano for donations.

But today, the man at the piano was Mack. He was focused intently, hitting the keys but not making music. As he banged away, his arms lifted up and down. His face shone. He was hopped up on something. People stopped to listen, threw a dollar or two into his hat on the ground, and then moved on. She heard one man say, "How can someone who earned fourteen million dollars become homeless?" Another answered, "I guess homelessness can happen to anyone, even professional athletes." They must've remembered Mack from his days on the ice during the Red Wings camps, Quinn thought.

As the small crowd dispersed after hearing enough of Mack's cacophony, Quinn quickly called Vernadeane and asked her to come by, hoping they'd be able to convince him to go into treatment. Vernadeane said she'd bring the mobile unit to Cass and Front as soon as she finished with her current patient, probably within 45 minutes to an hour. With help on the way, Quinn went to Mack and put her hand on his shoulder.

He startled at her touch and then looked at her with wide eyes, confused. "Quinn, you've come to listen to me play," he said.

She noticed he'd lost more weight, his eyes were red, and he smelled from lack of grooming. "I have, Mack. I haven't seen you around lately. What've you been up to?"

"The last couple of days, I've been practicing for my next concert. They just put the pianos out, so I'm behind schedule."

Knowing she had an hour to kill, she wondered how she'd get him into treatment. He seemed more agitated, constantly shifting on the piano bench and gesturing with his arms. Neon sneakers Quinn hadn't seen before pumped up and down on the pedals. Even though she understood homeless people sometimes turned to drugs as a refuge from life on the street, she cared about Mack and was worried about the direction his life was taking.

"Hey, how about you take a break from your practicing and walk with me down Front Street to see the pretty blossoms."

"Okay, but just for a while. I've got catching up to do with my piano."

As they set out, Quinn noticed Mack was unsteady on his feet and had developed a rolling gait, probably due to his toe amputations. Maybe whatever he was on was helping with his foot pain. They reached the alley next to Kilwins and saw a group of men playing cards at the weatherproof chairs and tables.

"Hey, fellas," Mack yelled, pointing to the mural on the brick wall. It was painted like a postcard and read *Greetings from Traverse City*. It showed area landmarks, including Old Mission Peninsula, The Commons, The State Theater, plus beach scenes and cherry orchards. "You like my latest magnum opus?" he asked.

They rolled their eyes. Quinn recognized two of the men from the Pines, but even their common homelessness didn't seem to connect them with Mack. He was an outsider.

As she steered Mack away from the group, she saw Vernadeane loping down the sidewalk toward them.

"We're parked right on the plaza in front of the bank. Let's see if we can get him into the mobile unit for an exam and hopefully some treatment."

Chapter 24: May 21

Connie had worked two double shifts at the laundromat and was wiped out. The rich snowbirds were returning from their winter havens and were dropping off laundry by the bags. Clothing from their travels. Bedding that needed freshening after lying dormant in their "cottages" during the off-season. For once, she longed for a real bed she could stretch out in for the night. A place where she could really sleep.

But Connie Jordan didn't have a real bed. She'd become homeless when she left her boyfriend after he beat her up the last time. While her black eye had faded mostly to yellow, the mask hid her fat lip. She'd couch-surfed for a while in her friends' living rooms, but that had gotten old for them as well as for her. She'd thought about going to the mission but feared the shame she'd feel. Being a local, someone who knew her from high school would find out her situation. She'd embarrass her family, who had no idea what she was going through. Besides, going to MCM wasn't an option anymore since it had closed with the pandemic.

With no other place to go, she'd opted to become a "rubber tramp." Someone who lived out of their car. It wasn't as bad as it sounded because the laundromat owners allowed her to use the facilities while she worked. It was the night hours that were challenging. Finding a place to park her rusty 1999 Honda CR-V that'd become her home. Well, not really. A vehicle isn't a home. At least by living in her vehicle, she felt in charge of her life.

She didn't have many possessions, but she could keep them safe there, locking the car doors when she left if she remembered. Her sleeping bag, extra blankets, and change of clothing were organized neatly in the back, along with a few toiletries. She kept a pile of paperbacks there, too, that she'd gotten from the Little Free Libraries that dotted city neighborhoods. She'd read them at night by her battery-run book light when she couldn't sleep, which was often. If it got too cold at night, she'd turn on the engine and flip the heat to high until the car warmed up. She even felt some pride in supporting herself on the pay from her minimum-wage laundromat job and her SNAP food benefits. Both kept her in food and gas. She charged her old flip phone through the Honda's cigarette lighter. New cars didn't even have them.

Her biggest challenge was where to park her car each night. While Traverse City was safe enough, Connie didn't want to become predictable. It'd become more complicated since the pandemic when townships passed ordinances that made sleeping and living in your car illegal. Cops cruised the local parks, kicking out the rubber tramps who'd tried to find safety there. But predictable she had become, choosing to park and sleep at Walmart. The store had a reputation for permitting overnight parking in their vast lot, and she was comforted that she wasn't alone. She'd met another rubber tramp who covered his car windows with pizza boxes for privacy. Someone else had a small dog he walked in the evening. He'd told her he lost his home and wasn't about to give up his dog, too. Walmart also allowed people traveling in motorhomes and fifth-wheel RVs to overnight in their parking lots. The scene was especially strange at night, with beaters housing the homeless next to luxury coaches.

Walmart's hours suited her, too. They were one of the few stores that opened early. At 6 a.m., she'd go in to use their bathroom. She was also able to get something hot from their food bar for breakfast and pick up a couple of sandwiches and fruit for later in the day. The store didn't close until 11 p.m., giving her time to use their restroom before she settled in at night.

Tonight, Connie had gone in for last call and picked up a bag of pretzels to snack on while she read. When she returned to her car, she pulled her Honda away from the other campers and the bright lights that kept her awake. She laid out the sleeping bag on her car seat, reclined it as far as it would go, and pulled the warm fleece blanket over her body. She pulled out Michelle Obama's book *Becoming* and began to read. She hadn't believed her luck when she pulled the hardback out of the Little Free Library on 9th Street. Most of the time, the best she got was ratty paperbacks. Obama's book was already inspiring her. She was adjusting her book light and beginning to read when movement in the dark caught her eye. She raised slightly and watched a figure walk towards her car. At first, she wasn't nervous, just aware. People coming and going in the parking lot was part of the reason she felt safe here. She raised further and recognized the kid. The one who'd washed his clothes at the laundromat. She lifted her left arm to depress the door lock with her elbow, but she was too late.

Chapter 25: May 22

The investigation had become more complicated with the addition of a third victim. For the last ten days, the combined team from the sheriff's department and TCPD had been following up on the evidence and were finally getting together to share their findings. Gilda, Quinn, Flint, Buzz, and Vernadeane were present. Earlier that morning, Chief Yeager had been called to a disturbance in the Walmart parking lot, so he was running late.

"Okay, let's get started," Gilda said. "I know you folks have been working round the clock to catch this guy, and I appreciate your efforts. Who wants to go first?"

"I will," Quinn replied. "I saw Connie Jordan three days ago, and she said the kid on the convenience store tape was the same guy who'd washed his clothing at the laundromat where she works. No hesitation at all in her decision."

"Anything else?" Gilda asked.

"We've also identified the convenience store victim from pictures of his tattoos that Doc Roberts took during his autopsy," Quinn continued. "He was known as Moose and lived in the Pines. Those who knew him said he was a loner and pitched his tent away from the others. No one knew anything more about him, except his tatts were distinctive works of art, making the partial identification possible."

"Another anonymous person, like Riley," Flint said.

"Quinn and I encountered him in the Pines just after the department cut down the tree branches. He was angry and felt we were exposing them," Vernadeane added.

"Okay, at least we have a start," Gilda said. "Did Doc say anything about Moose having his throat cut or finding a pill on his tongue?"

"Negative on both," Quinn replied. "Doc thinks the kill started as an accident and turned into murder after the kid saw he'd run over a homeless guy. That hypothesis also fits our idea that we've got hate crimes against the homeless. Let me show the surveillance tape so you can see what I mean."

Quinn projected the image on the conference room screen. They watched as the kid backed his car out of the 7-Eleven parking spot and turned the steering wheel tightly to the right to avoid a dumpster. When he feels the back end of his car rising, he gets out and looks.

"Okay, I'm gonna stop the tape right here. Doc and I think the kid changes right here. Look at his expression," Quinn says, using a pointer to touch the kid's face. "Pure hatred when he sees he's run over a homeless person. He then goes into a killing frenzy and runs back and forth over the body. This murder wasn't planned like the other two. More likely, it was a spontaneous action fueled by hatred for homeless people."

"Uffda. We've got a real whacko here. Now, if we could just identify him."

"Hang on. We've got new information from Michael Stafford's murder that might point us in that direction," Buzz said. "Results from Trace Evidence indicate the fibers we found in Michael Stafford's neck wound matched the fibers found in the debris from the dryer vent. It's another confirmation that the kid who washed his clothes at the laundromat is our guy."

"Good police work," Quinn said. "What about the DNA swabs? Anything there?"

"Nothing," Buzz replied. "The residue had been too degraded by the washer."

"What about results from the passenger manifests for the California flights?" Gilda asked.

"Getting to it, sheriff. Of the eleven one-way tickets flying from LAX through O'Hare into TC, three were couples who'd been visiting relatives on the West Coast and returned home because of COVID. Four were businessmen who'd been doing extended work projects in Southern California and also returned due to the pandemic. None of them are suspects."

"That leaves one passenger," Gilda said.

"Right. A 19-year-old male from Santa Monica by the name David Lathrop."

"Here we go," Flint said.

"We couldn't find a single listing for any Lathrop in Traverse City, so we started looking back in Santa Monica at the address provided on his ticket."

"What'd you learn?"

"The address turned out to be for a David Lathrop Sr. We called the number for the senior Lathrop, and it was the 19-year-old's father. He was cooperative but concerned. Right away, he asked what this was about."

"Hmmm."

"I told him we wanted to ask his son some questions, but we couldn't locate any Lathrops in TC. Senior said his ex-wife lived in Traverse City. They'd sent David here because they thought it would be a better place to weather the pandemic. After their divorce, Senior said his former wife had gone back to her maiden name, Susan Pugh. He didn't have her address but knew she'd recently moved to a new loft apartment at The Commons. Gave us her cell number."

"That it?"

"Not quite. I asked whether David had been in any trouble while in California, and the father hesitated. He went on to say David graduated from high school but had some run-ins with the law. At first, he had minor shoplifting incidents, stealing money from his mother's purse and setting fires in their backyard. Then, in his late teens, the kid became agitated and developed serious anger issues. Dad said he'd also been arrested and released for beating up classmates who'd bullied him," Buzz said.

"This is getting interesting," Quinn added. "Let me guess. They put him on Olanzapine to manage his symptoms."

"You got it. Zyprexa. 15 mg. The little blue oval pill."

"Shit. You get ahold of the mom?" Quinn asked.

"I did. After I talked to Senior, I called the mom right away and asked whether David was home. Before Susan answered, she expressed concern and wanted to know what this was about. I told her we just wanted to ask him some questions. She told us he wasn't there but gave us his cell phone so we could call him ourselves."

"Oh, man. We've gotta find this kid before he does it again," Gilda said.

Just then, Gilda's phone rang. "Sheriff Hanson," she said. "Yeah, what can I do for you, Chief?" She listened and finally said, "Sonovabitch. We'll be right there, Hank." She clicked her phone off and stood up. "We're too late. He's done it again. Another homeless person. This one is a woman living out of her car parked in Walmart."

"Our killer is ramping up," Quinn said. "It's just ten days since he killed Moose."

Chapter 26: That Afternoon

Buzz, Quinn, Flint, and Gilda piled into the Sheriff's Jeep Grand Cherokee and headed to the crime scene. Buzz tried David's cell phone again. When he didn't answer, Buzz called the mother to get an update on her son's whereabouts.

"I haven't seen him in the last 48 hours," she said. "But that's not unusual," she added. "He often keeps weird hours."

"Any idea where he is?" Buzz asked. "Friends he hangs with. Special places he frequents."

"No clue. I don't think he's been here long enough to develop friendships. I think he's been lonely since coming to Michigan. I sense that he walks and drives around a lot. Sorry, I'm not more help," she said.

"He has a car?" Buzz asked.

"He drives my car, a 2019 cream-colored Acura MDX."

"Okay, let us know when he comes home," Buzz said and hung up. He immediately called dispatch and put out an APB for the Acura, which matched the description of the car that peeled out of the 7-Eleven parking lot.

They reached Walmart, and it was easy to tell where the action was with all the flashing lights and crime scene tape. The medical examiner's van and CSI team were already there. Gilda screeched to a stop, and they all jumped out and ran to the scene.

"We got another one," Ted Roberts said grimly. No corny ME jokes today. "Same MO. Throat slit with a jagged-edged knife. Blue pill on the tongue. This one's a female, though. Looks like one more homeless person living out of a car."

"Have a TOD, doc?" Gilda asked.

"About 36-48 hours ago. Rigor mortis has mostly passed, and secondary relaxation has set in. Decomposition's begun, enhanced by being shut in a car. We're getting temperatures now."

They watched as the ME's technician made a tiny incision in the vic's upper right abdomen and passed a thermometer into the tissue of the liver to measure her core temperature. He'd already taken ambient temperatures of the vehicle's interior when they'd entered the unlocked car. Computer calculations back at the lab would give an exact time of death.

When the tech cut, Gilda groaned and backed away. "Eew," she'd moaned. "I don't understand why you have to carve her up more. Why can't you just get the core temperature through the neck opening?"

"Think about it, Sheriff," Ted said. "Inserting the thermometer into the existing wound might contaminate the evidence. We could've taken a rectal reading, but I decided this was more respectful to a female victim in front of a whole cadre of male officers."

As Gilda lurched away from the open car door where the forensic work was being done, Quinn moved in to get her first close look at the vic.

"I know her," Quinn said, crossing herself. "It's Connie Jordan. The laundromat worker who called in the tip about the kid who'd washed his clothes there."

"Oh, my god, it is," Buzz said. "We're so close."

"Not close enough," Quinn said, thinking of one more homeless person murdered since the mission closed. "We've gotta get ahold of the kid's clothes. I think it's time we get a warrant. I want his phone, too."

"There are fibers in Connie's neck wound, too," Ted said. "We'll expedite to see if they match the others."

"Okay. While CSI finishes up, let's go inside Walmart and check with their security people," Gilda said. "I've worked with them before. Besides eyes on the inside of the store, they keep cameras on their parking lot, too. We should be able to get pictures of the car.

They went upstairs and entered the security department. Banks of large screens were mounted around the room at double depth on the walls. Men seated in mobile office chairs rolled back and forth between computer monitors and keyboards at each workstation. Several were grouped around one set of screens focused on the area of the parking lot where the crime scene was. They looked up when the threesome entered.

"Afternoon, Sheriff," Security Chief Orin Zull said. He nodded at the two detectives. "Looks like all hell's broke loose out there."

"Got a homeless woman murdered, Orin. Someone who's been living out of her car. Hope you can help us."

"She's been a regular in our lot. We've already been working on the tapes for the last couple of days. You have a TOD yet?"

"ME says 36-48 hours."

"So that puts the murder at late Thursday night or early Friday morning. Let's see what we've got."

The security guys already had the tape queued up to the correct approximate spot. They rolled it on all screens so everyone could watch and give input. A few minutes into the surveillance footage, a light-colored SUV pulled up next to a Honda beater.

"That's him," Buzz said. "I can tell by the Acura's caliper logo on the front grill."

They watched as a male got out of the automobile and walked towards Connie's CR-V. He was dressed in jeans and a cotton tan worker jacket.

"Same stuff he had on at the laundromat and convenience store," Quinn commented.

He also wore a baseball cap and a COVID mask. His right hand hung low at his side, holding something, but they couldn't make out what.

"Fucking masks. Can't see any of his face," Gilda said.

"FC2'll be able to enhance the images," Quinn reassured.

"And who around here wears a Dodgers cap," Buzz added. "It's our California guy."

They watched as he pulled open Connie's driver-side door. Didn't look like it'd been locked. It was hard to tell in the dark what was happening, but there seemed to be a short struggle. Connie's hands had gone into the air for a few seconds. It appeared she was trying to get up from her car seat. Then she quickly fell back, like he'd pushed her back, maybe. Her arms continued to flail, though. The man next leaned into the car, and they could see him hovering over her. His arms were moving inside the car. Probably when he was slitting her throat. Then the action stopped, and the kid just stood there looking. Finally, he pulled something from his pocket, and he stooped, his arm going inside the car. They couldn't see what he was doing, but they guessed he'd placed the pill on Connie's tongue. The kid quickly slammed her car door, ran to his mother's Acura, and took off.

"That's it. We've got him. Orin, thanks. We'll need to take the tape with us," Gilda said.

They left the security department and walked through the parking lot. They noticed the ME had left for the morgue with Connie's body, numerous cop cars had moved on to other calls, and only one CSI van was left, further processing the interior of her car.

"Let's head to FC2 and get the paperwork going for warrants. See if we can line up a judge to sign them," Quinn said. "This is one case where we want our ducks in a row."

Chapter 27: May 23

The team hadn't had any luck finding David Lathrop overnight, so Quinn decided to head out with Ruby to take pictures of spring flowers. They'd just passed Bingham Road on M-22 going up the Leelanau Peninsula when her phone rang.

"Macarthy," she answered curtly, not wanting to be disturbed on her day off.

"Quinn, it's Buzz. Where are you?"

"Out taking pictures of blooming trees and flowers. It's Saturday, in case you forgot."

"Susan Pugh just called and said David had come home sometime during the night but had taken off again on foot. I think we need to get over there."

"I hear you. Let me drop my dog off at home and stop by the office to see if the warrants are ready. Meet you at the Commons."

"I'm already in the parking lot at FC2. I'll wait for you here. Gilda's on her way, too. Maybe we should also alert CSI."

An hour later, they arrived at Building 50, where Pugh's luxury loft was located. The entourage of three detectives and three CSI techs parked in front and entered the massive building, not exactly sure where her apartment was. Luckily, with the help of signage, they found her space and knocked on the door. She'd been waiting for them and opened immediately. She was an attractive woman in her late fifties, but the stress of dealing with her son was evident. Worry lines creased her forehead, and her eyes were red, either from crying or lack of sleep.

"You've got to find my son," Pugh said. "I'm worried he'll harm himself."

"We're concerned, too," Quinn said. "Unfortunately, we've also got some compelling evidence he's involved in the murders of several homeless people."

"No way! I know he hated those people in the Pines, but I don't think Davey's a killer."

"We can get to that later, ma'am," Buzz said. "Right now, we've got warrants to search your apartment, especially David's room, for clothing, medication, and his phone. Another one for your car, the Acura MDX. Is that here?"

"Yes, it's down in the parking garage," Pugh replied. "What medication are you talking about?"

"The Olanzapine he's been prescribed," Gilda said.

"How'd you find out about that?"

"We talked to his father, David Lathrop, Sr. In Santa Monica."

"Shit! He's gonna kill me for not keeping Davey on a regular medication schedule. But my son's an adult now. Nineteen years old. He should be able to manage his own medication."

They walked away from Pugh towards David's bedroom and bath. The CSI team went downstairs to work on the Acura.

Buzz and Gilda went into the bedroom and quickly picked David's tan fleece-lined jacket from the floor. A dark substance stained the right sleeve from the elbow to the wrist. They packaged it in an evidence bag for testing. Gilda found a Dodgers baseball cap on the edge of a dresser and bagged it, too. Next, they spotted a phone on the nightstand attached to a charger. Donning nitrile gloves, Buzz removed it from the bedside table and tapped the screen. It was locked. He looked over at Pugh, who'd been leaning against the door jamb watching them dismantle her son's room.

"You know the passcode?" he asked.

"Yes, it's on my plan, so I set it up. Try 101761. My birthdate."

Hoping David hadn't changed the code without his mother knowing, Buzz punched in the numbers. He stepped back in surprise when a skull with antlers came up on the screen.

"Jesus," Gilda said. "What's this kid into?"

"Think it might be an album cover," Buzz said as he read *Skeletonwitch. I am of Death (Hell has arrived).*

Buzz toggled to Settings and then Location Services. He scrolled through the recent listings and found what he was looking for: a map of the Walmart parking lot at 11:48 p.m. on May 21.

"Got him," Gilda said as she held out an evidence bag for Buzz to drop the phone into.

They walked into David's bathroom to see how Quinn was doing processing evidence there. She'd already bagged a bottle containing the remains of a 90-day supply of Olanzapine. She also confiscated a toothbrush and comb containing some of David's hair for DNA analysis. Now Quinn was working on the sink. She'd sprayed it with luminol, and the whole basin glowed blue, indicating the presence of blood. She was painstakingly swabbing the blue areas and placing them in sterile tubes for transport. She was just about done when CSI walked into the room.

"Look what we found under the seat of the Acura." one tech said as he held out a small, serrated folding pocketknife inside an evidence bag.

"What a hiding spot for a murder weapon. I'm not sure the kid was thinking straight. You get anything else off the vehicle?" Gilda asked.

"Lots of trace. Blood, too."

"Okay, let's get this stuff back to FC2," Quinn said. "I'm calling in the whole staff so we can process this evidence within the next couple hours. Also, get a plan going for finding David."

Chapter 28: Mid-Afternoon

One reason Quinn loved working at FC2 was the dedication of the staff to crime fighting. On a beautiful Saturday, all but one had responded to her message to come in on their day off. The only non-responder was in Chicago for his daughter's wedding. Everyone had arrived and was ready to work within thirty minutes. Someone ordered pizzas and subs so they could stay through the afternoon. Even though they had to prepare the forensic samples before running tests on them, they finished processing most of the evidence around 3 p.m. and sat down in the conference room to share their findings.

Doc Roberts started, "First, let me say I'm amazed at the work ethic of this crew. To give up your weekend to get this murder solved is something. I haven't been here long, but I'm proud to be part of this outstanding lab."

"Weekend?" Yancy Irving from Trace Evidence quipped. "We working tomorrow too?"

Everybody laughed.

Doc continued, "With our own rapid DNA lab, we were able to extract identifiers from David's toothbrush and hairs on his comb. I know we haven't met yet for Connie Jordan's autopsy results, but two findings are especially relevant. We found major defensive wounds on her hands and arms. She fought for her life, and the perpetrator's body should show evidence of that. She must've clawed him, and we found skin under her fingernails that matched the DNA from David's toothbrush and hair."

"What else did you discover?" Gilda asked.

"When we cast the wound in Connie's throat, the serrations matched the knife found under the Acura's driver's seat," Doc said. "Interestingly, it didn't match the serrations for the knife that killed Michael. The two were very similar, but not exact. We still have to find that second murder weapon."

"Who else has results to share?" Quinn asked.

Yancy said, "The fibers found in the neck wounds for both Michael Stafford and Connie Jordan matched the fleece lining of David's coat. It clearly puts him at both scenes."

Quinn turned to Buzz and asked, "You find anything out about the Olanzapine we found in David's bathroom?"

"Yeah. The imprint codes from the pills in Michael and Connie's mouths were the same as the ones we found in David's bathroom."

Bea Hillman from the FC2 Multimedia Department spoke next. "I've found two more links connecting David to the crime scene. I enhanced the surveillance tape from Walmart's security camera and put it through facial recognition. It was a perfect match to both his driver's license and a high school yearbook picture we found online."

"Wonderful work, Bea. What was the second piece you found?" Quinn asked.

"I went through David's iPhone more completely. Found that his GPS history put him not only at the Walmart crime scene but also at Boardman Lake early the morning of April 7, when Michael Stafford was killed. The kid hung out near the Pines on several days, too, including March 5, when Riley was murdered. I then decided to trace David's whereabouts throughout The Commons. He visited several trails there, but three he frequented often. I've printed out maps for each. Maybe they'll be helpful when you start the physical search for him."

"Thanks, Bea. I think we're about ready to get going with that," Quinn said. "Anybody have anything else?"

"What about the blood samples you took from David's bathroom sink? You have any luck with that?" Buzz asked.

"It's in the works," Yancy said. "Blood DNA takes a bit longer to process. Should have it tonight or early tomorrow."

"Thanks, everyone," Quinn said. "We definitely have enough evidence to identify David as our killer of these homeless folks. I think that's all for today. Enjoy the rest of your weekend."

As the team closed their labs and left FC2, Quinn, Gilda, and Buzz worked on their next steps. First, they familiarized themselves with Bea's printed maps of The Commons. While they'd responded to police calls there before, none of them had walked the trails that David seemed to frequent. Next, they called Susan Pugh to see if she'd heard from her son, and she hadn't. Finally, they called in available officers from the TCPD and the Sheriff's Department to organize themselves and get ready to execute the search process before darkness set in.

Just as the threesome walked to Gilda's Jeep, Buzz turned and asked, "Should we call in the dogs too?"

Chapter 29: That Evening

State Police Trooper Nick Wagner and his Belgian Malinois sniffer dog, Grit, had joined the search team heading to The Commons. The breed was known for its keen sense of smell and ability to sniff out explosives, animal scat, and even cancer. Following David Lathrop's wanderings in The Commons normally wouldn't be a challenge for Grit, except they only had the young man's outerwear jacket. They stopped by his mother's apartment to get something riper and ended up with an undershirt.

Grit strained at his leash after they allowed him to scent David's clothing outside Pugh's apartment. They expected the dog to head outside Building 50, but instead, he went downstairs to the underground tunnels that connected the buildings of the old Traverse City State Hospital. At one time, the tunnels had been filled with steam pipes and electrical conduits. Some tunnels were also used as shafts to transport fresh air throughout the asylum. When the Minervini Group started renovating the historic buildings in 2000, the tunnels were retained to run data cables, hold fire suppression pumps, and age cheese and champagne.

When Grit pulled to enter the Building 50 tunnel, the searchers hesitated. They knew the asylum had a reputation as one of the most haunted places in Michigan after it closed in 1989. Urban explorers regularly got spooked when they visited the abandoned campus. Eerie sensations in certain areas only contributed to the legends. Disembodied screams that echoed through empty halls. Lights that turned themselves on and off at random in unwired buildings. A shadowy figure said to creep around the tunnel basements.

So, when the searchers held back, it was because of the creepy tales they'd heard. Quinn rubbed at her scar. Buzz whispered, "Jesus," as he looked into the subterranean underworld. The primary entrance was damn scary-looking. The arched brick ceiling and walls above the flat brick floor created instant claustrophobic feelings. Sparse lighting cast shadows throughout the lengthy chamber. The tiny white door at the far end gave the appearance of a blank eyeball staring back at them.

Unable to contain Grit any longer, they breathed deeply and followed him inside, moving cautiously on the uneven brick surface. He appeared hot on David's trail until he suddenly stopped a third of the way in. He sniffed around and whined, pulling hard to return to the entrance.

"What's with the dog?" Gilda asked.

"I'm not sure. I've never seen him like this before," Nick said as he shoved David's undershirt at Grit's snout, hoping to re-scent him.

"Maybe the haunted tunnel got to him," Buzz said.

"Or maybe it was the kid who got scared and decided to turn back," Quinn replied.

Whatever the reason, Grit did an about-face and returned to the entrance. Back in the lobby, he sniffed the floor and ran for the outdoor exit. Everyone felt relieved in the fresh air as they followed the dog down Red Drive towards the Historic Barns Park. On their right, sitting on a hill, they passed the Cistern, which had supplied water to the asylum residents. It had become an art sculpture of sorts with colorful graffiti painted on it. They would've noticed the sounds of bubbling hidden streams and the smell of fresh pines if they hadn't been running so hard. Usually, it was a bit of peace in the heart of the city, but not today. They were chasing a killer.

Grit once again came to a halt at the entrance to another trail. A small wooden sign designated it as the fairy trail. Tiny dwellings made of natural materials dotted the dirt pathway. A bird nest fashioned from sticks and tree limbs marked the entrance.

"Is the dog spooked again?" Buzz asked.

"I don't think so," Nick replied. "He senses change with this new trail."

Nick opened his canteen and poured water into a portable dish he carried for the dog. After lapping the water vigorously, Grit turned and sat. Nick passed the undershirt towards the dog's snout, and he turned towards the trail, moseying slowly into the dark woods of the fairy trail. He sniffed the first miniature mansion and moved to the next, a mossy castle made for swamp fairies. The third tiny dwelling was 'White o Mornin' Bed and Breakfast.' Grit stopped walking and lay down.

"What's he doing now?" Gilda asked.

"David's been here. Grit thinks this is the destination," Nick said.

They all stopped and looked around to see if they could spot the kid. A couple of officers stepped into the dense foliage to see if he was nearby. Quinn stooped down and took a closer look at the miniature. The bed and breakfast was outfitted with furniture made from twigs, leaves, moss, and other natural items. On top of a pinecone bed sat a black tactical folding knife covered in blood.

"Holy shit," Quinn muttered. Donning gloves, she turned to Buzz and said, "Hand me an evidence bag. I think we've found the other murder weapon."

While they bagged the knife, the officers fanned further into the woods, looking for other evidence or signs of David Lathrop. Grit stood up and sat in front of Nick, a sign that he was ready to go again. Nick gave his dog another drink of water, a re-sniff of the undershirt, and took off down the rest of the fairy trail, now at a torrid pace. Buzz, Gilda, and Quinn followed, leaving the other officers behind to process the scene.

They passed the labyrinth and ran alongside Red Drive, almost retracing their original steps. Just before Greenspire Middle School, Grit made an abrupt left turn onto the Garfield Trail and then a quick right onto the second Streamside Loop trail. Grit slowed, and Quinn knew where they were heading as they walked deeper into the woods.

"He's going to the Hippie Tree," Quinn said.

"What's that?" Buzz asked.

"It's a huge willow tree that, over the years, has been spray-painted with psychedelic colors. Much of it has rotted and fallen apart. Legend has it the tree got its name from hippies in the 1960s and '70s who used it as a meet-up spot to meditate," Gilda replied. "That's the whimsical interpretation."

Buzz looked puzzled. They'd begun creeping along at a snail's pace as Grit carefully lifted one paw after another as if he was ready to pounce on some hidden prey. "There's more to the story?" Buzz asked.

"Yeah," Quinn said. "Some associate the Hippie Tree with supernatural, otherworldly powers. One especially sinister legend maintains the tree is a portal to hell that can be accessed by walking in a certain direction around it."

Grit suddenly stopped and went into a down position. A foot beyond the dog, David Lathrop lay curled up at the base of the tree. At first, they thought he was dead. But when his foot moved, Gilda drew her Glock. He looked up at them, his face dirty and tear-stained.

"Get up, son," Buzz said. "Your spree is over."

Chapter 30: May 27

It was Ian Doyle's first day back at his office as Traverse City Bureau Chief for the downstate newspaper, *The Chronicle*. He'd worked at his Crystal Lake home since the pandemic had begun and was ambivalent about rejoining a city still rife with COVID. He and Quinn were meeting for lunch at the Little Fleet, where they could eat outdoors. While they'd kept in contact through texts and phone calls, they hadn't seen each other in person since March. Despite social distancing rules, they hugged and laughed when they saw their unkempt hair peeking out from their Tigers caps.

"So good to see you," Ian exclaimed. "I'd begun to worry we'd never return to normal."

"We all thought that, but it's great the rules are starting to lighten up, at least here in the Northwoods," Quinn said.

They ordered from one of the food trucks, sat at a picnic table to wait for their lunches to come, and began talking.

"Outstanding work on catching the young homeless killer, Quinn."

"Had some good detective work and a few breaks along the way. Still, four people died in the process."

"Where's the kid now?"

"In the county jail awaiting arraignment."

"You think he'll plead not criminally responsible?"

"I'm expecting it since he's currently waiting for a bed in a psychiatric hospital for evaluation and treatment. Both Vernadeane and Doc think he experienced a psychotic break as a result of withdrawal from the Zyprexa."

"Too bad the mother can't be held for not keeping him on his medications."

"Yeah, pretty hard to do that when David is an adult. At least by age."

Their food came, and they sat down and savored the spicy sandwiches they'd gotten from the Crocodile Palace.

"How's the house coming?" Quinn asked. "You were nearly done last time we talked."

"It's finished. Last of the workmen cleared out over the weekend."

"You happy with the results?"

"Over the top. The new addition with a master suite and home office made the place. We're doing a final cleaning, hanging some pictures, and construction will be history. I hope you'll come to visit soon."

"Can't wait. I don't know how you stood all that upheaval for two years."

They finished their meals and started walking up Front Street. Window shopping longingly, taking in the delight of being outdoors together, and stopping at the street piano to hear a blue-uniformed Interlochen student play Chopin's Raindrop Prelude. The young woman had drawn quite a crowd. Quinn couldn't help but remember when she'd been here almost ten days earlier, and Mack was junked up on drugs, pounding away on the keys. She and Vernadeane had gotten him to Street Medicine, but he'd walked out at the suggestion of rehab. Nobody had seen him since.

"You been out shooting lately? Lots going on with spring flowers popping and the bird migration in full swing?"

"Not much, and I miss it. Been too busy with the homeless murders. Patrick and I did get out a couple of weeks ago to visit the new peregrine falcon breeding center going in north of the city."

"Huh, hadn't heard about that."

"Yeah, it's pretty exciting. A sheik from Dubai is hoping to repopulate the peregrine falcon population in northwestern Lower Michigan. They've been successful doing it near the Detroit River and Western Lake Erie and think our area will be even better due to the cooler climate and nearby dune habitat. He's building quite the complex near the tip of Old Mission. Can't wait to learn more."

"Sounds interesting, Quinn. Right up your alley."

Chapter 31: June 3

In one of the courtyards at FC2, they'd erected a large tent so they could hold as many meetings outside as the weather allowed. Everyone was sick of masking, so gathering outdoors where COVID rules were relaxed seemed like a good solution. The tent had also become the team's favorite spot to eat lunch and take breaks. Today, they were meeting there so Gilda could update them on the David Lathrop case.

"Lathrop Senior arrived in Traverse City with his attorney and son's psychiatrist as soon as he learned Davey was taken into custody," Gilda said.

"That must've cost a pretty penny," Flint added.

"When his doctor saw the state the kid was in, he raised hell and immediately got him transferred to the emergency room so he could begin treatment."

"Why the ER?" Quinn asked.

"There are no beds available in any of the psychiatric hospitals right now. It could be weeks before one opens up," Vernadeane replied.

"So, did the shrink have input into what was going on with Davey?" Buzz asked.

"Yeah, he said the kid was having acute symptoms of sudden withdrawal from his antipsychotic medication. The dizziness, headaches, agitation, and profuse sweating were part of it, but worse was the kid's developing psychosis. Davey completely lost touch with reality, heard voices, and exhibited intense anger. By the time the father and psychiatrist arrived, the kid was actively hallucinating," Vernadeane explained.

"Jesus," Quinn said. "And all this was happening in a jail cell?"

"You got it," Vernadeane answered. "Any more recent news on what's happening since the kid was hospitalized?

"Uh huh," Gilda replied. "Davey was stabilized during the ER stay and released back into police custody on Monday."

"Geez Louise, so he's back in jail," Flint said. "That doesn't seem right."

"It's the best that we could do. He'll be under constant medical supervision until a psych bed becomes available," Gilda said. "Remember, David Lathrop is still a murderer responsible for the deaths of four homeless people."

"That it?" Buzz asked.

"One more thing. David was arraigned yesterday via Zoom," Gilda said. "It was a very intense hearing with both the psychiatrist and Senior giving the kid's history and treatment. Both put considerable blame on the ex-wife for not keeping their son on his medication."

"Let me guess," Buzz said. "He pled guilty to an NCR charge."

Gilda nodded.

"I know we want David to pay for the homeless murders, but it sounds like Not Criminally Responsible fits the kid," Quinn said. "At least he'll be kept away from the public and given psychiatric care."

As the team gathered their belongings to leave the meeting, Gilda's phone rang.

"Sheriff Hansen," she answered. She listened and nodded her head several times. Finally, she told the caller to notify the ME and CSI to meet them at the scene.

"We got a DB in the woods behind Centre Ice," Gilda said. "Looks like another homeless man. Let's go."

"How could that be?" Buzz said as he grabbed his jacket. "We already caught the killer."

"Not all dead homeless people are murdered," Vernadeane snapped.

As they exited the building for the short trip down Garfield and Hammond to Centre Ice, Quinn felt bile rise into her throat. For the second time in two months, her jawline scar began to tingle and itch. She absently brushed her hand against it, praying her gut was wrong about who the dead body belonged to.

As the investigators disembarked from Gil's Jeep, they wound through the crowd of medical and emergency personnel. The ME's van was already there, and they could see the CSI's camera flashing in the distance. Quinn led the way, but when she caught sight of neon sneakers on the victim, she cried out and began to run. Vernadeane followed closely in her footsteps. Quinn knelt and cradled Mack's body, weeping openly. No one stopped her from disturbing the scene.

Finally, Ted Roberts began dictating into his lapel mic, "Fifty to sixty-year-old Caucasian male found deceased in the trees behind Centre Ice Arena. Nearby sleeping bag and backpack of personal possessions indicate the vic may be homeless. No identification on the person. No signs of violence at the scene. Spotted by the lawn maintenance crew ninety minutes ago. Said he hadn't been here late yesterday when they were planting shrubbery. The Centre Ice manager reported the vic hung around the rink during hockey season and went by Mack. Rigor mortis is set, indicating he's been dead for two to six hours. Bluish-purple skin tone suggests possible overdose, as do blue fingernails and frothy foam around the mouth. No drug paraphernalia on the person, but tin foil litter was found near the backpack."

As they lifted Mack's lifeless body into the van, Quinn wailed, "Oh, Keegan Cammack. How could we let this happen to you? *Ar dheis De' go raibh a anam*. May your soul be at God's right hand."

Chapter 32: June 12

Quinn had taken a week off work to sort out her feelings about Mack's death and plan his memorial. She'd be damned if she'd let him be buried in a pauper's grave. COVID was still preventing large indoor gatherings, so she'd planned a small outdoor service at the Catholic cemetery. She expected a few law enforcement friends of hers to attend, plus some who knew him from Centre Ice. Her brother Rowan, the FBI agent working out of the Cleveland office, also decided to come because he and Keegan had played hockey together at WMU. Her parents were going to rent a cabin near the Platte River for the last two weeks in June but found out it was available, so they came north early. Being avid Red Wings fans, they decided to attend the service too. Quinn expected there to be fifteen to twenty at best.

Ian wrote a eulogy for Keegan Cammack in his downstate newspaper, *The Chronicle*. It ran throughout the Detroit area. *The Record-Eagle* picked it up through the wire services. It told of Mack's illustrious career for fifteen seasons as a professional hockey player with the Red Wings and other teams. His downfall that began with repeated blows to the head, several concussions, and eventually Chronic Traumatic Encephalopathy. Depression, difficulty thinking, memory loss, and emotional instability led to drug use and then homelessness. He closed the eulogy with both a plea and a charge to find solutions to the dual problems of opioid overdose and homelessness.

So when the hearse containing Mack's body, and Quinn, Gilda, Patrick, Rowan, and her parents as passengers, wended its way through the winding cemetery paths, Quinn was surprised at the number of people walking towards the burial site wearing masks and sporting purple ribbons for homeless awareness. Her eyes were already red from crying, but the sight of this tribute to Mack started the tears again. The shiny black hearse pulled close to the grave, and the funeral directors helped pull Mack's coffin onto a wheeled cart. They all walked alongside it, their hands touching the burnished cherry casket until it was placed on the bier. The director set a spray of red and white roses on top of it. Everyone took seats, and the priest began the short service. Quinn tried to pay attention, but her thoughts went to viewing Mack in the coffin before they'd closed the lid. He'd looked so dignified. Clean, freshly shaven, with a new navy blue suit, crisp white shirt, and green tie. His neon sneakers were the only reminder of his homelessness. Quinn jerked to attention as the priest began the benediction, and Mack was lowered into his final resting place. They all stood and, one by one, gently tossed the red and white roses they'd been given earlier onto the casket. By the time all the attendees had filed past to pay their last respects, the open maw was a sea of Red Wings red and white.

As Quinn, her family, and friends stood at the gravesite and watched, they heard a text tone go off. She turned and saw Buzz look down at his phone, then nod to Gilda and Vernadeane to follow him.

"There's another disturbance at the library," Buzz whispered.

"Jesus," Gilda added. "It's only been open ten days, and already we've had eleven calls. What is it this time?"

"Someone set fire to toilet paper in the bathroom," Buzz replied. "It was a minor incident, and they were able to put it out without calling the fire department, but they can't get the person who did it to leave."

"Sounds like another homeless person seeking shelter," Vernadeane said. "Let's go see how we can help."

Before the pandemic, the library was one of the places homeless people went when the Middle Coast Mission closed in the morning. They also went to a nearby church for breakfast. The Boys and Girls Club building was open too for computer use, games, and conversation until 2 p.m. when school let out, and the kids came for enrichment activities. When COVID shut down MCM and all the other regular haunts homeless people frequented, they had no place to go. With the library resuming hours on the first of June, it became the de facto day shelter. But the library hadn't been prepared for the onslaught of problems the reopening caused. While most homeless people peaceably came to read and use the computers, a few ruined it for the others. Obvious drug use and smoking at the library entrance deterred regular patrons from going in. Loud, colorful language disturbed the interior quiet. Several loyal volunteers had quit when they couldn't wake up an intoxicated individual and had to call an ambulance.

As they pulled the squad car in front of the library, the director was waiting for them. Buzz, Gilda, and Vernadeane ran towards the entrance.

"He's barricaded himself in the handicapped stall in the men's bathroom," the director said. "I'm afraid he's gonna set us on fire again."

Buzz and Gilda flew inside but found a different story. The homeless man had opened the door to the stall and was sitting on the toilet with his pants down, unrolling toilet paper onto the floor into an increasingly large pile. He must've heard their sirens. The director had been right about the possibility of another fire. The guy was so drunk they could smell the whiskey on his breath almost as soon as they'd entered.

"Come on, buster," Buzz said. "Pull up your pants, and let's get you outa here."

While they escorted the man to the back of the squad car for his probable stay in the drunk tank, Vernadeane attempted to soothe the director about the increasingly violent problems at the library. She promised to get a police officer assigned permanently there. But when she brought up getting the staff trained in using naloxone for overdoses and how to handle incidents empathically, the director scoffed, "Pfft. Not what I signed up for," and walked away.

Chapter 33: That Evening

Driving home after settling the account with the funeral home, Quinn wasn't sure she was up to a house full of family and friends. They were bringing dinner, saying she had to eat and they didn't want her spending the evening alone. They'd been so supportive, but they didn't understand all she was going through. They'd chalked up her friendship with Mack to empathy for homeless people. Gilda worried Quinn blurred professional boundaries with someone she might have to arrest someday. And her dad. If she heard him warn her one more time to be careful around homeless men, she'd explode.

Quinn knew they'd also been concerned about her moodiness since Mack's death. She could read it on their faces and in their actions. They tried to soothe her during crying bouts. Seeing her express such pain made them uncomfortable. Her sudden, intense anger had thrown them off guard, too. The outburst at the funeral director, when she insisted on burying Mack in his neon sneakers, had shocked Gilda. As did her snapping at Patrick when he suggested they head out in nature to take pictures, something that'd always brought her peace.

But her close friends and family had missed what was going on beneath the grief and anger. Quinn didn't fault them for not understanding because she hadn't spoken up. She was just figuring it out herself. Her real struggle was not being able to do anything about Mack's situation. Feeling helpless at not getting him into treatment or finding him housing. She knew it went further than Mack, though. A miasma of despair kept her discouraged about these same issues in the community. No real solutions to the affordable housing crisis. The drug scourge impacting so many lives. When she added in the continuing pandemic, the helplessness felt overwhelming. Quinn knew she'd been bogged down by these concerns for a while, but Mack's death had brought them to the surface.

When Quick drove into her garage and entered the house, Ruby jumped all over her, wound up from all the visitors. Her friends had set up chairs and tray tables in her fenced side yard. Hannah and Ian had brought homemade lasagna, Patrick made a fresh green salad, and Gilda provided Moomers and fudge topping for dessert. Rowan had picked up a case of Harp's Lager, knowing it might be more palatable to some than Guinness. While they didn't eat in total silence, talk was at a minimum because they didn't know what to say without triggering Quinn's emotions. Her dad Sullivan finished his meal and began fiddling with her wood-burning chiminea, finally coaxing a fire to life. Patrick tossed the Chuckit Flying Squirrel to Ruby and let her retrieve it. Everyone was finally relaxed, settling in as the evening's last light waned.

Quinn started it off, her voice quivering, fighting for control, "Thank you for all your support during this tough time. You are family to me. I know you don't get how I became close to Mack. It's something I don't fully understand myself. I remember the first time I heard him shout, 'Hey, right winger, good game!' and I raised my stick to him. Then, talking with him in the Blue Line Bar, I saw he was so full of life despite his circumstances. Humble too, not letting me buy him lunch or even share my French fries."

They stared into the dancing flames of the chiminea as Quinn talked. Only chirping crickets and a wood thrush's *pit, pit, pit* punctuated the silence.

"But I could tell Mack was hurting despite his enthusiasm for the game. The pain from the concussion symptoms and CTE. Headaches, memory loss, messed up thinking, and emotional problems. All were a result of the sport he loved."

Living in a hockey town and following Quinn's playing in the women's league, they all knew what concussions could lead to. Luckily, with newer protocols and better headgear, players were experiencing less of that.

"Throw in being homeless and having to live in the elements, Mack didn't stand a chance," Quinn continued. "I can see why drugs became his escape of choice. Except for Street Medicine, Vernadeane, and me, he had no social support. What else could he do?"

Quinn was letting them in. She'd already told them more about Mack than she had before. They continued to listen, noticing tears shining on her face in the glow of the fire.

"But here's the honest-to-God fucking truth," Quinn said, her voice low and intense. "I feel responsible for Mack's death. Couldn't convince him to go into rehab. Incapable of finding him affordable housing. But, guys, he's not the only one. There are hundreds more just like Mack suffering from the same shit in our community. If I couldn't help one man I cared about, how can I make a dent in reaching others? The situation feels so hopeless."

"Jesus, Quinn," Gilda said. "I'm beginning to think you have some kind of savior complex. Look at what you've already done."

Quinn glared at her.

"Yeah," Patrick added. "You're a damn good detective. Consider the work you did on the Lathrop case for a start. Also, all the volunteering and training you've done with the Homeless Alliance. One person can only do so much."

"Well, it's not enough. We've got to do more," Quinn insisted. "Advocate more effectively for homeless folks. Get our local government on board with affordable housing projects. Step up our work to stop the influx of drugs into our community. Maybe if we all got on board, we could make a difference. We've supported each other on projects before. Why not this? Perhaps as a way to honor Mack's memory."

"Here we go. Another 'it takes a village' rah-rah speech," Gilda said.

"You're either with me, or you're not."

The two women stared at each other for seconds that seemed more like minutes. Quinn's eyes burned with anger at her friend's second snarky remark.

Finally, Gilda said, "I'm sorry, Quinn. We're with you all the way. But sometimes, we feel just as helpless as you."

Chapter 34: June 15

Quinn was in catch-up mode after returning to work from bereavement leave. She'd just gotten off the phone with Patrick, who'd asked if she would be up for a photo shoot in the next week or so, and she said she would be. He seemed as warm and friendly as ever. She missed seeing the goof regularly since they weren't currently working a case together.

The Medical Examiner had gotten back the lab results from Mack's autopsy. Doc suspected Mack had died from an overdose of fentanyl when CSI found tin foil near the deceased's body. Fentanyl users typically crush their pills and place the drug dust on tin foil. Then, they hold a flame under the foil and inhale the smoke using a straw-like tool. The drug was completely odorless, making it perfect for homeless people to use inside their tents without detection.

So when Doc Roberts found Quinn alone in her office, he came in to personally share the toxicology report on Mack's cause of death.

"Mack died from an overdose of synthetic opioid, this one a fentanyl-laced product," doc explained. He went on to say an IMF, or Illicitly Made Fentanyl, was manufactured as a powder, then mixed with drugs like heroin, cocaine, or methamphetamine and made into pills resembling prescription opioids. "They're the most dangerous types of drugs, Quinn. And the most common involved in overdose deaths."

"This wasn't pharmaceutical fentanyl, right?"

"Correct. It was not prescribed by a doctor to treat pain. It was a trafficked illegal drug. Cheap, too, making it a popular choice among homeless folks. Fifty to a hundred times more potent than morphine."

"Seriously? What about Mack's brain? Did you see evidence of CTE in the autopsy?"

"Yes, unfortunately. There was degeneration of the brain tissue and abnormal deposits of tau and other proteins throughout his brain."

"What does that mean?"

"In a healthy brain, tau has a role in maintaining the structural stability of the organ. In a diseased brain, the tau disassembles and forms clumps that kill brain cells. Mack's brain was advanced in that process, and most likely the cause of headaches, decline in memory, poor impulse control, and maybe even suicidal behavior."

"So, Mack might've killed himself?"

"Not an intentional suicide, but he was not well enough to make wise decisions."

"Mack was really ill."

"He was, Quinn. I wouldn't have expected him to live much longer."

Quinn wasn't sure if the autopsy report made her feel better or worse about Mack. At least the results took her off an emotional plane and gave her some medical understanding of what her friend had been going through. Maybe she could cut herself some slack about being responsible for his death. It was clear Mack was too far gone physically to be helped. At least she'd done her best to be a supportive friend. So far, no one had bought into her ideas about working on the homeless situation in Traverse City. Nor had they been enthusiastic about stepping up their efforts to stop drugs flowing into the community. Probably felt they were already overwhelmed with drug busts, sniffer dogs, and education programs in the schools. She felt she was still good with Patrick and Ian but hadn't had any contact with Gilda since the dinner following Mack's service. It wasn't like her to be this standoffish. Maybe she was embarrassed at her sarcastic comments. It wouldn't be the first time.

Chapter 35: June 29

Quinn had taken the day off, using some of the comp time she'd accrued during the Lathrop case. Her parents were leaving their rented cottage in two days, and she wanted to spend some time with them before they went home. They were retired and in their early eighties. Her dad was in excellent health and physically active. Her mom, however, was crippled with rheumatoid arthritis and used a walker to get around. She was content to spend her time reading and watching television, but her dad was going stir-crazy with a sedentary lifestyle different from the years he'd spent as a Highland Park PD detective.

She'd arrived early in the morning at their rental near Boekeloo Road, not far from Platte Point. They'd planned to tour the Point Betsie Lighthouse just north of Frankfort and then see Ian and Hannah's newly renovated home on Crystal Lake. Afterward, the five of them would share a meal at The Manitou. But her mom had begged off at the last minute, saying she wanted to save her energy for lunch.

"She's doing that more and more, Pix," her dad Sullivan said.

"I wonder if she's trying to care for you in her own way. Knowing you need time for yourself away from all the household responsibilities you've taken on since her illness."

Quinn pulled into one of the few roadside parking spots near the Point Betsie Light, and she and her dad grabbed their cameras and headed down to the beach. She and her brothers had gone together to surprise him with a 40x zoom point-and-shoot camera last Christmas, hoping it would spur him to a new hobby that'd get him outside in nature. Turns out, it had.

The beach was nearly empty due to high winds. Surf kicked up along the rusty metal breakwater. They snapped pictures of the swirling waves and the views beyond. Two kite surfers soared above the roiling swells. Eventually, Quinn and her dad headed up to the quaint, red-roofed lighthouse for more photography. Inside, they climbed the steps to the Lantern, the active navigational aid that guides ships entering the Manitou Passage. The vista was stunning. Waves crashing along the shoreline. The brilliant turquoise waters with Platte Point and the Manitou Islands in the distance. Quinn ached to take pictures from the catwalk, but it wasn't open.

They'd not been gone two hours when Sullivan said, "I think we should head over to the Doyle's house. I don't like leaving your mom alone too long."

"Sure, dad. It's really close by."

They drove to the Doyle's cottage on Hurdmans Bay, a short distance from M-22. As they pulled into the driveway, she hardly recognized the place. The new addition blended right in with the original cottage, all of it re-sided in barn red vinyl with white trim. Hannah and Ian had seen them arrive and met them at the front door.

"Where's Mrs. Macarthy?" Hannah asked.

"She doesn't have a lot of energy these days," Sullivan said. "She wanted to save it for lunch, so we'll pick her up and then meet you at The Manitou when we're done here."

Ian and Hannah took Quinn and her dad on the tour. Sullivan snapped pictures so he could share them with his wife later. The great room and kitchen they'd demolished walls to create. A massive fireplace at one end. State-of-art kitchen at the other. They'd also knocked down walls between two small bedrooms to make one large guest room. They moved on to the addition they'd put up on the extra half lot that came with their purchase. A large master suite that included a sitting area and bath. Another room off the suite served as Ian's home office.

"Now you've gotta see this," Ian said as he opened sliders to the lakeside.

"I insisted we have a screened porch like we did in Royal Oak, but there wasn't room."

"So, we now have a screened gazebo," Ian said, showing off the last part of his project. The gazebo was stained to match the house siding and was flanked by composite decking. A new grill stood ready to be used, and comfortable outdoor furniture filled the gazebo.

"You, guys. This is amazing," Quinn said. "I can't believe you did it yourself."

"Well, mostly. At first, anyway. When I got the TC Bureau Chief job, I got a raise, and I started hiring out more. We got sick of living in the mess full time," Ian said.

"Listen, Dad and I are gonna head back to get mom. Let's meet at The Manitou in an hour."

Quinn and Sullivan returned to the rental and found mom dozing in her chair. Sullivan immediately got his iPad and wirelessly transferred all the pictures he'd taken from Point Betsie and the Doyle's home. After Quinn's mom awakened, they headed to lunch.

Located in the middle of nowhere, The Manitou screamed Northern Michigan with its log siding, woodsy atmosphere, and fishing lodge appearance. Ever mindful of COVID, they opted for eating on the outdoor patio. They quickly ordered drinks and their entrees, all choosing one of the fish favorites from the menu. Whitefish, perch, or walleye.

"So, you've enjoyed your stay in the Platte area?" Ian asked Quinn's parents.

"Yeah," Sullivan answered. "It'd been nice getting away from the big city, which is about a month behind you coming out of the stay-at-home order."

The server brought their lunches, and everyone dug in, savoring the fine meals.

"I hear you've been hanging out with Arabian royalty, Quinn," Ian said as he ate.

"Not sure he was royalty. Are sheiks part of the royal family?"

"Often in that part of the world, they are. They can also be the head of a tribe or family."

"What'd I miss, Pix? You never told me about meeting a sheik."

"Oh, dad. It was nothing. Patrick learned about a new peregrine falcon breeding facility being built on Old Mission, and we went snooping. We met the owner, Sheik Badr-Uddin, and he told us about the Arabian history of falconry and how the new center will introduce the sport to our county. That's all there is."

"Not from what I hear," Ian said. "According to Patrick, the sheik invited you to dinner."

"Ugh. Wait till I get ahold of him," Quinn continued. "The sheik noticed I was interested in the falconry center. Offered to take me to dinner and tell me more. End of story."

"You be careful, Pixie. I don't know whether I like the idea of you going out alone with one of those, uh..." Sullivan stopped himself short of calling the sheik one of those pejorative terms Arabs are sometimes known by.

"Dad," Quinn scolded, knowing what he was thinking. "I'll be fine."

"Don't worry, Mr. Macarthy. "I'll look into this Sheik Badr-Uddin. Make sure he's okay."

Everyone laughed except Quinn, perturbed by how they all seemed to be into her business.

The server brought key lime pie for dessert, and everyone enjoyed the finishing touch to their meal. Quinn glanced at her watch and saw it was nearing 4 p.m.

"I've got to get my parents back to their cottage and then head to TC for an appointment before tonight's meeting at the governmental center. You still coming, Ian?" Quinn asked.

"I'll be there. Gonna do a big spread on it for the paper," he replied.

"You got two more things on your schedule for today, Pix?" Sullivan asked. "You're gonna be knackered before the day is over."

Chapter 36: That Evening

Quinn pulled her car into the lot at the Governmental Center on Boardman Avenue. Before heading inside, she parked next to the river to check out the ducks swimming below. The building was shared by the city and county, and tonight's meeting included both. She slipped on her mask as she entered the commission chambers, immediately noticing it had been rearranged for social distancing. Ian waved her over to a seat he'd saved, six feet away from him.

"Well, look at you," he said. "How'd you swing that with the salons still closed?"

"My hairdresser's a gem. Did it out of her home. Never had a haircut feel so good."

"Looks good, too. I was beginning to think you were some kind of rocker."

Mayor Janet Perkins rapped the gavel to get everyone's attention. This was her fourth term as Traverse City mayor, and she was known for a hard-ass attitude that got things done.

"Tonight's meeting is our first in-person session since COVID. We've rearranged the room to comply with social distancing mandates. Also, please keep yourselves masked, including when you're talking. COVID numbers are still high in the county. Any questions?"

No one said a thing. A few squirmed in their seats and adjusted their masks as they waited for the mayor to continue. Some were nervous about being in a group setting with the pandemic still raging. But everyone knew how important the topic was and set their fears aside to come.

Mayor Perkins continued, "Our last intergovernmental meeting was a disaster. Not only was it our first via Zoom, but it was also out of control, with people expressing anger, frustration, and ignorance about our topic: Homelessness in Grand Traverse County. When

COVID hit, and the mission closed, hundreds of our people were sent outdoors without shelter. But, the problem has been brewing before the pandemic, with the number of homeless people rising due to a lack of affordable housing in our area. So, tonight, we're going back to basics. We're here to listen to three local experts educate us on what they know about homelessness. We're going to ask questions to deepen our understanding of the situation. We're not doing any voting or decision-making tonight because we first need to be on the same page about the facts. Any questions?"

At first, Quinn thought everyone would keep quiet again, but then she noticed one man squirming in his seat, itching to comment. She realized he was the same person from the Zoom call who'd supported shutting down encampments in the township parks. He raised his hand.

"Please stand and say your name. Speak loudly because we're not using mikes tonight."

"I'm Duane Davies. Garfield Township. I wonder why you're calling these homeless folks "our people" when most of them come from other places to take advantage of our services?"

"Ah, Mr. Davies," Mayor Perkins said, working to keep the sarcasm from her voice. "That's an excellent question and one that will be answered by our first speaker."

While Davies sat down red-faced, Vernadeane came forward, switched on her computer, and projected her presentation notes onto the screens around the chamber.

"I'm Vernadeane Novak, a cop with the Sheriff's Department. I'm also a licensed social worker providing support services to those falling through the cracks in our community. Homeless folks and those with mental health or substance use disorders. Tonight, I'm going to discuss the myths that exist about homeless people and then counter them with the truth according to facts and statistics. We need to understand why people are homeless and why they can't get out of homelessness."

Vernadeane then worked through her PowerPoint. Looking straight at Duane Davies, she said, "The first misconception people have about homelessness is that offering support services exacerbates the problem by drawing unhoused individuals from elsewhere. But the facts tell a different story. There are approximately 260 people in our five-county region experiencing homelessness, and 97% of those are locals."

Vernadeane continued to the other myths, such as homelessness would be solved if people would just get a job. "In reality," she said, "over 45% of unhoused folks have at least one income source, such as disability or social security. Another 17% are employed full or part-time. They just aren't making enough to secure housing."

The third myth Vernadeane debunked was that homelessness is rare among children. "The reality is that 30 families with kids currently experience homelessness in northern Michigan. The numbers are even worse when you consider the TCAPS statistics for kids lacking a fixed, regular, nighttime residence, who don't have adequate clothing, shoes, or hygiene products."

Vernadeane concluded her presentation with the last myth that people are homeless because of mental health or substance abuse issues. "Many believe mental illness and substance abuse cause homelessness when they are more likely the effects," Vernadeane explained. "Substance use is a coping mechanism. When you live on the streets, life is really hard. Mental health issues get worse, and so does substance abuse."

Mayor Perkins called the next speaker, Dr. Shelby Nealon. "I came to Traverse City for the first time ten years ago for my residency in family practice through MSU. I've since made TC my permanent home. I currently head the Street Medicine program that runs a local health clinic and mobile medical unit for the unhoused people in our area. The point I want to get across tonight is that homelessness is a health issue."

Dr. Nealon opened her computer and projected a single page onto the screens. She then read through a recent CDC study that pointed out the differences in health challenges between unsheltered and sheltered people:

Eighty-four percent of unsheltered people experience physical health problems, compared to nineteen percent of sheltered people.

Seventy-eight percent of unsheltered people experience mental health problems, compared to fifty percent of sheltered people.

Seventy-five percent of unsheltered people experience substance abuse conditions, compared to thirteen percent of sheltered people.

Fifty percent of unsheltered people experience tri-morbidity, meaning they have co-occurring physical health, mental health, and substance abuse challenges, compared to two percent of sheltered people.

"The bottom line is that homeless people are a lot less healthy than sheltered people," Dr. Nealon concluded. "The mortality rate among homeless people is 3.5 times higher than among those with housing. It's deadly to be a homeless person."

The last person Mayor Perkins called to speak was a man who worked at the Middle Coast Mission. "Hi, everyone. I'm Jack Kreps, and I volunteer at MCM. Even though COVID shut down the shelter, there's still a lot going on behind the scenes. Yesterday, I delivered sleeping bags and tarps to the Pines. After the heavy thunderstorm a few days ago, everything was soaking wet there. We took the soggy bags and replaced them with new ones. We'll take the wet bags to the laundromat, wash and dry them, and rotate them back in if they're still usable."

Quinn noticed a few people wrinkling their noses, perhaps at the idea of handling unsanitary sleeping bags from homeless people.

"When the mission was open, I did a variety of jobs. Checked in the guests as they arrived. Cleaned up the dining room when the guests were done eating. Played board games with the guests in the evening. I even learned to play chess from one of the regulars."

Jack stopped when he heard the word 'guest' being whispered and laughed at in some spots of the room. He looked at the Mayor, unsure whether to continue. She nodded at him.

"I'm not sure, but it seems like a few of you don't know why we call our homeless people guests. I even heard a few laughs along with the whispered words. The unhoused visitors to the mission ARE our guests. We welcome them into our shelter home like we would neighbors in our private homes. We also call them guests because the word shows dignity and respect, something we try to impart to these folks who get little of that on the street."

Once again, Jack paused his talk, unsure how it was being received. Finally, he continued when a few people nodded vigorously, and a few more began to clap.

"I'm often asked how I started volunteering and what I get out of it. My church takes two of the weekly shifts during the mission's open season, typically from October 15 through April 30. I liked helping during those two weeks but wanted more, so I became part of the regular volunteer force. When I first started, I felt helpless and sad. Then, I just learned to do my job. Completing whatever work was assigned. Listening to the guests and their stories without judgment. It didn't take me long to realize these people are desperate for a positive human connection. I've learned so much. I was surprised at how homelessness affects such a wide range of individuals. Sometimes, I get frustrated there isn't yet a long-term initiative to solve these problems, but I know meetings like this are a beginning. It's all been an eye-opening experience for me, and I keep coming back."

The room was silent when Jack ended his talk. Even the naysayers' whispered remarks had been curbed. The mayor remained seated for what seemed to be minutes before she stood and addressed the group.

"I want to thank our speakers for coming tonight. Your information has been helpful, at least for me, in busting some of the preconceived ideas I've had about homelessness. I know we have some brochures about MCM if anyone is interested in volunteering there.

Mayor Perkins looked down at her watch before continuing.

"It's almost 9:15. I'd hoped we could have a short Q&A following the talks tonight. Or maybe even begin thinking about next steps. But my gut tells me to save that for our next joint meeting in September. So, let's all head home. Spend some time absorbing what we've heard tonight. You know where to find me if you have questions or comments. Peace, everyone."

Chapter 37: July 2

It'd been four weeks since Mack died, and Quinn's emotions continued to be all over the place. She tried to hide her grief from her friends, but the anger that leaked out occasionally let them know she was still hurting. When Patrick suggested they drive around farm country to see if any cranes had colts yet, she snapped at him, saying he should know it was too early. He'd just stared at her, obviously hurt. And then there was Gilda. Quinn was having a difficult time forgiving her for the snarky comments she'd made at the dinner following Mack's service. Gil even had the gall to comment, 'leave the social work to Vernadeane' when Quinn asked if she wanted to join Ian and her for last week's intergovernmental meeting.

Quinn had also tried to reconnect with her Catholic faith during the grief cycle. That's what religion was for, wasn't it, to bring people comfort during hard times? She'd gone to church a few times and found some solace in the rituals of the mass. Ultimately, though, she'd come away emptier and angrier than before. While she'd probably always be Catholic on some level because of her family background, she was buying in less and less to the tenets of her religious upbringing. Too many folks were left out or relegated to minor roles. Women and gays, especially.

Ultimately, she stuffed what feelings she could and continued to work on helping the homeless and stopping the influx of drugs into their community. It seemed like focusing on those concrete actions eased her grief some. Finally, Quinn decided a talk with Flint might give her some direction, so she headed down the hall to his office.

"Uffda, Quinn. You scared the crap outa me," Flint said after she walked into his office unannounced.

"Sorry. It looks like you're in the middle of something important."

"Nah. Just finishing up some paperwork before I go to lunch. You wanna come with?"

"Sure, where you headed?"

"I was thinking about the farm market up the road. They have outdoor seating, cold sandwiches, and dark sweet cherries have just come in."

They took Quinn's Outback for the five-minute drive. A few people were buying produce at the stand, but no one was eating outside, perfect for talking in private. Quinn ordered a tuna salad sandwich, a bag of chips, and a cup of cherries. Flint went for the cherry chicken salad, a bowl of cherries, and a pop.

"I feel kinda sad," Quinn said. "It's Cherry Festival week, and it's been canceled due to COVID. This is usually the busiest week of the year, and nothing's happening except the Fourth."

"Yah, sure. Lots of people are missing out financially, too. So, tell me, Quinn. It seemed like when you walked into my office, you wanted to talk about something."

"I did. When Gilda introduced you after first arriving in TC, she said that you'd been involved in a lot of drug stings when you were in Minnesota. That right?"

"Oh, yah. I went undercover often for MPD. What's your interest?"

"I think you know I befriended a homeless man, Keegan Cammack. Went by Mack. He passed recently due to a drug overdose. Doc Roberts identified the drug as a fentanyl-laced, synthetic opioid. An illicitly made fentanyl versus one prescribed by a doctor. I'm interested in learning more about its use."

"It's a nasty drug, Quinn. Fentanyl is 50 times more powerful than heroin and deadlier than any drug on the streets. It's ripping through homeless encampments and either killing residents or trapping them in homelessness."

"Trapping them? How so?"

"By the drug's addictiveness. Many people started using the drug to cope with their homelessness. I had one victim tell me she started using fentanyl because she couldn't sleep at night in the camp. She told me passing cars would rev their engines, and people would cry out, making it impossible to sleep."

"Mack said that was happening in the Pines too."

"This vic told me someone offered her the drug, and after smoking it a bit, she'd get five hours of peaceful sleep. But quitting became impossible. Unless she got the drug in her system every few hours, she'd vomit, have diarrhea, the chills, muscle cramps, and bone pain. We treated her 13 times with opioid reversal medication before she finally succumbed."

Quinn just sat there after listening to Flint's story, anger creeping through her body. Her heart raced, and her muscles tensed. She felt feverish as perspiration formed on her forehead.

"You okay, Quinn? You don't look so hot right now. Maybe you should drink some water," Flint advised.

"I'm okay. Your story just brought back Mack and his struggles." She drank from her water bottle and sat there recovering. Then she asked, "What can you tell me about the illegal drug trade? You know, the smuggling that brings fentanyl here in the first place."

"For cripes sake, why would you want to know that, Quinn?"

"I need to know the whole story of how these drugs get here. We can't stop the influx without knowing that information."

"These smuggling operations are part of organized crime. Leave that work to the DEA. They're not something you should be nosing into on your own."

"I'm not, Flint. Truly. I'm just trying to understand."

"Okay, if that's all. Well, uh, to begin with, we know IMFs are primarily manufactured in foreign clandestine labs, mainly in China and Mexico. India's emerging as a source, too. Then they're smuggled into the U.S. through Mexico."

"What about Russian involvement?" Quinn asked.

"We're seeing some activity in Russia too. They have a thriving chemical industry which is pretty unregulated, so precursor substances are easily obtained by Russian criminals to produce synthetic drugs for both domestic and foreign markets."

"Hmmm. Anything else on Russia?"

"Some. Opiates originated in Afghanistan are also being smuggled to Russia, then onto Europe via the Central Asian states."

"Seems like there're lots of supply routes."

"Yah, sure. Hard to pin them down because the supply lines and money laundering routes are in constant flux due to intercartel warfare."

"Huh, hadn't thought of that."

"Drug trafficking is one of the most profitable criminal enterprises, Quinn. These organized crime networks exploit porous borders and are helped by corrupt officials. They also exploit vulnerable people to act as couriers. Added to the massive increase in cargo and passenger traffic, the border guards have become overwhelmed. Why all the questions about Russia?"

Just then, Quinn's phone bugled, and she saw it was Vernadeane. "Hey, what's up?" she answered. Then she listened and said, "Be there shortly."

"What's going on?" Flint asked.

"I gotta go. Something's happening over in the NoBo district with a homeless man. I'll drop you off at FC2 on my way. Thanks so much for your help, Flint."

Chapter 38: Later that Afternoon

The North Boardman Lake District, commonly known as NoBo, was an eclectic mix of homes, government buildings, brewpubs, shopping, and the Boardman Lake Loop Trail. Middle Coast Mission was located there, too, and sometimes caused anxiety among the homeowners in the district, especially with trespassing and crime. Police had been called there when a woman was accosted by a homeless man wielding a knife. Drug paraphernalia was often found on the grounds of F&M Park. And today, Vernadeane had called Quinn to help diffuse a situation of a man reportedly exposing himself in front of her young child. When they arrived and questioned those involved, they learned the man had just opened his fly to urinate when the mother and child came upon him. There'd been no intent at indecent exposure or any other sexual crime. They'd been able to calm everyone down and effectively resolve the problem. They'd empathized with the mother, who finally understood with the mission closed, the man had few other choices.

They were just departing the scene when Quinn spotted Ian walking towards her.

"You've been listening to the police scanner again, haven't you?" Quinn asked.

"It's always on when I'm in TC. Gotta compete with the local newspaper," Ian laughed. "You wanna grab an early dinner or a snack? I've got some news about your sheik."

"I've already had lunch but could do ice cream. How's that sound?"

"What's your brand this week?"

"How about Buchan's West Bay? They've got amazing homemade flavors and a nice outdoor picnic area where we can talk."

Ian nodded, got into his vehicle, and followed Quinn to Buchan's on M-22 just inside Leelanau County. They parked, walked inside to order, and then sat at a turquoise picnic table enjoying their treats: Quinn a waffle cone with mint chocolate chip and Ian a Snickers flurry. They were quiet while they ate.

"It was Buchan Good!" Ian laughed when they finished. "I love their logo. Makes me feel so naughty."

Quinn laughed, too, and then asked, "What's the scoop on Sheik Badr-Uddin?"

"You expect me to top that?" Ian said, still playing the ice cream theme. "Okay, have you heard from him since he offered to wine and dine you?"

"I haven't. I won't be surprised if I don't either. I think his offer was just a pleasantry."

"Maybe. Anyway, I learned the man's a legitimate sheik and falconer. He purchased the Old Mission property four years ago. Actually, from what you've told me, you and Patrick only saw a fraction of it. It's eighty acres, and he paid just over six million for it."

"Wow," Quinn exclaimed. "He wasn't kidding about his country being rich."

"I looked into the property, and it's a beauty. Heavily treed, rolling meadows, lots of open fields, and, get this, 300 feet of frontage on Grand Traverse Bay."

"That'd sure jack up the price."

"According to the property deed, he built a 2500 square foot house and several outbuildings deep in the woods shortly after he purchased the land. I tried to find it on Google Earth, but nothing showed up. Just dense forests. Maybe that's where he lives."

"I'm still curious what he's doing here. Seems weird for him to come all this way to start a breeding center for falcons."

"Not weird at all. The Middle East is the second largest source of foreign investment in U.S. commercial real estate after Europe. Most of the money comes from the oil companies."

"Seriously?"

"Yeah. One research firm that monitors property transfers tracked almost $1.4 billion in commercial property sales to Middle Eastern investors in the last year."

"Huh. Wonder why I've never heard about this."

"Probably because reading the financials isn't your cup of tea. Plus, foreign investors, especially from the Middle East, often operate quietly and confidentially."

"Hmmm. You learn anything else about the sheik?"

"Some. Until ten years ago, he was the chief trainer at the Jebel Ali Falconry Center outside Dubai. The center was owned by the royal family. Prince Farouk Al-Kirdar Haboori. I found several articles about the sheik and Haboori going back fifteen years. Training paradigms they'd set up. Festivals they'd run. Even prizes they'd won at various competitions all over the world. Then, beginning in 2010, I couldn't find another thing on the two working together."

"Huh. Wonder if they had a falling out. Did you find anything out about the Prince?"

"Ultra-rich. Seems to sink his money mostly into his falconry enterprises. Quite the playboy, too. Runs with the rich and famous in the Middle East and Eastern Europe. Pictures I found show him with one beautiful starlet after another."

"Hmmm."

"I think I'm gonna head back to Crystal Lake."

"Any big plans for the holiday weekend?"

"Nothing. Hey, I keep forgetting to ask. You getting excited about the baseball season?"

"I wouldn't call sixty games much of a season. I suppose it's better than nothing, though."

Chapter 39: July 4

Call it coincidence, serendipity, or a twist of fate, but when Quinn got home from meeting Ian, there was a message from Sheik Badr-Uddin on her answering machine. She rarely used the landline and almost missed the flashing light coming from her study. She immediately thought it was her father because he often called on her home phone. She'd also put the landline number on her business cards, hoping to ward off robocalls from disturbing her workday.

The sheik's message said he was going to fly his peregrine Saturday morning at the construction site, and she was welcome to join him. He said she didn't need to call him back. He'd be there regardless. Interesting, she thought. Was he aware that Saturday was one of America's biggest holidays? Fortunately, she'd made no plans for the Fourth due to COVID. She wasn't even on call. So, on Saturday morning, Quinn plugged the directions into her GPS and headed up Old Mission.

The construction site swarmed with workers, obviously not a holiday for them. Quinn could also see the progress that'd been made since her last visit nearly two months ago. The exterior of both buildings appeared completed. A large white, heavy-duty pole tent had also been erected in a meadow a distance from the construction site. She noticed a royal blue, six-seater canopied golf cart speeding in her direction. She didn't recognize the driver but saw he was a large, well-muscled man. As he pulled up and stepped out of the cart, she could see he was about 6'4" tall and probably weighed at least two hundred fifty pounds.

He bowed slightly and said, "I am Abdul Salaam, Servant of the Peace. I will take you to Sheik Badr-Uddin." Then he motioned for her to take a seat.

She climbed into the second row of the cart, not having time to reply to Abdul Salaam's terse introduction. He immediately sped off towards the tent. She looked around at the cart's accessories. The tinted windshield, camel-colored leather seats, and what she thought were falcon perches attached to the third-row seating. The cart had as much legroom as her Subaru. While she was taking it all in, she noticed a small military rifle sitting on the seat next to Abdul Salaam. Probably a M4 carbine. Servant of the Peace, my ass, she thought. He must be the sheik's bodyguard. Suddenly, she felt uncomfortable. She hadn't thought to bring her Glock because she'd felt no danger. Now, she wasn't sure.

As the cart pulled up to the tent, the Sheik walked towards her, smiling with outstretched, welcoming arms. She relaxed some, hoping she wasn't seeing a wolf dressed in sheep's clothing. Badr-Uddin was again dressed in a white, ankle-length robe, but this one appeared lighter weight. He still wore a red-checkered keffiyeh on his head. She wondered how he stood it in the summer weather. Quinn hoped she wasn't being disrespectful in her khaki cargo shorts and striped no-iron linen shirt.

"So glad you could come today, Miss Quinn," the sheik said.

"Thank you for inviting me. I'm excited to see your birds fly."

"Let's get started then. This is Thamina, my four-year-old peregrine. Her name means Priceless in my language," the sheik said as he walked over to the perches holding two birds.

The falcon was a beauty. Blue-gray upperparts with heavily barred sides, belly, and leggings. Its head was typical for a peregrine, with a black hood and sideburns.

"Why are her eyes covered?"

"The hood cuts out most of the bird's sensory intake, allowing her to remain calm. Would you like to see her fly?"

"Would love to!"

The sheik spoke his native language to Abdul Salaam, who took a leather lure with two quail wings attached and fastened it to the end of a long rope. Then he ran down the meadow, perhaps four hundred feet away. While the assistant did that, the sheik pulled a long leather glove onto his arm, held it next to Thamina, and made a kissing sound. The falcon jumped onto his fist, and he removed the bird's hood. The peregrine saw Abdul Salaam twirling the lure at the far end of the meadow and exploded into the air. The assistant twisted and twirled the lure in elaborate sweeps. Thamina swooped for the prey, but Abdul Salaam kept it out of her reach. After repeating the charade several more times, he hurled the simulated prey high in the sky. The falcon quickly grabbed it and returned to the sheik. He rewarded her with a real quail heart and let her enjoy her meal. Finally, he spoke soothing words to her as he petted her, hooded her eyes, and gently returned her to the perch.

Quinn was nearly speechless at the spectacle but managed to say, "That was amazing."

"How about if we have some lunch? You hungry?"

"Yeah, sure."

Abdul Salaam quickly laid out a cold lunch of hummus, pita bread, falafel, kebabs, and fresh fruit. He poured lemonade infused with mint for them to drink.

"Thank you. This looks wonderful," Quinn said as they began eating. "Do you only fly peregrines?"

"Mostly. I also have an older gyrfalcon that I fly in cooler weather. Gyrs come from the Arctic and don't do well in hot temperatures. I keep her at my air-conditioned home."

"Are peregrines better adapted to our climate?"

"Yes, especially in Michigan. They've made a huge comeback after they died out from DDT poisoning before the pesticide was outlawed in the 70s. You'll find peregrines in nature, but also in the city, where they build nests on human constructs, like buildings and bridges."

"Aren't they still on the endangered species list in Michigan?"

"They are. It's one of the reasons I chose your beautiful state for my center. It gives them an extra level of protection."

Abdul Salaam suddenly jumped up and pointed to the sky as four pigeons landed on an electrical wire.

"And that's another reason I came to Michigan. An endless supply of rock pigeons. They're a favorite prey of peregrines. Ready for another show?"

Before Quinn could answer, the sheik was up and moving towards the falcon perch, pulling on his leather glove as he did.

"This is Taufan, my three-year-old. He's king of the sky."

"Does his name have a special meaning?"

"It does. Taufan means strong storm. He terrorizes the sky whenever he's up there."

"He's almost the same age as Thamina, but he's smaller than she is."

"Yes, falcons are sexually dimorphic, meaning the females are larger than the males."

As he spoke, four more pigeons came to the wire. Both the sheik and Abdul Salaam laughed, knowing what was about to happen.

The falcon hopped on the sheik's gloved fist, and when he unmasked the bird, Taufan burst into the sky. At the sight of their predator, the pigeons erupted from the wire and scattered throughout the blue. The chase was on. Taufan flew high above the eight pigeons who were fleeing in every direction. He finally decided which bird would become his meal, tucked in his pointed wings, and pick up speed. Dropping from the sky at 200 miles an hour, Taufan grabbed his target and slammed the pigeon to the ground, snapping the bird's vertebrae with its curved beak. They watched from the tent as Taufan consumed his catch.

"Holy shit," Quinn whispered. "What an athletic performance. I've never seen anything like that dive!"

"It's called the stoop. Peregrines are the fastest animals on the planet."

When he was sure Taufan had completed his meal, the sheik whistled, and the falcon flew low to the ground, into the tent, and onto Badr-Uddin's gloved hand. He stroked the falcon's back and talked to him in his native language. Taufan ruffled his feathers. The sheik took a small cloth and wiped the blood and pigeon feathers from the bird's face. Then he hooded the falcon and placed him on the perch next to Thamina.

"You obviously love these falcons," Quinn said. "But, um, they seem like an unusual pet."

"Why, because they aren't warm and fuzzy like that cute red dog that's on your phone?"

"That's Ruby, my mini-goldendoodle. I didn't mean to be offensive, but I hadn't thought of falcons as pets. I can see, though, that you have a special relationship with your birds."

"They are not affectionate animals, like your Ruby, but we definitely have a partnership."

"Do you worry they won't return when you send them off after prey?"

"Not at all. While I have a close relationship with my birds, I do not own them. They are not my slaves and are free to leave any time they want. But we have trust between us. The birds know I provide them with good food, safe habitat, and security. They want to return, and I trust that they will. We are equals."

"Hmmm."

"Shall we finish our lunch? We never got to our fruit."

As they returned to the table, Quinn had a hard time making conversation. The spectacle of the falcons had left her tongue-tied and thoughtful. She looked at the sheik and noticed he had a scar running along the side of his face. She wondered if his tingled too. As he lifted fresh strawberries to his mouth, she saw more scars on his hands, and the end of his index finger was missing. Then she thought of the bodyguard. His muscles and size. The M4 carbine he kept within reach. She realized the sheik's story must go deeper than falconry.

Chapter 40: July 27

Quinn returned to FC2 and quickly went to the locker room to shower and change into a fresh uniform. She'd been standing out in the heat all morning working with the Michigan Army National Guard, who were providing free drive-thru COVID testing at the fairgrounds. All county law enforcement officers were involved in keeping order for the line of cars that snaked to M-37. At least she didn't have to wear the white PPE hooded coveralls and heavy plastic face shields the Guards wore.

"You're back," Flint said, walking past Quinn's office just as she settled into her chair and was listening to messages. "How'd it go?"

"Hot, but good. I can't believe the number of folks clamoring to be tested."

"Yah, sure. I heard this morning the county just had its sixth death from COVID."

"Six months into the pandemic, and some are still not taking precautions."

"Maybe we can at least flatten the curve some," Flint said.

Before the conversation went further, Vernadeane rushed into Quinn's office, her face ashen.

"Gilda just called. There's been a suicide at the jail."

"Not Davey Lathrop?" Quinn asked.

"She didn't say, but let's get over there."

Young Lathrop had been lodged in the Grand Traverse County Jail since his arrest at the end of May, except for a short stay in the ER to stabilize his psychosis. He'd been waiting for a bed to open up at the Center for Forensic Psychiatry south of Ann Arbor, which is responsible for all court-ordered mental health evaluations, but one hadn't yet become available. The wait for admittance was often long, an average of 127 days for most.

In addition to working with the homeless population, Vernadeane was also an advocate for the mentally ill in jail, who made up nearly 70% of the inmate population.

"There have been 40 suicide attempts inside the jail since 2011, and this one is the second one in four years resulting in death, both by hanging," Vernadeane ranted as they drove. "With less mental health funding and the continued closure of psychiatric hospitals, people who should be going to mental hospitals are now going to jail."

When they arrived at the jail, Gilda met them near the entrance and said David wasn't the latest suicide victim. Luckily, the senior Lathrop had remained in Traverse City and was a staunch advocate for his son's care. While many mentally ill inmates sat in jail for months with no medication and were expected to behave, David was under his personal psychiatrist's care.

Leaving Vernadeane at the jail to work with Gilda on the latest crisis, Quinn returned to FC2 only to find Ian in her office with an update on the sheik. She'd already told him about her experience flying falcons with Badr-Uddin. Also, the curious details about the sheik's scars and missing fingertip, as well as his presumed bodyguard and M4 carbine. Ian said he'd try to look deeper into the sheik's past. Maybe talk to some foreign correspondents from *The Chronicle* who had Middle Eastern contacts.

"So, you've learned more about Sheik Badr-Uddin?"

"I have. From a friend at the State Department, I learned about the sheik's visa."

"Seriously? You mean the U.S. State Department?"

"Yeah, that's the one. Badr-Uddin's visa is a U Nonimmigrant Visa."

"Never heard of that before."

"Me either. This visa type is for victims of criminal activity. Here, let me read what the website said. I copied it to my phone. The

U Nonimmigrant Visa is for *'victims of certain criminal activities that occurred in the United States or violated U.S. laws...victims must have suffered substantial mental or physical abuse due to the criminal activity and possess information concerning that criminal activity. Law enforcement authorities must also certify that the victim has been, is being, or is likely to be helpful in the investigation or prosecution of the criminal activity.'* Whaddya make of that?"

"Whew, not sure," Quinn said. "But it might account for his need for protection. Also, it could be the reason for his scars and missing fingertip."

"That's what I think too. What about the last part?"

"You think the sheik might be some kind of spy or confidential informant about this so-called criminal activity?"

"Makes me wonder," Ian replied.

But for the rest of the day, Quinn put homeless people, Davey Lathrop, and the sheik out of her mind as she rushed home to host friends for the Tigers home opener. Normally, she would've driven to Detroit to attend the game with her dad and brothers. It was as much of a family tradition as St. Patrick's Day in Corktown. Opening Day, nicknamed April in the D, was also accompanied by great hoopla.

It had become abundantly clear in the middle of the pandemic that these times were anything but normal. The season had been postponed from April to July. Stadiums would be closed to fans. Heavy protocols had been mandated to protect the teams. To minimize the spread of the virus by travel, teams would only play opponents from the same division in the American and National League. She'd read that the document detailing the health agreement between MLB and the players was over a hundred pages long. Pitchers could no longer lick their fingers to improve the grip on the baseballs because it might spread germs. Players had to take their temperatures three times a day, followed by testing if they got a reading over 100 degrees. Social distancing was required throughout the dugout and locker room. Quinn wondered whether all the rigamarole associated with a shortened season was worth it. She decided it was. After all, baseball was America's pastime.

Quinn took care of Ruby when she got home. She ran the dog around the fenced yard and threw the Chuckit Flying Squirrel. Quinn next set up tray tables in her living room so everyone could comfortably eat and watch the game. Gilda arrived first with a huge green salad. Ian and Hannah came next, bringing salted caramel brownies and ice cream for dessert. Patrick showed up last bearing Jet's Pizza, the closest they could get to the square, deep-dish Detroit-style pizza in Traverse City. As they served themselves and found a seat in front of the television, Quinn brought around frosted mugs of Harp's Lager.

While they enjoyed their food and the pre-game show, the reality of the 2020 season sank in. No one in line at the ticket booth on the plaza. The stadium empty of fans. Miggy standing off by himself, waiting to take batting practice. The dugout players masked and standing six feet apart. No hugging, back-slapping, or playful banter. Then, perhaps the saddest part of the new season, the first without Al Kaline, who'd died April 6. The team wore commemorative black patches with Mr. Tiger's No. 6 on their uniform sleeves. Even the announcers Matt Shepard, Kirk Gibson, and Jack Morris seemed less enthusiastic in their reportage.

And then the game got underway. Michael Fulmer was Detroit's starting pitcher against the Kansas City Royals. It took him 15 pitches to get through the first inning.

"He's gonna burn through his pitch count if he keeps this up," Ian said.

"At least he didn't give up any runs," Gil added.

"Let's see if we can get some offense going," Quinn said.

Turns out, that's exactly what happened, with Detroit scoring five runs in the second, including a homer from Jacoby Jones. But

Fulmer's pitch count continued to climb, and he was pulled after only 2.2 innings.

"Jesus," Patrick said. "Let's see if Funkhouser can do better."

"Gotta win Opening Day," Quinn encouraged.

Funkhouser ended up pitching just one inning and gave up five earned runs. Detroit paraded four more pitchers through the end of the slugfest, which Detroit lost 6-14.

"Longest fricking Opening Day I've ever watched," Hannah said.

"Three hours and twenty minutes of torture," Gilda added.

"This the last year of Gardenhire's contract?" Patrick asked.

"Yeah. Maybe he'll decide to retire," Ian said.

"Guys, guys, what's the matter with you? This is just the first game of the new season. Why're you talking doom and gloom this early?" Quinn asked.

"Because I have a feeling that this game may portend how the rest of the season's gonna play out," Ian replied.

Chapter 41: August 15

Quinn walked by her study on the way out the door and decided to play the sheik's new message one more time. It hadn't made sense. He'd said the new falcon racecourse was ready, and he'd be flying Thamina and Taufan Saturday morning if she wanted to stop by. She'd never heard of falcon racing but was game to learn. She hesitated at her closet, where she kept her gun safe, then decided against taking her Glock.

It'd been six weeks since Quinn had visited the sheik on July 4th. Again, bodyguard Abdul Salaam was waiting for her at the entrance, his M4 carbine on the seat next to him. Quinn jumped into the second row of the golf cart without invitation, and they sped over the vast meadow. She found the property quieter today, with most of the workers putting the finishing touches on the interior of the first structure, the propagation center. The second building on the property had been completed, too. Twice as large as the first, the training center was white-sided and roofed with a generous number of large openings covered in mesh wire. Probably so the birds could get ample fresh air and sunlight, Quinn thought. She noticed the interior was an open space, and she could see several falcons flying free within. Finally, Quinn and the bodyguard arrived at a large event tent enclosed on all sides.

"Miss Quinn. I'm so glad you decided to come," Sheik Badr-Uddin said in greeting.

"I've never heard of falcon racing, and my curiosity got the best of me."

"Falcon racing is a relatively new sport. While there are various kinds, my focus here is on the Telwah, which is a classic line race. The falcons fly close to the ground over a 400 or 600-meter course to reach the catcher at the end, twirling a lure. The fastest bird wins."

"Huh," Quinn muttered, thinking but not saying this didn't sound much like falconry.

As the sheik talked, Quinn took in the surroundings. There were six hooded peregrines on perches inside the tent. The perches were covered in green artificial turf to protect the birds' feet and were spaced six feet apart. She noticed each bird had a tiny ring attached to its leg. The tent was also filled with electronic equipment, most of which she didn't recognize except the computers. Robed technicians and falcon trainers were busy at work in the air-conditioned room.

Outside the tent, straight down the closely mowed meadow, a wide alley covered in smooth pea gravel stretched for 400 meters. Two pieces of electronic equipment were placed at the beginning and end of the lane. One bore the name Microgate. The other she recognized as a FinishLynx, a camera system capable of shooting 5,000 frames per second. She'd seen pictures of them before detecting photo finishes at horse races. On the sides of the meadow, stadium seats were being installed. While the work had been halted for today's demonstration, photographers and people writing on clipboards sat in the completed sections.

"You ready for this, Miss Quinn?" the sheik asked.

"I am. Sounds like the race is a point-to-point sprint against the clock. Is that right?"

"Yes. There will be several heats using six of my peregrines. The one with the best time is the winner. Today's race is a trial run for both the birds and the new equipment."

"I recognize the FinishLynx from the Kentucky Derby, but what's the Microgate piece?"

"It's a laser sensor used to detect the exact time the falcon crosses the start and finish lines."

Just then, a falconer emerged from the tent holding one of the sheik's peregrines on his fist, which was covered with a roll of the green artificial turf. He unhooded the bird, raised it in the air, and passed a scent object in front of the falcon's nares. The peregrine came alive and looked down the course at the catcher, who'd begun twirling a rotating rope with a pigeon wing lure attached. He danced around, yelling words Quinn didn't understand. The falcon immediately took off, flying close to the ground towards the lure. The Microgate clicked off the seconds it took for the bird to reach the end sensor and the twirling prey.

"Nineteen seconds," the sheik shouted.

"Is that a good time?" Quinn asked.

"Not really, but Maeveen is still learning, so it's okay. She'll get better now that we have an official course where she can train."

They watched as the falconer retrieved his bird, gently sprayed it with cooling water, and rewarded it with a whole pigeon. Then, the sheik's five other birds took their turns. Taufan came in first with a time of just over sixteen seconds and a top speed of 110 kilometers per hour. The sheik personally retrieved Taufan and rewarded him with a whole pigeon heart, part of falconry tradition. He thanked everyone in the tent for their work making the dry run successful. The sheik motioned Quinn towards the golf cart and got in beside her while Abdul Salaam drove them along a winding path through the woods. They emerged to a pristine beach along Grand Traverse Bay, where a large wooden pergola had been erected to shade visitors from the sun. A servant was laying out lunch underneath the structure. While he wore traditional flowing robes and a keffiyeh, the servant's holster holding a gun loosely at his waist seemed out of place. In the distance, Quinn noticed a large modernistic home standing on a hillside with panoramic vistas of the water. Must be the sheik's residence, she thought. Several outbuildings were nearby. She wondered whether they housed people or falcons. Nearly out of her view, workers were building another structure along the shoreline.

"Have a seat and begin eating," the sheik said. "What did you think of the race?"

"I enjoyed it," she answered. "I wondered what the ring on the falcon's leg is for?"

"Oh, it contains a miniature computer chip that connects to the electronics to provide accurate data on the falcon's speed and flight distance. It weighs less than three grams, so it doesn't affect the bird's performance."

"Huh," Quinn said. Then, searching for the words to say what she was thinking without offending her host, she continued. "It, um, doesn't seem to match what you've told me about the history of falconry in your country. Nothing like the hunting demo you showed me earlier."

Badr-Uddin nodded as he generously spread humus over a pita. "Let me address your question by saying traditional falconry is facing some challenges."

"Seriously?"

"Yes. The first involves extinction. In my country, falcons are threatened by the increasing scarcity of their prey, loss of habitat due to urban sprawl and deforestation, and climate change in the Arctic regions."

"I understand the last two because they're affecting wildlife here too. But what do you mean by scarcity of prey?"

"In the Middle East, falcons feed on a ground bird called the houbara bustard, which falconers have nearly hunted to extinction."

"Ah, so you bring your birds here to feast on our rock pigeons instead," Quinn joked.

The sheik laughed and said, "That's not our intent at all. We've made some huge changes to our sport to preserve it. First, we've outlawed hunting bustards and wild falcons. The only falcons used for sport now are captive-bred birds."

"Our country has the same law."

"It does. It's why breeding centers have popped up all over the world. To support the sport. We've also made a huge shift in focus to keep our ancient tradition alive and sustainable."

"So, you've changed from hunting falcons to racing them?"

"Correct. High-stakes falcon races protect the birds, their prey, and the environment. We use the same falconry training techniques developed by our ancestors and apply them to this new form of our hobby."

"Makes sense. So, have falconers bought into this new sport and its rules?"

"For the most part. Our festivals only allow captive-bred falcons to participate. A few still prefer wild caught falcons even though it's against the law."

"Hmmm," Quinn said, noticing the sheik's olive-toned skin had darkened as he spoke.

"Unfortunately, there's a thriving black market for wild falcons."

Quinn hated the words black market and instinctively reached for her jawline scar. They reminded her of the case she'd worked a couple of years ago to bust a Russian syndicate selling counterfeit pesticides. During a pursuit, she'd taken a bad beating from one of the middlemen involved. While Meyer Garfield had been sent to prison, and his partner, Kyle Watkins, had drowned in a related fishing accident, they'd never caught the mobster heading the syndicate. Even though the case was in the past, any talk of black market dealings sent her back there. Finally returning to the present, she listened to the sheik talk about the black market trafficking of wild falcons.

"Due to our oil reserves, few places in the world have money to spare, like the Middle East. Unfortunately, where there is that much money, trouble follows."

"I hear you."

"Some of the most-prized falcons fetch up to $500,000, hardly indicative of the sport's humble desert beginnings. Those amounts are very enticing to those who don't come from money and are trying to eke out a living."

Quinn nodded and waited for him to continue.

"Trafficking these birds is a serious enterprise for governments across the globe, the Russian mafia, and desperate Bedouin trappers."

"Any idea the numbers involved?"

"I can't give you an exact amount, but I've read falcon trafficking is second only to smuggling weapons across the Gulf."

Chapter 42: August 25

Quinn was on her way to Crystal Lake to meet Ian about his latest project. It was a beautiful sunny day, and US-31 going west was packed. She'd heard the pandemic had brought sizeable numbers to Sleeping Bear Dunes. People trying to create distance and space in the COVID era had already set a new attendance record for the national lakeshore. As she drove, her mind wandered to something that'd niggled at her since her last meeting with the sheik. Maybe longer. She hadn't said anything to her friends, but maybe she'd broach the topic today with Ian.

What bothered her related to Russia. In a couple of recent conversations, Russia had come up. First, when she'd talked to Flint about his experiences working stings in Minnesota, he told her about drugs being illicitly manufactured and smuggled through the Russian syndicate. Then, learning from the sheik that the Russian Mafia was involved in wild falcon trafficking made her jawline scar tingle. Could these two situations be connected? Did more than one syndicate operate out of Russia? Maybe she was being overly sensitive to references to the Russian Mafia because of the counterfeit pesticide case. Reaching the Doyle home, she quickly set aside her thoughts. She noticed Hannah reading in her screened gazebo.

"Hey, Quinn. Good to see you."

"You look relaxed and comfortable. Whatcha reading?"

"Finally, getting to *Where the Crawdads Sing.*

"Oh, it's amazing. My mom left me her copy when they were here in June."

Ian came to the French doors, greeted Quinn, and beckoned her inside.

"What's this project you're cooking up?" Quinn asked as they settled into his home office.

"I've been thinking about starting a street magazine for the homeless population."

"How cool! Tell me more."

"The idea started to percolate during the last intergovernmental meeting. When we heard the presentations about homelessness, I began to think these folks have stories to tell. And it seems that no one asks to hear them."

"So true, Ian. Mack was always eager to talk. What've you got in mind?"

"I guess I need to start by meeting with those who might be interested. Perhaps hold some writing workshops. Most likely, they don't think of themselves as writers."

"You want to go into the Pines? You need a police escort before entering. I can do that."

"Thanks. I was hoping you would. There's a conference room we could use at my downtown office. Accommodates around twelve. That should be enough space."

"Maybe we could feed them too while we're there."

"Wonderful idea, Quinn. So glad you're on board."

"Anything else in your plans?"

"One more thing. Whaddya think about homeless folks selling the magazines as a way to earn money?"

"Hmmm. Sure would be an alternative to panhandling."

"I think so too. So what's going on with you? I can tell something's on your mind."

Quinn shared her worries about Russian involvement in falcon trafficking and fentanyl smuggling. Hesitatingly, she even voiced whether these Russian markets could be tied to their counterfeit pesticide case two years ago.

"Say his name, Quinn. I know you've been avoiding it. It'll help you heal from the ordeal if you face the monster head-on."

"I know, but I hate going there. Even thinking about Russian involvement in these situations makes me crazy."

"I know, hon. Say his name anyway."

"Pavel Pilecki," she whispered.

Pavel Pilecki was the head of the Russian syndicate that operated out of Eastern Europe, mainly through Belarus, a transit country used to smuggle merchandise between Asian and European markets. He'd been responsible for trafficking counterfeit pesticides throughout the East Coast and Midwest. Quinn's oldest brother Rowan, an FBI agent out of the Cleveland office, had been chasing him for years to no avail. Worse than the smuggling, authorities were certain he'd ordered the hit that killed George Watkins, who'd been running the counterfeit operation stateside. In the last year, they'd finally made connections between Watkins and Pilecki through sources on the dark web. But Watkins wasn't the only man Pilecki had ordered killed. Currently, he is third on Interpol's Ten Most Wanted list for heinous crimes, including murder and torture.

"Pavel Pilecki," Quinn whispered again.

"You okay?"

"Yeah. I hadn't wanted to open this can of worms. Felt safer to keep it under wraps. I'm worried it's gonna turn out to be worse than worms. More of a Pandora's Box."

"I hear you, but we're not going to catch this bastard unless we do."

"I know. Will you look into Pilecki? See what you can find out about what he's been up to recently. Like what you were doing when you checked out the sheik's background. Maybe you can call in some favors from your foreign contacts."

Chapter 43: September 10

To zoom or not to zoom. That was the question meeting planners faced during COVID. The city commissioners had finally received word from public health officials that the percentage of positive cases in the county had declined again, so they could go ahead with their second intergovernmental meeting on homelessness. They'd been warned not to let their guards down, though, especially with flu season approaching. Schools had reopened, too, but with two weeks of online learning before transitioning to face-to-face education. Everyone was waiting to see how the gradual lifting of restrictions would affect pandemic numbers.

Mayor Janet Perkins opened the meeting with instructions. "You can see by our setup we're still masking and socially distanced. Please don't move any of the chairs. Also, notice the microphones set up around the room. Behind them, the floor has been taped off in six-foot increments. Please maintain those distances if you get in line to speak. Any questions?"

The room was filled to the allowed capacity, but no one had anything to say.

Perkins continued, "Our last meeting was educational with three speakers. Social Worker Vernadeane Novak busted myths about homelessness, Dr. Shelby Nealon described how homelessness is a health issue, and Jack Kreps described his work volunteering at Middle Coast Mission. I'd like a show of hands to see how many attended that meeting."

At least eighty percent of the audience raised their hands.

"Good, good," the mayor said. "At least we're on the same page with information. In tonight's conversation, we're going to get community input on what we can do to address homelessness in our area. It'll be more of a brainstorming session. But before we get to that, I'm going to call on Ozzie McKay, executive director of Middle Coast Mission, who has a very exciting announcement."

"We all know that Traverse City, like many cities around the U.S., has a severe housing shortage and unaffordable rents. Ultimately, these two problems are the root of homelessness. Tonight, I'm here to announce that MCM has just signed an agreement to purchase the sixty-room Beachcomber Motel in East Bay Township, which has been closed for the last three years. We've been able to do that using Low-Income Housing Tax Credits from the state and a tax break from the city. We're very excited to be moving towards a permanent solution to our city's housing crisis by turning the motel into apartments for those facing chronic homelessness. I'm gonna turn this over to a couple of others involved in the project for more details."

"Hi, everyone. I'm Vernadeane Novak from the Sheriff's Department. The East Bay development we're undertaking will finally offer a lifeline to those who have endured the hardships of homelessness. The project comes under the category of permanent supportive housing, which means it will go beyond housing alone. It will also include wrap-around services, such as mental and physical healthcare, counseling, job opportunities, addiction recovery services, and a connection to the community. Before we open the discussion to the audience, we have one more individual involved in the project who'll speak."

The audience watched as a large bald man with a long white beard and the upper build of a former football player moved toward the microphone. He had a kind face and rosy complexion. He wore a blue t-shirt bearing the Habitat for Humanity logo and overalls.

"Hi, y'all. I'm Carlisle Wertz, construction foreman for Habitat for Humanity Grand Traverse. As you may know, Habitat for Humanity is all about putting God's love into action by bringing people together to build homes so that everyone has a decent place to live. We'll be using local volunteers and people from the homeless community to renovate that old motel into affordable apartments these folks can call home."

"Okay, thanks, everyone," the mayor said, taking back the mic. "We're going to entertain questions and comments right now, either about the East Bay project or homeless solutions in general. You can line up behind the mic nearest you, and I'll point to you when it's your turn. Please state your name and the city or township where you live." Perkins recognized the first speaker from the last meeting and decided to get his comment over with.

"I'm Duane Davies from Garfield Township. This apartment plan sounds like a good idea, and it seems to be well-funded, but what about those so-called wrap-around services? Won't they be expensive?"

"I'll answer this," Vernadeane said. "We know we could put people in an apartment and take the subsidy, but it's the wrap-around support that KEEPS people housed. According to a study by the Homeless Alliance, managing homelessness in this area costs about $2.5 million a year. That number includes $1.3 million to fund hospital expenses and over 400 police and ambulance responses. In contrast, the East Bay apartment plan with wrap-around services would cost $945,000 per year. Not only is it a humanitarian solution, but it makes economic sense."

Perkins pointed to the next person in line to speak.

"My name is Judith Shaw from Traverse City. How will you determine who gets the housing first?"

Again, Vernadeane spoke. "The apartments will be geared towards those earning 60% below the area median income who are homeless, have a disability, or are fleeing domestic violence. Those people will be housed first."

"I'm Pastor Rick Greenman, also from Traverse City. I'm wondering if there's been any discussion about turning the Middle Coast Mission into a year-round facility."

MCM executive director Ozzie McKay answered, "There's been discussion about that on several occasions, but it's not as simple as it seems. First, our land use permits don't allow for a year-round operation of the mission. Also, the facility itself would need significant upgrades, such as adding air conditioning for summer operations. Plus, we're looking for permanent housing solutions, not temporary ones like the shelter provides."

"My name is Deanna Wentworth from Traverse City. I live in NoBo, and I'd hate to see more burden put on my neighborhood if the mission went year-round. There have already been many incidents that happened when MCM releases its guests every morning at 8 a.m., a time that coincides with school starting. I don't want to get into specifics, but having the shelter near our neighborhood is already a problem."

Applause erupted from several parts of the audience. Several shouted, "Here, here," and "Yes." One person even yelled, "How about that murder that happened in NoBo?"

Mayor Perkins pounded on her lectern and shouted into her mic for order. Then she said, "We appreciate the input from our neighborhoods and empathize with their experiences. It's important, though, that we work together to find compassionate responses to problems on both sides of the issue. Let's take another question or two before adjourning for the evening. Yes, you there in the Hawaiian shirt."

"I'm Randy Nestell from East Bay Township. I'd like to see something done to make the Pines a healthier place to live. Maybe it's time to revisit having some restrooms and sinks installed. Seems like having a place to use the bathroom and wash one's hands is not only hygienic but a human right."

Chapter 44: September 29

Quinn sat on her patio reading while Ruby stretched out asleep on the lawn. She knew Ian was stopping by after he finished work, she just didn't know when. She'd left the French doors to her condo cracked so she'd hear the doorbell, but he surprised her by coming around to the side gate. Ruby sprang to life at the familiar face and immediately dropped the Chuckit Flying Squirrel at his feet. Setting the stack of papers he'd brought on the table next to Quinn, Ian obliged the dog until she flopped on the ground, exhausted. As Ian sipped the Guinness he'd gotten from Quinn's refrigerator, she took the top document off the pile and began to read.

"Ian, is this the first issue of your street magazine? It looks great."

"Go ahead and look it over. I'm anxious for your feedback."

She was quiet as she flipped through the twenty-page zine, skimming the articles and looking at the artwork. A piece about the unidentified homeless man who'd been killed by a hit-and-run driver on Division Street. His death had started a conversation about pedestrian safety and prompted a donation of reflective vests distributed among the homeless community. A poem describing survival as homeless folks experienced it. A line drawing showing tents spread throughout the Pines. A first-person account of what it's like to live out of a van. Tributes to homeless individuals who'd died over the past year, including Mack.

"This is really amazing! These folks can write."

"It's hard for them to think of themselves as writers. Many are writing stories for the first time in their lives."

"Your writing clinics are working. Have you started selling the magazines yet?"

"Yeah, they're going like hotcakes, especially at downtown venues like Horizon Books. Outside Walmart, too, where lots of homeless people shop and park their cars. People seem hungry for real news about the homeless community."

They sipped their stouts and watched the sun set behind Quinn's condo complex. The solar lights near her garden slowly brightened enough to make out the details in her yard. Quinn reached for her sweatshirt as the chill set in on the late September evening.

"So what's all this other stuff you brought?"

"Research, Quinn, research. You asked me to look into Russian falcon trafficking as it related to Pavel Pilecki, and I did."

"Seriously? You found all this?"

"Yeah. Not sure what's relevant, but maybe we can put some pieces together."

"Huh."

"First of all, Putin is big into..."

"Wait. Putin? As in Russian President Vladimir Putin?"

"Yes, that's the one. Now, as I was trying to say, Putin is big into falcons, especially gyrfalcons, who were once prized by Russian tsars. He's begun a huge project to breed and export falcons."

"I'll be damned."

"He's established a whole network of falconry nurseries across Russia. An especially popular location is on the Kamchatka Peninsula near Norway and Finland. All of them are engaged in breeding sakers, one of the most endangered and rarest of falcons. Also, gyrfalcons, or gyrs as they are commonly called, and peregrines. There are about a dozen nurseries in all."

"And Pilecki is involved in this project?"

"Quinn, slow down. Let me tell the story. The nurseries mostly sell their birds to Arab countries because of their history and current interest in falconry. Putin has even gifted several falcons to the kings and princes in the Middle East, including, get this, Prince Farouk Al-Kirdar Haboori."

Quinn looked blank for a few moments. Then her eyes widened, and she crossed herself.

"That's the prince the sheik trained falcons for at his center outside Dubai. The rich playboy prince who runs in Middle Eastern and Eastern European circles. Right?"

"That's the one."

"You still haven't..."

"Stop and listen, Quinn. I'm trying to get to it before you explode. Prince Farouk and Pavel Pilecki are buddies. They socialize together in the high life, and both are avid falconers. There you have it. Your connection."

Quinn went silent at the news that her hunches had substance. She'd been drawn towards the idea that Pilecki might be involved yet fighting the knowledge at the same time. Not wanting it to take hold of her again and send her back to the emotions she'd worked so hard to escape.

"You've not found anything about them being involved in bird trafficking, have you?"

"Not yet, but I'm still looking."

"What're the rest of the documents you have in your stack, Ian?"

"Pictures from the press of Pilecki and Prince Farouk."

Quinn stared at the pictures of the two men as Ian flipped through them. The prince dark-complected and handsome. A traditionally large Arab nose and wide mouth. Thick brown hair and eyes. Pilecki was more round-faced, also big-nosed but thin-lipped. He wore a spade beard, fitting for a Russian. Attractive too. Fair skin and eyes the shade of ice water. Piercing, even from the page. The pictures showed both men at parties escorting beautiful women. Another, a desert scene, revealed them both holding falcons on their leather hand perches.

"Oh, my God! That's her!" Quinn exclaimed when Ian turned to the next document. "The attendant who cared for George Watkins in the assisted living facility. She went missing, along with his computer, after he was murdered. Do you know who she is?"

"Yes, it's Mika Pilecki. Pavel Pilecki's sister."

Chapter 45: October 9

Patrick had been in the FC2 building for an end-of-the-day meeting and stopped by Quinn's office on his way out.

"Hey, you," Quinn said as he sat down beside her. "What're you doing here?"

"DNR had a meeting in your auditorium about some new policies, and I just wanted to say hi. Haven't seen you in an age since we're not working a case together."

"I know. I miss our outdoor time together."

"I was out patrolling farm country yesterday and saw sandhill cranes staging for migration. A flock of about fifty birds was off Harrand Road."

"Hmmm. Hope we can get out to photograph them soon."

"Me too. They'll be around for a while yet. You catch the Tigers' last game of the season?"

"Of course. I'm not just a fair-weather fan, Patrick. Hopefully, next season will be better with a new manager and getting COVID under control."

They chit-chatted for a few more minutes, and then Patrick left, sensing Quinn had somewhere else to be. After Patrick left, Quinn raced home to Ruby, who was having a special visitor that evening. As a young dog, she'd gone through Search and Rescue Scent Training. Her SAR training had focused on the traditional tracking method, where the dog follows a specific human scent deposited on the ground from where the victim was last seen. While Ruby was skilled at her job and found every victim she'd searched for, the work wasn't plentiful. She'd tracked down three seniors with dementia who'd wandered from their nursing homes and two toddlers who'd escaped fenced yards when the gates were inadvertently left open. She'd also located a snowshoer lost in the woods at Sleeping Bear. Six cases in five years wasn't enough to keep Ruby's skills sharp.

So Quinn had begun mulling over adding a different kind of scent training to Ruby's repertoire. When Mack died of an overdose of synthetic opioids, and Quinn pledged to stop the influx of drugs into the city, she considered that she and Ruby might work together as a drug detection team. It'd be a way to honor Mack and help her community at the same time.

She'd first spoken to State Police Trooper Nick Wagner, who owned the sniffer dog Grit, about whether there was a need for more drug detection work, and he jumped at the idea, saying she could work as much as she wanted. Quinn had also talked to Gilda about whether she could use some hours from her workday to help the Sheriff's Department with drug detection. Gil was delighted at the thought of getting the extra help.

Nick told Quinn that Ruby would have to go through some formal training and testing, but it would be expedited because of her prior certification as a SAR dog. Nick was also willing to get them started with the process. They'd begun working with Ruby on some foundational skills. They'd gotten her used to a new toy, an 8" oblong rubber scent probe, similar to the retriever rolls Quinn used to teach Ruby to fetch, except that it had holes and an end cap. Once she was comfortable playing with the toy, they began to add cotton balls soaked in various essential oils to the probe's interior. Anise and clove to begin with. Nick would hide the probe somewhere in Quinn's neighborhood. He'd then give Ruby a whiff of the oil and turn her loose to find the hidden probe. She'd found it every time and was rewarded with her favorite toy, a Kong stuffed with peanut butter.

Tonight, they were stepping up the game by using real drugs. Marijuana, this time. Nick had parked his Tahoe at the condo clubhouse and stuffed a cotton ball saturated with a tincture of cannabis into the vehicle's wheel well.

"We're intensifying Ruby's training tonight not only by using a real drug but also by putting it in a place where criminals often hide them. No scent toy probe this time. Don't be disappointed if she doesn't find it the first time," Nick cautioned.

"She'll do well. I'm confident she's getting it," Quinn said.

Nick stooped over Ruby and passed a cotton ball soaked with a tincture of cannabis in front of her nose. "Ruby, go find."

Ruby took off at a normal walking pace, her head high and snout pointed up. Quinn had her on a retractable leash to give her some freedom yet have her under control. The dog acted as she typically did on her daily walk, sniffing bushes, relieving herself, and constantly wagging her golden retriever tail. They were approaching the clubhouse, and Ruby kept going. Suddenly, at the far edge of the parking lot, she stopped, sniffed the air, and went right to Nick's Tahoe. She stood there a minute, circled it, sniffed the left rear tire, and sat.

"Good girl, good girl," Nick said in a high voice while he petted Ruby.

"She did it!" Quinn squealed as she pulled the peanut butter Kong from her pocket.

"Ruby's a natural. It won't take much more until she's ready for her certification testing."

Chapter 46: October 15

Quinn was at her desk when Vernadeane called to give her an update on the Lathrop case.

"I just got the news that Davey Lathrop was admitted to CFP today."

"CFP? Refresh my memory. What is that?"

"Sorry. Sometimes, I forget not everyone lives and breathes the mental health system. CFP is the Center for Forensic Psychiatry in Saline, just outside Ann Arbor. It's where Davey has been waiting to be admitted for his criminal responsibility evaluation."

"Oh, yeah, I remember now. How long has it been since his arrest and incarceration in the county jail?"

"From May 23 until today. A hundred forty-five days total."

"Jesus. The kid and his family must be going nuts."

"They have been. I saw Davey a couple of weeks ago, and he was bored out of his mind. I think the only thing that got him admitted was his father threatening a lawsuit."

"How long will his stay be in Ann Arbor?"

"The evaluation is supposed to be completed within 60 days, but many go longer?"

"Do you think he'll ever stand trial for the homeless murders?"

"Hard to say, but it's possible if therapy and medication can help him reach competency."

"Thanks for the update, Vernadeane. Are we still on for later this afternoon?"

"Yeah. See you in a couple hours."

Following the phone call, Quinn stopped off at her condo to let Ruby out and get some lunch. She discovered a message from two days ago on her answering machine. It was from Sheik Badr Uddin: *The weather is cool enough to fly my gyrfalcon Zohra. Abdul Salaam*

will be at the falcon training center at 10 a.m. Saturday to take you to
my home if you're interested.

Click. That was it. Of course, she was interested. She hadn't seen
the sheik since mid-August and was eager to see his gyrfalcon for
the first time. She also hoped to learn more about his connection
to Prince Farouk Al-Kirdar Haboori and perhaps the prince's buddy
Pavel Pilecki.

At 3 p.m., Quinn picked up Vernadeane, and they drove to
Middle Coast Mission, which was reopening for the first time since
COVID. Although check-in didn't begin until 4:30, there was
already a line. People were desperate for a place to stay after seven
months of living outdoors when the shelter had closed. For Quinn,
seeing these unhoused folks brought back memories of Mack and
how he'd suffered from homelessness, brain injuries, and the opiate
addiction that finally killed him. She pushed aside those painful
recollections and focused on the tour the MCM director was giving
of the facility's improvements since COVID began.

The first new safety protocol was that all guests would have their
temperatures taken upon arrival. Anyone with symptoms would be
sent to an isolation room where alternative lodging would be found
for them. Everyone would also be tested for COVID every two
weeks to keep the population safe. Volunteers still served meals in
the dining room but in shifts of 28 people so they could socially
distance. Guests continued to sleep in bunk beds except that they'd
been wrapped in plastic sheeting and outfitted with curtains to
prevent viral spread. The biggest change to MCM was to the social
space, which wasn't large enough to allow safe distancing. Volunteers
had erected a 40 x 60 heated event tent on the property. It contained
comfortable seating, Wi-Fi, and televisions so guests could safely
enjoy themselves during the evenings until bedtime. Impressed with
the changes put in place, Vernadeane and Quinn headed back to the
entrance and began checking in guests.

Chapter 47: October 17

Quinn was surprised when Abdul Salaam deposited her at the sheik's beachfront pergola. She'd expected to watch the gyrfalcon fly at the training center like the peregrines had. But she was most astonished by all the work completed on the property since her last visit. The shoreline dock system and boathouse were finished and filled with several watercraft. A fifty-foot luxury motor yacht was berthed inside. A twenty-five-foot Chris-Craft cabin cruiser was docked next to it. It was like the antique wooden boats she'd seen in the Les Cheneaux Islands in the Upper Peninsula. Quinn also noticed three Dauntless Rams of varying lengths moored at the end of the extensive dock system. She knew what they were because they were the same models used by law enforcement to police the Great Lakes. Several men in robes and keffiyehs patrolled the area, their high-performance firearms obvious.

Near the sheik's home on the hillside, more building had taken place in an open area cleared of trees. She could make out a large structure with a curved roof and a wide front door. Two helicopters sat inside. One appeared to be a single-rotor utility copter. The other was larger with both main and tail rotors, reminding her of the MH-60 Jayhawks the Coast Guard used for rescue and military ops. Outside the hangar was a forty-foot circular helipad marked with an H in the center. The area bustled with activity, and she could make out armed guards there, too.

Quinn was puzzled by the new structures. First of all, how had the sheik managed to build them when construction was at a standstill due to COVID? The County Road Commission had delayed several of its summer projects, and most residential and commercial construction work had gone unfinished due to a lack of contractors and supplies. And then there was all the security. It went far beyond Abdul Salaam, the sheik's bodyguard, with protection at the shoreline and the helipad. The sheik felt in danger. She wondered if it had something to do with his U Nonimmigrant Visa that Ian'd discovered. There was more going on than she understood. But before she could figure it out, the sheik came walking towards her with the most beautiful bird she'd ever seen.

It immediately reminded her of the Snowy Owls she'd photographed when Up North winters had been colder. The bird was pure white with some fine brown streaking on its head. It was larger than any of the peregrines she'd seen. Quinn's eyes were drawn to the bird's densely feathered thighs, which gave the impression the gyr was wearing pants.

"Miss Quinn. So glad to see you again. Meet my gyrfalcon, Zohra."

"She's beautiful. I suppose her name has a special meaning like the other falcons you own."

"Yes, of course. Zohra means jewel of the sky," he said as he stroked the bird's cheek and set her on the perch inside the pergola.

"She's not wearing a hood like the other falcons you've shown me."

"No, Zohra is very calm. I've had her for eleven years since she was just a chick. We trust each other implicitly."

"Where does she come from?"

"A region in northeast Russia."

"The Kamchatka Peninsula, perhaps?"

The sheik's face darkened into a scowl at hearing Quinn mention the specific place where Zohra was born, but he didn't respond.

"Would you like to see her fly and hunt? I think she's hungry."

"I would. I was surprised that we weren't meeting at the training center, where you've flown the other falcons."

"Zohra no longer hunts for competition. She's my pet and lives in my home, much like your Ruby does. Speaking of Ruby, how is your furry friend?"

Quinn told the sheik about Ruby's history as a Search and Rescue sniffer dog and her recent training as a drug detection dog.

"Ruby left yesterday for a week-long training camp to prepare for her final certification. I really miss her."

"I imagine so. Shall we get started with Zohra?"

They walked outside the pergola and north up the beach towards some low dunes dotted with abundant grasses and scrub vegetation. Without a word, the sheik lifted his fist, and the gyr cast off into the sky. They watched her circle above the dunes.

"She doesn't seem to be flying as high as your peregrines," Quinn said.

"You're right. Peregrines are known for their high-altitude dives to catch their prey. Gyrs hunt differently. Watch, and you'll see."

Zohra glided above the dunes, her fan-shaped tail and steady wing beats powering the flight. She soared on the thermals the warm October sunshine provided. At first, Quinn thought the gyr lacked the intensity of the peregrine, but she was wrong. At a leisurely pace, Zohra dropped from the sky and flew horizontally above the dune grasses, flushing prey as she flew. Seeing a small ring-necked pheasant, Zohra rose into the sky, turned, and dove straight down onto the prey, killing it instantly. The gyr looked back at the sheik, who raised his arm in the air. Immediately, the falcon grabbed the dead prey, flew back to the sheik, and dropped it at his feet. Waiting. The sheik laughed and nodded to Abdul Salaam, who came forward and expertly excised the heart from the partridge and gave it to the sheik. He placed it on the ground next to Zohra, who quivered with excitement as she consumed the trophy from her kill. While she ate, Abdul Salaam gathered the rest of the partridge and waited for the sheik to make the next move.

After the gyr finished her meal, the sheik said, "Let's head up to my house. It's time to get Zohra back inside. I assume you'll be able to stay for a pheasant dinner with Ruby being away at camp. I think we have some things to discuss."

Chapter 48: That Afternoon

They'd settled Zohra into her indoor mew and had some lunch when the sheik suggested a boat ride. Even though it was mid-October, the temperatures had risen to the low seventies.

"Let's not waste a sunny day," the sheik said. "Besides, the fall colors along the shoreline are spectacular."

"Sounds wonderful," Quinn said. "How do you like the seasonal changes in this part of our country?"

"I enjoy that about living here. It's nice being able to get Zohra and the other falcons outdoors in the cooler months, especially winter."

They walked down to the boathouse, entered the Chris-Craft, and settled into the leather swivel chairs at the rear. As Abdul Salaam expertly backed the boat out onto Lake Michigan, Quinn watched two semipalmated plovers hopping around in the shallows. She could hear their chatter above the quiet hum of the boat's inboard motor. *Che-che-che.* She wondered if the small shorebirds had begun their southward winter migration. She turned her attention to the lake, watching the V trail spread on the flat water behind them. She also noticed one of the Dauntless Rams following them with two armed guards standing on the stern, their weapons dangling from shoulder slings.

As they cruised the shoreline, they took in the resplendent fall colors on the hillsides beyond the low dunes. Splashes of red and orange from the maples. Striking yellows from quaking aspen and larch. Deep browns from the oaks. The sheik got up, walked a few steps down to the galley, and retrieved a jug of cherry ginger cider from the refrigerator. As he poured two glasses, Quinn noticed it was from the Taproot Cider House in Traverse City. The sheik seemed to be assimilating into local culture in some ways, Quinn thought, but wondered whether he would ever shed his long robes and keffiyeh now that he no longer needed protection from the desert heat. Or did he wear them as a sign of modesty and religious devotion? Regardless, Quinn decided it was time to broach the questions she'd been hoping to ask.

"The last time we met, you commented that trafficking birds is a serious enterprise for governments across the globe, the Russian mafia, and desperate Bedouin trappers. You said the illegal falcon trade was second only to weapons smuggling in the Middle East. What else can you tell me about this trafficking business?"

"Hmmm. What made you bring up such an unsavory topic, Miss Quinn? Are you not enjoying our ride to watch these lovely colors?"

"I'm enjoying it, I promise. And I'll tell you why I've asked after you answer my question."

"Harrumph, if you insist," the sheik said. "The illegal falcon trade is a complex interplay between history and money."

"By history, I assume you're referring to the stories you told me earlier about desert Bedouins using falcons to hunt food for their families."

"Yes, there's that. Plus, as falconry became a favorite pastime for Middle Eastern royalty, the demand for these birds increased."

"How does one go about catching a falcon?"

The sheik laughed, lightening the mood that had become serious with Quinn's inquiry. "I remember how I caught my first falcon as a young boy. It was a simple process. My brother and I walked into the desert. We brought along ground squirrels we'd caught and planned to use as lures. Once we were far away from our village, we lay down on the ground and covered ourselves as best we could with sand, leaving our heads and arms free. We then held the squirrels up and waited. It only took ten or fifteen minutes before a prairie falcon came and grabbed the squirrels. The first few times, the falcons were faster than we were and got away with our lures. Finally, though, we got our timing correct and were able to seize the falcons before they escaped. Our success brought great rejoicing."

"What a story! But that's not how falcons are caught for trafficking now, is it?"

"No, but it's similar. Trappers now drive into remote desert areas on motorbikes or in pickups during trapping season, which goes from late August to November. They often camp for weeks at a time. When they spot a bird, the trappers release a pigeon or quail that has a small trap made of looped iron wire on its back. The falcon swoops to the lure, but its talons get tangled in the trap. It takes off but soon tires from the weight of the prey. Finally, it lands, and the hunters throw a net over the grounded falcon, capturing it for sale."

"That's where the money aspect of falcon trafficking comes in."

"Yes. Trappers can expect to get anywhere between $1,000 and $30,000 per bird, depending on the breed. That's a lot of money for poor desert folk."

"I thought the trend in falconry was towards captive-bred birds. Didn't you even tell me the sport has outlawed wild falcons?"

"That is true, Miss Quinn," the sheik said, his voice rising. "The practice of hunting with wild falcons was outlawed due to the toll it took on various species, some of which are threatened with extinction."

"Those laws sound like they aren't being enforced."

"They're not. In some Gulf countries, lawlessness is rampant due to ongoing war. And even though testing has shown no difference in speed and prowess between captive-bred and wild-caught falcons, a demand still exists for the latter, especially among tribal sheiks and royalty. Wild-caught falcons are more prestigious in wealthier circles."

"So, how do the trappers smuggle the birds?"

"You are so full of questions, Quinn Macarthy. I'll answer this one, and then it's time to hear why you're so interested in this topic."

"Fair enough."

"Smugglers stuff swaddled and drugged falcons into suitcases with false bottoms, mailing tubes, car seats, even down their trousers before traveling by car or plane to invitation-only sales in private homes. Whatever the method, smuggling falcons is always traumatic for the birds, and many don't survive, often dying due to suffocation in transit."

"How awful!"

"Truly. Gyrs often fare the worst because they've come from Russia's far-eastern Kamchatka subarctic region, which has cold, snowy winters and cool, wet summers. Many don't make the transition to the desert climate, dying from the heat and disease. Despite these challenges, gyrfalcons are in highest demand because of their white color and beauty. Their sales sometimes bring up to $100,000 per bird."

"Unbelievable, but sad."

As the Chris-Craft pulled into its slip at the sheik's compound, his staff secured the boat to its moorings, scoped out the surroundings for any danger, and accompanied Quinn and Badr-Uddin to his hillside home.

Chapter 49: That Evening

The sheik's chef had prepared a delectable meal for them, expertly roasting the pheasant Zohra had caught. He'd made root vegetables, mashed potatoes, and Brussels sprouts as side dishes. They'd finished a bottle of Pinot Noir when the sheik suggested they move to the living room with its expansive views of Lake Michigan. The sun had already set, but the sky was still deep blue with streaks of pink and gold.

"I'm ready to hear what's made you so interested in falcon smuggling, Miss Quinn."

"Yes, I will tell you the story. But please, just call me Quinn."

"I can do that if you'll call me by my given name also. Badr." He pronounced it Baa-der, with the second syllable short and clipped.

Quinn was quiet for a moment while she gathered her thoughts and decided where to begin. She told the sheik about the counterfeit Avipel case she'd worked on two years ago. How they'd traced the source of the imitation pesticide to the Russian mafia. That they'd captured one of the middlemen in their bust. How the main U.S. liaison to the syndicate, George Watkins, had mysteriously died, and they'd later learned he'd been murdered from a massive injection of the heart stimulant epinephrine. That his foreign-speaking nurse and computer had gone missing after his death.

"What's wrong with your jaw, Quinn? I notice you have a scar there that you've been rubbing. Were you somehow injured while you worked the case?"

"I was assaulted during the takedown of the middlemen, but the scar comes from a previous injury during my rookie year."

"It must bother you the way you're pawing at it."

"It prickles when I'm nerved up, like now. But let me get back to my story."

Quinn resumed talking but worried it appeared she was getting off track. She told Badr of her homeless friend Mack and how he'd died of illicitly manufactured fentanyl, presumably smuggled through the Russian syndicate.

"Your story has more than one thread, Quinn. Perhaps we need to cork our second bottle of Pinot Noir. Counterfeit pesticides and illegal fentanyl. Do they fit together?"

"I'm getting to that, Badr. Don't you see? They all relate to the Russian mafia."

"Okay, I understand. But what do they have to do with falcon smuggling?"

"You said the Russian mafia was involved in falcon smuggling, just like they're involved in counterfeit pesticides and fentanyl trafficking."

"Yes, but this organization is way more complex than you're depicting it. It's not a solitary entity. When the former Soviet Union dissolved in 1991, more than 6,000 gangs emerged under the rubric of the Russian mafia. These mobsters now operate in more than fifty countries around the world with thirty Russian crime syndicates working in at least seventeen cities in the U.S."

"You seem to know a lot about the Russian Mafia. What do you know about mobster Pavel Pilecki? And his relationship with Prince Farouk Al-Kirdar Haboori."

At the mention of both names, the sheik went silent, his face darkening, his eyebrows arching. Quinn could tell from his expression that she'd crossed the line. Their budding friendship had entered new territory. Perhaps it'd even been destroyed.

"How did you come by this information? Have you been nosing into my past? What would make you betray our amity?"

"That was never my intent. When I first met you, I was really interested in your work. Still am. But I was also curious. You seemed out of place here. I wondered what would make an Arab from Dubai settle here in the Northwoods."

"So you started snooping into my identity?"

"That's what I do, Badr. I'm a detective. I look into things that seem off."

"And did you learn that I spent several years in charge of the Detroit River International Wildlife Refuge working to re-nest peregrines in the Erie Basin?"

"I learned that your new center here is related to that downstate program, but I didn't know that you ran it."

"Small detail omitted, I'd say. I'm on a legitimate mission as a guest of the United States to help repopulate peregrines in Michigan. Our goal is to get these falcons off the endangered list."

"You say you're here as our country's guest. How does that relate to your U Nonimmigrant Visa? For victims of criminal activity occurring in the United States or that violated U.S. laws. For those who've suffered substantial mental or physical abuse due to the criminal activity. I've noticed your scarred hands, Badr. And your missing fingertip."

The sheik reached for the half-gone bottle of Pinot Noir and topped off his glass. He moved the wine towards Quinn's, but she put her hand over the top, indicating she'd had enough.

"And there's more to question, Badr. What about your bodyguard and all the security you're building into the compound? You're obviously in some kind of danger."

The sheik nodded slowly, his face expressionless. He got up and walked towards the bank of windows overlooking the dark lake. He turned to Quinn as she continued peppering him with questions.

"I want to hear what you know about Pavel Pilecki and his relationship with Prince Farouk. I've learned they're buddies. Playboys on the Eastern European and Middle Eastern social scenes. Both are avid falconers. I also recently learned that Pavel Pilecki's sister, Mika, was most likely the nurse responsible for administering the heart stimulant that killed George Watkins, the American liaison to Pilecki's group. They were recently photographed together in Belarus, Pilecki's home base."

The sheik asked, "You think I can help you find and capture this woman?"

But Quinn was on a roll with her inquiry and resumed, "And what about your relationship with the Prince? I know you were the head trainer at his falconry center outside Dubai. The two of you were well known for setting up training protocols used throughout the Gulf states. You also were renowned for winning top prizes at worldwide competitions. Then, suddenly, somewhere around 2010, I believe, there was nothing in the news about the two of you. Did you have some kind of falling out?"

The sheik sighed and sat back down on the loveseat he'd been occupying. He poured himself another glass of wine and raised the bottle towards Quinn. Again, she nodded no. Finally, after taking several gulps that drained his glass, he looked straight into her eyes.

"Your detective work is very good, Quinn Macarthy."

Chapter 50: The Next Morning

Quinn opened her eyes, acutely aware she wasn't in her own bed. As daylight streamed in through the windows, she took in her surroundings. The 50" large-screen television hung on the wall. Nearby, a teak desk piled with paperwork and a computer. The rich maroon Turkish floor sofa she was lying on. And then she remembered. The dinner and discussion she'd had with the sheik the night before. Too much Pinot Noir. No wonder she had a red wine headache. She'd agreed she wasn't fit to drive. Badr had sent Abdul Salaam to retrieve the overnight bag she always kept in her car. But she'd fallen asleep in what must be the sheik's den before he returned. She rummaged in her bag for the bottle of Extra-Strength Excedrin and downed two tablets. She sat up slowly, working to keep the nausea at bay. She headed to the bathroom off the den with her bag and turned on the water. As she soaked her head under the steaming shower, she recalled last evening. The revelations she'd made about Badr's connections to Prince Farouk and Pavel Pilecki. His anger at being the source of her sleuthing. Quinn knew she had to regain Badr's trust if they were going to accomplish anything together. She worried she might've ruined the only hope she had to catch the rogue mobster that'd plagued her the last two years. She dressed in the fresh clothing from her overnight bag and stepped out of the bathroom, beginning to feel human again. She followed her nose towards the kitchen, where she found Badr humming at the stove and cooking breakfast.

"Good morning, Miss Quinn. I imagine you are hungry," Badr said.

Quinn looked at him and nodded, disappointed that he'd reverted to addressing her formally. "I see you're cooking instead of your chef. It smells delicious."

"Sometimes I tire of everyone hovering over me, so I sent them all away for the day. Thought it would be easier to talk if we had some privacy."

He set breakfast on the table and sat down. Freshly squeezed orange juice. A bowl of sliced melon. Eggs scrambled with tomatoes, peppers, and spices stuffed into pita pockets. Hot cinnamon tea. They dug into their meals without conversation.

Finally, Quinn said, "This is all delicious. You are an excellent cook, Badr."

"Thank you, Miss Quinn."

She winced at the decorum that had returned to the sheik's speech. He was silent as he gathered up the dishes, wiped down the table, freshened their tea, and sat back down.

"I will tell you my story now," Badr began matter-of-factly. "My father was a falconer employed in the aviary of Prince Farouk Al-Kirdar Haboori's father. The king. At an early age, I was singled out as having the gift for training falcons, especially the peregrines and gyrs. I was eager to join the apprentice team, but at age sixteen, the king sent me away to study wildlife ecology and conservation at Bangor University in Wales. From there, I did postgraduate work at the University of British Columbia in Vancouver in ornithology, specializing in breeding birds from high-elevation habitats."

"No wonder your English is excellent."

Badr inclined his head slightly and said, "I returned to Dubai at the age of twenty-two, finally prepared to work with the birds I loved."

"With all the education, did you still have to serve an apprenticeship?"

"I did. Book learning's not the same as hands-on training."

The sheik rose and began to pace around the large, sunlit kitchen as he spoke. He seemed almost unaware that Quinn was present, telling his story by rote, as though he'd mulled it over in his mind many times.

"The falconry world was changing by the time I came back. The focus had shifted from hunting to sport, from using wild-caught falcons to breeding captive-bred birds. New regulations had been enacted to prevent the import and export of all but ones captively bred. I began to understand that I'd been sent away to learn these new methods. The royal family was on board with the changes because they knew they would save falconry from becoming a dying sport. The prince, just five years older than me, had been educated abroad too, but on the business side of falconry. We worked together to develop breeding protocols, first using artificial insemination and then progressing to natural propagation. We tested our captive-bred birds and found they performed equally well against birds from the wild. Our training facility became second to none, the premier place in the Middle East to acquire captive-bred peregrines and gyrfalcons."

"Why those two breeds?"

"As falcon racing spread, larger, stronger, and faster birds were in demand. Gyrs, being the largest raptor, were prized for their power. Peregrines for their ability to stoop at speeds of 240 miles an hour. The best falconers preferred those two breeds."

The sheik set his tea down and motioned for Quinn to follow him as he walked through his living room, opened the front sliders, and went down the hill to the beach pergola. It was another sunny autumn day. Puffy, cumulous clouds scudded across the blue sky. It wasn't yet noon, but Quinn felt the temperatures must be near seventy. As they relaxed in the comfortable outdoor furniture, she looked around the hillside and noticed not a single armed guard.

"While using captive-bred birds had become the benchmark in modern falconry sport, not everyone was on board," the sheik continued. "Some enthusiasts in the Gulf still believed wild birds were genetically superior and spent hundreds of thousands of dollars for birds acquired by unscrupulous trappers poaching from raptor-rich environments such as the Kamchatka Peninsula. Several even argued the birds were better off cared for by wealthy Arab falconers in a training center than left to survive the harsh conditions of the Russian Far East."

"Prince Farouk wasn't part of that, was he?"

Ignoring her question, he continued, "Besides the prince's love of falconry, he also enjoyed beautiful women and life in the fast lane, as you Americans call it. Drinking, partying, staying out all night. He'd started dating a young starlet from Belarus and, by default, left the training center mostly up to me. I saw less and less of him."

"Mika Pilecki."

Badr nodded, got up from his beach chair, and walked towards the shoreline, still talking. Even though he'd not motioned for Quinn to follow, she did. He seemed to be in another place. As they made their way along the water's edge, Badr trudged through the shallows. Waves sending foam over his shoe tops went unnoticed.

"With the prince involved elsewhere, I began handling the business side of the center too. It wasn't my area of expertise, but I knew enough to get by. One day, I passed through the hatchling room and found a new brood of five gyrfalcons. I was puzzled because I always kept close tabs on which birds were breeding and when their chicks would arrive. I worried that I'd missed something as I focused my time on the commercial aspects. I tried to contact the prince, but he wouldn't return my calls."

"Huh," Quinn muttered, absently rubbing her jaw.

"So I began digging into the breeding manifests to see what I could learn about these young gyrs. I discovered this brood had no propagation papers on file, which is highly irregular. I poked through more documents and found export papers for some of our birds that I knew were fake because the numbers on the manifests didn't match the certifications we kept for our captive-bred falcons. I became suspicious that something illegal was going on. Something I'd not been informed about. Something I'd never want to be associated with the training center."

Quinn was sure Badr had seen the driftwood that'd washed up along the shoreline. It was right in their pathway and seemed impossible to miss. But the sheik was wrapped up in his story, paying attention only to the next step in his narrative. Quinn hadn't the time to warn him when his foot caught the edge of the log, and he flew headlong into the water, clutching his knee and writhing in agony.

Chapter 51: That Afternoon

Badr was resting on his living room couch, leg elevated, an ice pack draped over his bent knee. Quinn hadn't known how she was going to get the sheik out of the water and into his home after his distracted fall. But within seconds, Abdul Salaam had arrived on the beach in his golf cart along with several other armed guards, bringing medical attention. Had Badr lied to her about sending his security away? Or had they not listened to him and watched for his safety from afar? With the sheik settled, his chef brought them a charcuterie board piled with cured meats, pates, cheeses, breads, and fruit. Quinn got up and filled a small plate for Badr, but he only took a couple of bites before setting it aside, preferring to finish his story.

"I can't tell you the sense of betrayal I felt from the prince, Quinn. We'd worked together on building and running the Dubai training center from the beginning. I couldn't imagine where the treachery had come from with my family's strong connections to the royals."

"When did you begin to connect it to Pilecki?"

"I started paying better attention to what was in the news. Not just Pavel and Farouk doing the playboy scene, but what was being said about Pilecki outside that realm. His connections to the Russian mafia, especially. I had no idea he was on Interpol's wanted list."

"Hmmm."

"My concerns grew into fear. The breeding center and its falcons were my lifeblood. I couldn't let it go down to unscrupulous practices. When I heard that Russia was the only country that had failed to stop smuggling wild falcons, I worried that trafficked gyrs and peregrines were being laundered through our Dubai facility."

"You were entering dangerous territory, Badr."

"I'm afraid so. But I began taking precautions. I copied all the falsified documents I could find and hid them in a safe deposit box.

I socked away my income and savings in offshore bank accounts in case I needed to run. I tried talking sense into Farouk, but he called my accusations absurd. Said I had an overactive imagination. But among the lies and inconsistencies, I knew something wicked was going on."

Quinn waited while Badr collected his thoughts.

"One night, they came for me at my home. Warned me to stop snooping into things that were none of my business. They hammered my hands and cut off the end of my index finger. They ran a knife along my face until it drew blood. When they left, I had a hunch they were going to my center to get their brood of gyrfalcons. I guessed they already had a buyer for them."

"They could've killed you, Badr," Quinn said.

"I cleaned my wounds as best I could and stemmed the bleeding from my fingertip with a washcloth. Even though I was in pain from my injuries, I drove myself to the center, hoping to stop the robbery of the beautiful gyrs, but I was too late. They'd already taken four of the five, leaving behind the weakest chick who didn't appear she'd survive. I tended to the bird, hand-feeding her, hydrating her, and finally putting her in a portable incubator. My finger had bled through the washcloth, so I rewrapped it a second time, grabbed the incubator and a bag I'd packed for such an occasion, and set off for the United States Consulate."

"The gyr was Zohra, wasn't it?"

Badr nodded and continued, "It was the middle of the night, but they opened the gates and let me in, under guard. They immediately called in medical personnel to address my wounds. When I mentioned I had information about illegal falcon trafficking and Pavel Pilecki, they informed the ambassador, who arrived shortly afterward."

"So, did they give you asylum or put you in witness protection in exchange for information? Are you some kind of confidential informant?"

"Not fully. They were eager for my paperwork because it confirmed their suspicions about the falcon trafficking going on out of Russia. But my information didn't connect definitively enough with Pavel Pilecki, so it wasn't as useful as they'd hoped."

The sheik groaned as he shifted his knee position on the couch, obviously in pain. Finally, he was able to continue.

"They did, however, facilitate getting Zohra and me out of Dubai to America through the U Non-Immigrant visa as long as I continued to share anything I learned about falcon trafficking from Russia. They also advocated for me in getting the peregrine repopulation job at the Detroit River-Western Lake Erie Basin."

"What about this compound and all the security surrounding you? Is that provided by our government, too?"

"No, the land, buildings, and security are all mine. Bought and paid for with the savings I brought with me when I emigrated from the UAE. At first, life in the Detroit area was good with the large Arab population there, but I worried that's exactly where they'd come looking for me, so I sought out a place I could continue my work more discreetly."

"It must be lonely up here with little contact to your culture."

"Sometimes it feels that way. But overall, I feel safer here. I do get regular updates from the FBI on any unusual movements of the Russian mafia in this area, which has been rare. They're mostly confined to territories in New York, Chicago, Las Vegas, and Miami."

"You're in contact with the FBI?"

"Yes, Quinn. Both through your old friend Zoey Rogers in the Traverse City satellite office and your brother Rowan in Cleveland."

Quinn was stunned at this news and couldn't find words to respond. She and Zoey had been in the same Forensic Science Master's Program at Michigan State. Zoey had gone to Quantico following graduation for training with the FBI and then placement at the field office in Detroit and, more recently, the satellite office in TC.

"You're not the only one doing good detective work," Badr continued. "The Russian mob has tentacles with a wide reach, and I am determined to protect myself and my life's work. If that means staying in touch with the FBI, so be it."

"Huh," Quinn said, still speechless. "Do you know why Mika Pilecki was in the States?"

"I didn't even know she'd been here until you shared your story about her being George Watkins' nurse. When I hadn't seen Farouk and Mika in the news, I just assumed he'd moved on to his next starlet. I'm puzzled, though, why Pilecki would dispose of a top boss."

"Good question. I guess that Watkins knew too much about his organization. His computer went missing when Mika left the country. Probably contained a treasure trove of information and contacts."

"Huh."

"Badr, you've got to help us apprehend this guy. He's responsible for so much evil. Black marketing dangerous counterfeit goods like pesticides, smuggling illicitly manufactured drugs into our country, and trafficking wild-caught falcons."

"I hear you, Quinn. But I don't see how I can help. Besides, Pavel Pilecki never travels outside Eastern Europe, Russia, and the Gulf States. He knows where he's outlawed and takes every precaution to keep himself safe."

Chapter 52: November 12

Quinn hadn't seen Badr since mid-October, when the two of them had shared information about the Russian Mafia and Pavel Pilecki. She'd returned to her regular routines since then, but something different had begun creeping into the collective psyche. They were calling it the new normal, and it appeared to be pandemic-related. Leaf peepers still visited the Northwoods, for example, but their numbers were greatly reduced due to a cautionary attitude. Fewer people were willing to chance packed bus rides to travel between vineyards to taste the fruits of the fall harvest or view the vibrant color show. Those that did come stuck to their vehicles or rented RVs for the trip.

Quinn had embarked on her new responsibilities in drug detection after Ruby had passed her certification with flying colors. As Gilda promised, she'd kept the two of them busy with work at the airport and traffic stops. Quinn enjoyed the new work, but maintaining the rigorous safety protocols was getting old. The constant handwashing, masking, social distancing, and equipment disinfecting were tiresome. Her women's hockey league had just begun again, yet the players returned without the usual verve of hugging and back-slapping that accompanied a new season. Even on the ice, they feared person-to-person contact.

As the pandemic droned on, tele-everything became the norm for living with COVID. Working remotely grew into the standard business model. Schools went from in-person to distance learning whenever the infection numbers increased. Zoom evolved from corporate meetings to medical and mental health appointments. Other struggles affected people's lives, too. Temporary layoffs fueled high unemployment. Supply chain issues resulted in high food costs and shortages. Social isolation and anxiety crept into the nation's psychological well-being. And all these troubles played out against a contentious fall political campaign that resulted in electing a new president. One that trusted science and gave people hope that they'd somehow get through these trying times.

While Quinn had maintained social contact with her closest friends, her bond with Patrick had suffered. Before the pandemic, they'd been nearly inseparable in their pursuits around photography and winter sports. But Patrick had a mind of his own and could be contrary about following rules he felt weren't warranted. That had become painfully obvious during COVID when his righteous anti-masker stance put him at odds with others. And while they'd never talked politics, Quinn was pretty sure they'd canceled out each other's votes in the recent election. Still, she felt their friendship was worth saving, so she suggested they head to Kingsley, where the last of the sandhill cranes were leaving for their migration south.

"So, you still seeing your buddy, the sheik?" Patrick asked as they drove.

"He's not my buddy, Patrick. I've only been interested in watching him fly his falcons."

"Is that why you spent the weekend with him recently?"

"What??? Where did you get that idea?"

"I stopped by your house the weekend Ruby was at drug detection training camp. Thought you might want some company. You'd told me you were going to the sheik's Saturday morning to watch his gyrfalcon fly. When you didn't return, well, you know what I assumed."

"Patrick, you, of all people, should know I wouldn't be romantically involved with Badr."

"Badr? You're now on a first-name basis with the guy?"

They continued in icy silence and reached Harrand Road in Mayfield Township, west of Kingsley. Car windows down, they followed the sky-born calls and located masses of cranes staging in fields along the verge. Quinn and Patrick began taking pictures as sedge after sedge rose in unison against the backdrop of fall color into the gray autumn sky, their 1500-mile journey south to Florida underway. The cranes, necks outstretched and legs taut behind them, were amazing to watch. Their cacophonous bugling was so loud it made conversation difficult. As the last of the cranes took flight, they sat there silently, clicking through the pictures on the backs of their cameras to see what they'd gotten.

"You have time to catch dinner?" Patrick asked.

"I can't tonight but would love to another time. With the second COVID wave hitting Munson, Vernadeane and I are going to MCM to test the guests. Trying to keep the homeless population as safe as possible."

"A second wave?"

"Yeah. The pandemic response plan just moved to Level Orange, the second-highest step. Forty people are currently hospitalized in two isolation units that are nearing capacity."

"Huh. Wasn't aware of that."

"Maybe you should quit watching so much fake news."

Chapter 53: December 21

It was the Winter Solstice, the longest night of the year. Around the country, people marked the beginning of winter and participated in the annual silent walk that was part of National Homeless Persons' Memorial Day. Twelve homeless people had died this year in Traverse City. Four had been murdered. The rest had passed away from harsh living conditions, chronic health problems, or drug overdoses.

They'd started the evening at the Rare Bird because of its proximity to the governmental center, where the walk would begin. Gilda and Flint hadn't been able to attend due to being in charge of traffic and crowd control. Ian and Hannah had joined the group in solidarity with their friends' work with the local homeless population. The mood among them at the restaurant was subdued. They'd even chosen a booth at the back without much lighting. Nobody had much to say. Everyone knew Quinn and Vernadeane were especially affected by the walk because of their frontline work to combat homelessness. Quinn picked at the fried cheese curds she'd ordered. Vernadeane nursed a Big Lake Michigan Amber and pushed her beet salad around on its plate. Finally, they paid their tabs and walked up Eighth Street towards the Governmental Center on Boardman.

A group of at least a hundred folks had already gathered in the front of the building where a small podium had been set up. Everyone in the crowd held lighted votives, which flickered in the slight evening breeze. As Quinn waited for the ceremony to begin, she looked around and saw a few familiar faces. Men from the Pines there to remember Riley and Moose. The restaurant manager from Centre Ice who'd served Mack free cups of coffee. Paula Stafford, Michael Stafford's sister. Her four-year-old daughter Lexie in a stroller. The child's eyes lit up when she saw Flint walking towards her with a lollipop. Jack Kreps, a regular volunteer at the mission. And then Quinn saw Susan Pugh, whose son David Lathrop had murdered four homeless people. At first, Quinn's gut churned in anger, thinking how dare she attend this somber event. Then she remembered that, in some ways, Susan had lost a son too.

As Mayor Janet Perkins walked to the podium, twelve members from the crowd lined up behind her, holding votives that remained to be lit.

"Tonight, we are here to remember those who died while experiencing homelessness this year and in past years," the mayor began. "Cities across our nation are holding similar memorials on this longest night of the year as a reminder of how challenging it can be to survive winter, especially in our northern climates. But mostly, we've come to remember those who died in Traverse City due to being homeless. Their lives, their smiles, and their struggles. We're also here to raise awareness that it doesn't have to be this way. As I call the names of the twelve men and women we lost in 2020, a representative for each person will come forward to light a candle in their honor. Once all names are read, we will silently march downtown and back to remember these people."

The mayor read the first two names, whom the law enforcement teams didn't recognize.

As Perkins said, "Keegan Cammack," Quinn came forward to light Mack's votive. Her face glistened in the candlelight.

The mayor read three more names, anonymous too in the wider community.

Then she read, "Connie Jordan." A man and a woman wearing starched white uniforms came forward to light her candle. Quinn guessed the duo had been Connie's bosses from the laundromat. No ex-boyfriend to pay his respects.

Another three names Quinn didn't recognize. She was surprised there were so many homeless people she didn't know, especially with her close involvement with the community and her work at the mission.

Perkins next called Riley, followed by Moose. MCM volunteers Jack Kreps and his wife came forward to light their candles. Still unidentified with no known next-of-kin, Quinn was saddened at the lack of support many of these people had. If it weren't for the police, the mission, and the volunteers, she didn't know what would've happened to them.

Lastly, the mayor said, "Michael Stafford." Paula came forward holding Lexie in her arms. As she lit the candle in remembrance of her brother, the votive's glow highlighted the child's face smeared with lollipop juice and brought smiles to those who saw it.

The mayor led the way down Boardman Avenue, the twelve candle holders next, the crowd filling in behind with their votives. They wended their way past Grace Episcopal and The Coin Slot, turning onto Front Street into downtown. Quinn was surprised that the group had maintained absolute silence, only the sounds of their winter boots padding along on the sidewalks heard in the cold night. Patrick and Ian had walked beside Quinn, knowing she'd appreciate their support. While Mack was never far from her thoughts, the night had intensified her grief. The new hockey season wasn't the same without him there yelling, 'Hey, Right Winger. Good game.' The solstice memorial had also intensified her commitment to put away the drug trafficker who'd supplied the fentanyl that'd killed him. Whether it was through her drug sniffing work with Ruby or the law enforcement team stopping Pilecki's network, Quinn was resolved to get it done.

Chapter 54: December 31

Over the last few years, they'd become best friends. Gilda, Patrick, Quinn, Ian, and Hannah. Their get-togethers were legendary. Meeting at Kilkenny's after Quinn's hockey games to celebrate her victories. Summer picnics at the Lakeshore that ended up being gourmet events. A Halloween Bootleggers Ball held at a now-closed downtown speakeasy. New Year's Eve gatherings to close out the old and ring in the new. All were marked by amazing food, plentiful drink, and a wealth of laughter and hijinks.

Because of pandemic rules surrounding large gatherings, they planned to celebrate New Year's Eve 2020 at the Doyles' newly renovated cottage on Hurdmans Bay at Crystal Lake. Patrick, Quinn, and Gilda had traveled together in her jeep from Traverse City, arriving just after 6 p.m. When local weatherman Joe Charlevoix forecasted the evening temperatures to be in the low fifties and with no snow on the ground, they decided to take their party to the beach, wondering if the unseasonably warm December temperatures were part of the new normal.

With the change of plans, they scavenged through the Doyles' refrigerator for food more suitable for the lakeshore than the gourmet items they'd already prepared, saving that meal for later. The sun had set about an hour earlier, but the sky was still bright from the waxing gibbous moon when they arrived at Old Indian Trail. The pathway had gotten its name from a time when Native Americans used the route to access their fishing camps along Lake Michigan. They unloaded the jeep and began the two-and-a-half-mile trek through gently rolling dunes, evergreens, and hardwoods.

When they arrived at the beach, they were silent, observing the expanse of dark sea against an equally inky sky, only the nearly full moon casting a yellow pathway across the lake's glassy surface.

Tranquil waves barely made a sound as they reached the shoreline. Under the vault of stars and sky, they felt small and insignificant.

"I've observed this scene a thousand times, yet I'm always awed when I see it again," Quinn said.

"I hear you," the others chorused.

After a few more moments in silence, they spread out along the beach just south of Platte Bay to gather driftwood for a fire. No other people or fires as far as they could see.

They dropped the dry wood onto the sand, opened the beach chairs they'd carried on their backs, and sat in a circle as Ian added kindling to the driftwood and started a fire that roared and snapped.

"Anyone ready for a beer?" Patrick said as he opened the cooler and extracted the twelve-pack of Harp's Lager he'd carried in.

They all eagerly popped their cans and took their first sips. The absence of conversation and gaiety was glaring. They were glad to be observing the holiday together at the beach, but the mood was more melancholy than usual.

When the fire settled down enough for cooking, Gilda passed around paper plates, napkins, plastic utensils, and long roasting forks. Quinn and Hannah laid a red and white plaid vinyl tablecloth on the ground and added hot dogs, buns, condiments, and store-bought baked beans. Patrick opened a bag of marshmallows and placed it near the other food, along with packets of graham crackers and Hershey's chocolate bars. Soon, they were all roasting hot dogs, making s'mores, eating, and attempting conversation.

"I can't believe how warm it is for the end of December."

"You think the Lions are gonna make the playoffs this year?"

"How are things going at the newspaper these days?

"What have you been taking pictures of lately?"

Finally, with the meal completed and talk going nowhere, Hannah brought out her 32-key Yamaha melodica and began to play and sing, hoping others would join in. She started with an old camp song, *Kum Ba Yah*, but it turned into a solo. When she moved to *Scarborough Fair* and *Amazing Grace*, she got a couple more voices to join hers. It wasn't until she played *Auld Lang Syne* that all five participated. Deciding to quit on a high note, she packed away her instrument and respected the gloom that seemed to theme the evening.

They were all stretched out in their chairs, looking up at the starry night sky.

"Look! There's a meteor shower!" Quinn exclaimed."

"Huh," Ian said.

"I bet it's left over from the Ursids since they appear to emanate from the Ursa Minor constellation," Patrick added.

"Fitting for Sleeping Bear," Quinn said. "Makes me hopeful."

They watched a bit longer as two more meteors streaked across the heavens. It was a sparse display, though, in comparison to the Perseids, which had filled the sky last August.

Looking at his watch, Ian said, "If we're gonna watch the ball drop, we should probably head back to the cottage. It's nearly 10:30, and we have over two miles to hike."

They doused the fire, picked up their chairs and supplies, and began the hike through the dunes to Gilda's jeep. Arriving back at the Doyles' cottage, they settled around the large screen TV in their great room. Ian built a fire in their new floor-to-ceiling wood-burning fireplace, hoping to warm the mood before the year ended. He flipped on the remote to catch the local news, and the CherryT Ball drop at midnight. It was a virtual livestream event this year due to the pandemic.

"Before we switch to the downtown area, we have some sobering statistics to share," the news anchor said. "Michigan ends the year with 488,134 confirmed cases of COVID and 12,333 confirmed deaths."

They were silent as they took in the human impact of the pandemic, wondering what the numbers were for Grand Traverse County. Finally, the news feed moved to the empty downtown intersection, where the CherryT Ball was about to begin its countdown to the New Year.

"Why do they call it the CherryT Ball? I don't get where the 'T' comes in," Patrick said.

They all groaned, and Hannah finally responded. "It's a play on words, Patrick. The donations taken in from the ball drop support local charities. CherryT, as in charity."

Patrick continued to look blank but said, "Okay, thanks."

"You can be such a doofus sometimes," Quinn said.

Chapter 55: January 9, 2021

As the pandemic approached its first anniversary, two events early in the new year brought hope to a grieving and depressed nation. First, the arrival of at-home rapid COVID tests helped people get immediate medical attention if they tested positive. Then, after the FDA approved new emergency vaccines, many dreamed of avoiding the virus altogether. Although the vaccines had been tested less rigorously than prior ones, people hoped they would wipe out the coronavirus, much like Salk's vaccine did with polio in 1955.

Quinn had continued her hockey season into 2021, lackluster as it was. Coronaphobia had halved the number of teams in the women's league, and even though her red team was in first place, it had become monotonous playing the same few teams over and over again. She likened it to last summer's shortened baseball season when teams only faced those within the division. Moreover, without fans in the ice rink stands and no raucous celebrating at Kilkenny's afterward, Quinn was ready to hang up her skates for the year.

But on this sunny, crisp winter morning, Quinn was driving up Old Mission to visit Badr for the first time since mid-October when she'd watched him fly Zohra, and they'd exchanged stories about their connections to the Russian mob. He'd left her a message while she was at work, saying Saturday's weather would be cold, perfect for flying his gyr, and inviting her to join him again. She was excited but wondered about the long time between their communications, unsure under what terms they'd be meeting.

Abdul Salaam and Badr met her just outside the entrance to *The Peregrine Falcon Propagation and Training Center*. They'd traded their royal blue six-seater golf cart for a bright red utility task vehicle with an enclosed cab.

"Good to see you, Quinn," Badr said as he got out of the UTV and approached her smiling.

"You too, Badr. It's been a while. I see you've gotten a new vehicle."

"Yes. We quickly discovered our battery-operated golf cart wasn't suited for the climate here in winter. This works much better."

Greetings complete, Quinn looked around and could hardly believe how the property had changed since she'd been here last. A huge parking lot. The whole property was surrounded by ten-foot black Palisade fencing, which was aesthetically pleasing and resembled wrought iron. But the narrow spacing between posts that were topped with bent tri-point pales made clear the fence was for security. Mounted surveillance cameras added to the atmosphere of impregnability.

"You've done a lot here in the last three months," Quinn exclaimed. "How'd that happen when construction workers and building materials are in such short supply?"

The sheik laughed and explained, "When I worked on the Detroit River-Western Lake Erie project, I lived in Dearborn, which has the largest concentration of Arab Americans in the country. I made lots of friends there, some of Arabian descent and some not, and that's where I got my rudimentary staff to start the peregrine repopulation center up here. After the pandemic hit, more of my contacts were eager to come north to escape the city's high COVID rates. Because the work was mostly outdoors, it was especially appealing."

"How many do you have working for you?"

"Hmmm. I'd say around a hundred fifty."

"Seriously? Where are you lodging them all? Finding affordable housing in this area is nearly impossible."

"That's been the most difficult part. But the people who came here are resourceful, intelligent, and extremely hard-working. Together, we developed a plan for them to build their own homes and apartments after they completed their forty-hour week with me. Besides the eighty acres I own for the training center and my residence, I purchased another hundred-twenty acres of farmland just down the road south of here. The downstate transplants lived in temporary shelters while they built permanent homes for themselves and their families. All the structures are now framed in, roofed, and have windows, electricity, heat, and running water. They are currently in the process of moving in so they can finish the interiors over the rest of the winter. Right now, two apartment buildings are nearly completed, each having twenty-five one or two-bedroom units. Another thirty single-family homes are also underway."

"Amazing. You've built an entire village. Why haven't I heard about this before?"

"I'm not sure. It's been in the *Record-Eagle*, mostly under construction and zoning permits versus front page stories. I think news coverage has focused on other things this past year."

"I wonder whether your immigration status and involvement with the FBI has affected the project's lack of publicity."

Badr chuckled. "I don't know, but it's certainly possible. Why don't I give you a tour before we head to my home to fly Zohra and have some lunch."

Badr ran a plastic card through a security reader, which opened a gate and let Quinn, Badr, and his bodyguard inside the grounds. They started at the first building, the breeding center, whose exterior had been mostly completed the last time Quinn visited. Now it bustled with activity, both scientists and peregrines. The building was high-ceilinged, twenty feet at the top, sloping to fourteen at the sides. A hallway ran through the middle, with individual chambers for falcons on each side. The rooms measured ten feet by twenty feet, large enough for falcon pairs to move around and even fly with the high ceilings. Each was equipped with gravel flooring, perches, nesting ledges, and baths. Offices for scientists were located between the chambers and were equipped with one-way glass so breeders could watch their birds. A veterinary clinic suitable for treating both healthy and ill falcons was located at the far end of the breeding center.

"This is amazing, Badr," Quinn said. "How does it compare to the center you had with Farouk in Dubai?"

"Same kind of set-up but much smaller here. About half the size," the sheik said. "Let me show you the training center now that it's finished."

They went outdoors to the training building, which was twice the size of the breeding center. Its wide open interior and many mesh-wired windows gave it the feeling of being outdoors, letting in abundant fresh air and sunlight. The room was filled with perches, some holding young peregrine falcons. A 200-meter racecourse complete with timing devices ran down the center of the space.

"When do you begin training these birds to hunt?"

"Remember, Quinn, these are captive-bred falcons. We train them for sport racing, not hunting prey outdoors."

"So, you transfer the young ones from the breeding facility here for their next steps?"

"Exactly. They come here when they're four to six months old to socialize with other birds and people. We want them to be relaxed in their new environment."

"Huh."

"Once they become acclimated, we begin training them on the fist and then with a lure. Eventually, we transfer those skills to teaching them to race on our indoor short course."

"But they do move to the longer course outdoors, right?"

"Yes, after about six months here, we begin mixing the indoor work with outdoor training on the 400-meter course."

"Aren't you worried they'll fly away?"

"Not at all. Most birds are trained to get their food from us, so they have no reason to leave. They're always free to fly away, but they don't."

"Do you ever find birds with no aptitude for racing?"

"All the time. Those birds are given specialized training in outdoor hunting and are released into the wild. It's how we're repopulating the peregrines up here. Let's go outside. I have one more building to show you."

As they walked on the still-unfrozen ground, Quinn tried to make sense of all she'd learned. The idea of captive-bred birds had made sense when she'd heard how it reduced the scarcity of falcons due to overhunting and poaching. But now, seeing it in action, it seemed so unnatural, both the breeding aspects and the sport. Nothing like what she'd imagined falconry to be. Quinn finally concluded that captive breeding of falcons for sport wasn't much different from breeding horses or greyhounds for racing.

As the threesome trudged across the meadow, Quinn noticed the stadium seating had been completed along both sides of the 400-meter racetrack, along with concession stands and bathrooms. It reminded her of the old Hazel Park Raceway her dad used to take them to on Friday evenings to see live harness racing.

As they drew closer, Quinn saw the biggest change was the event tent had been replaced by a new building, the size of both the breeding and training centers combined. Quinn noticed the building's unique design. A high roof peaked on several levels, colorful geometric patterns on the exterior walls, and no windows.

"What an unusual-looking structure," she said.

"Yes, it was designed for the falcons. The building has no windows to prevent bird strikes. The striking colors also help the building stand out when they are airborne."

"What is this place?" Quinn gasped as they entered the palatial building.

"It's the Hospitality Center. It contains lounge areas and souks."

"Souks?"

"An Arab bazaar."

The interior of the building contained groupings of comfortable white leather chairs, loveseats, and low tables. Colorful, patterned rugs defined several conversation areas. Perches covered with green artificial turf were placed throughout. Large screen televisions were hung so visitors could watch whatever proceedings were happening throughout the compound. Computer terminals were placed on stands so the competitors and guests could follow race results and check their emails. Stalls lined the exterior of the lounge, probably for the bazaar, but most were currently empty.

"What will go in the souks?"

"A few will be food kiosks. We'll have a small museum displaying the history of falconry. There will also be a few retail stores. One will be a gallery selling art about falconry. Another will vend supplies falconers use, such as gloves, hoods, tethers, and lures. We will also have a gift shop selling the usual touristy items: jewelry, stuffed falcons, magnets, mugs with our logo, t-shirts, and hats."

"You've accomplished a lot, Badr. This place is amazing. I'm sure it'll draw loads of visitors interested in the sport."

"That's my hope. Now, let's grab the UTV and head over to my place."

Chapter 56: That Afternoon

They arrived at the sheik's residence, and he immediately retrieved Zohra from her outdoor mew. Quinn, the bodyguard, and Badr walked to the low dunes where he'd flown her before. They watched the bird take off, flying low above the grasses and flushing prey. Finally, the gyr dove at a fat grey squirrel, killing it instantly.

"Hah!" Badr exclaimed. "I bet that's the one that's been raiding my bird feeders!"

The sheik raised his arm, and Zohra flew back to him, dropping the squirrel at his feet. So like a retriever, Quinn thought as she watched. Badr excised the squirrel's heart and fed the trophy to his gyr. He signaled Abdul Salaam to dispose of the squirrel, knowing it wouldn't make a suitable meal. On the return walk to his home, Badr petted his bird and praised her for the capture. He returned Zohra to her outdoor mew instead of bringing her into the house, knowing she preferred being outside in the cold winter months. The chef had already laid out lunch, and Quinn and Badr sat down and quietly ate before moving to his living room. Abdul Salaam brought in a pot of hot cinnamon tea, poured two steaming cups, and left the two of them alone to talk.

Blowing on the tea before taking a sip, Quinn asked. "So now that your falconry complex is nearly finished, what are you working on?"

"The falconry festival. With its May dates fast approaching, there's still lots to organize."

"Why are you holding it in the spring? Most festivals up here are held in the summer when tourists can avail themselves of these activities. I think you'd get a better turnout then."

"I understand what you're saying, but the festival must happen at a time when it's best for the birds, not the vacationers. Even in the Northwoods, the summers are too hot for falcon racing."

"Okay, I get it. I know you'll have the 400-meter outdoor falcon races, but what other events will the festival include?"

"There'll be training demonstrations showing newcomers how to get started in falconry. Techniques as well as laws regulating the sport. We'll also have an auction for qualified buyers wanting to purchase one of our falcons. I'm firming up plans for a beauty pageant, too."

"A beauty pageant for falcons? You've gotta be kidding me."

"Don't laugh, Quinn. The beauty contest is one of the most popular events at festivals in the Middle East. Birds are judged and awarded points based on seven criteria: head, shoulders, upper part of the chest, back, legs, claws, and color. The falcon receiving the highest score wins the prize, which has been up to $800,000 at the Dubai pageant."

"Unbelievable, Badr. Why are you waiting to firm up plans?"

"I ran an ad in the *North American Falconry* magazine about our festival. I got a response from a premier falconry breeder in Washington State. *Evergreen Falconry,* it's called. They specialize in breeding gyrs, peregrines, and hybrids."

"Uh-huh."

"The owners, Naomi and Daryl Duncan, want to enter their gyrfalcons in our beauty pageant and then sell some of the gyrs and hybrids at the auction, too."

"You have a problem with that?"

"Some. Mostly about pride. I want this festival to focus on the work we're doing with peregrines in this part of the country. I already know the gyrs will steal the show at the beauty pageant. They always do. But I don't want their birds to compete with ours at the auction. Sounds a bit silly, now that I think about it."

"I'm going to switch topics, Badr. It's not hard to notice that your home and the center have high levels of security. Will the festival put you at risk? Are you worried Farouk and Pilecki's minions might find you here?"

"I'd be lying if I answered with a definitive no, but I'm not too concerned, especially with my new location. My security team and system are second to none. I've not advertised the festival in any of the international falconry journals. I also have protection from the FBI. I don't know what else I can do to keep myself and my enterprise safe. Despite any imagined threats, I must go on living my life according to Allah's plan."

Quinn nodded as she took in Badr's last comment. It was the first time he'd made any mention of being Muslim. She wondered how he practiced his religion without there being a mosque or Imam in the area. Or at least that she knew of. Then it dawned on her how the community the sheik was building might already be providing that religious support.

"So tell me what's going on with you," Badr said. "How is your new drug detection work going with Ruby?"

"She's a natural, and I'm enjoying getting outside to use a different set of policing skills."

"I imagine every time you crack a case of illicitly trafficked fentanyl, you think of your homeless friend Mack."

Quinn was stunned by Badr's remembering, which brought tears to her eyes. She nodded, understanding that was how grief worked at times, creeping in unannounced.

Finally, changing the subject, she said, "I brought along a list of names I'd like to run by you if you're willing. They're foreign names we've not been able to track down."

Quinn handed him the list, and Badr put on his reading glasses and began perusing the names.

"Where'd you get these names, Quinn?" he said, looking up.

"My friend newspaperman Ian Doyle just emailed them to me. He said he got them from a foreign correspondent who thinks they might be tied to Pilecki."

Badr sighed, shook his head, and picked up his pencil. He placed a tick mark next to one name. Then he continued down the list and ticked off a second.

"These two are both Sovietniks," Badr said, passing the list back to her.

"Sovietniks?"

"Sovietniks are also known as Councilors. They are the closest, most trusted individuals to the Pakhan, who is the Boss or Godfather, as they're known in Italian-American Mafia crime families. Miss Quinn, your investigation worries me. You're getting dangerously close to the Russian mob and Pavel Pilecki. I know you're concerned about my security, but I think you need to focus on your own, especially if you begin digging into those two names."

Chapter 57: January 20

Vernadeane had just finished the jail visits she made two or three mornings a week. She'd call on each of the inmates, especially ones with mental health issues. She'd look over their records to see if they'd had any struggles over the last few days. She'd check the logs to make sure they were up-to-date with their medications. But mostly, she served as a sounding board for whatever they wanted to talk about.

On her way out through the waiting room, she noticed a familiar face at the check-out window. David Lathrop Senior, father of the young man who'd committed the four murders of homeless people.

"Mr. Lathrop, I don't know if you remember me. I'm Vernadeane Novak, the social worker for the Sheriff's Department. Davey's not back in jail, is he?" she asked.

"No, no. I'm just picking up the last of his belongings. His transfer to the Center for Forensic Psychiatry came so fast that I didn't have the chance to get his things before he moved to Ann Arbor."

"Is he still at CFP? I'd expect his evaluation would've been completed by now. It's certainly been sixty days since his admission."

"Yeah, more like ninety days. Once they finished his evaluation, they couldn't find a proper placement for him until just recently."

"I'm so sorry. Everything takes so long with the shortage of psychologists and beds for these folks with mental health issues."

"It's been a long haul. I didn't think Davey was ever gonna get the care he needed."

"Do you have time to give me an update?"

"I guess. The evaluation had good and bad results. Davey's showing early signs of schizophrenia. He's stable now with medication and therapy but will probably live the rest of his life institutionalized. He was found not criminally responsible for the murders."

"Would you like to talk more about this? Perhaps over a cup of coffee?" Vernadeane asked. "There's a place we could walk to a couple of streets over."

David Senior nodded and followed Vernadeane up Washington to Cass and then into the Omelette Shoppe. It wasn't very busy on a Wednesday in January, and they quickly found a corner booth where they could talk privately. They both ordered coffee and something to eat, David one of their pecan rolls and Vernadeane a cup of tomato basil soup. He fidgeted while they waited for their food, so she asked a question to keep the connection going.

"Mr. Lathrop, did you see any signs that Davey hated homeless people?"

"Oh, yeah," he answered, a bitter anger creeping into his voice. "And I know exactly how it started."

"Uh huh," Vernadeane murmured.

"When Susan and I were still married, we lived in Ocean Beach, California, about three hours south of where I live now in Santa Monica. At least where I used to live before COVID hit, and we decided to send Davey here."

Vernadeane nodded, her brows furrowed in concern.

"Susan's parents lived there and babysat Davey before he started school and during the summers while we worked. The kid was smart and curious from the get-go. He'd read everything he could get his hands on: books, road signs, even bumper stickers. I guess that's where it all started. With a bumper sticker."

"Hmmm," Vernadeane said, inviting more.

"Ocean Beach had always been a funky little town with people holding a lot of different opinions they spouted off about publicly. The hottest topic during this time was the growing homeless population. Encampments had grown up around the Ocean Beach

Pier and were setting off protests. Cops hauling away the trolls, as they were called. Others who defended their right to camp there."

"Let me guess. Davey's grandpa was against the homeless population," Vernadeane said.

"You're right. Russell Pugh was a ruthless hothead who often spouted his negative opinions in public places. He belonged to a closed Facebook group known as the Ocean Beach Troll Bashers. It had over 250 members whose main job was to foment violence against homeless people."

"How'd you learn about this group if it was closed?"

"It became public knowledge when the man accused of killing several homeless men was caught."

"OMG!" Vernadeane exclaimed. "Not your father-in-law?"

"No, no. His biggest weapon was his mouth."

The server brought their coffee and food, and they were quiet for a while as they ate. After a few minutes, Vernadeane restarted the conversation.

"You said earlier that Davey's problems began with a bumper sticker."

"Yeah, Russell had an anti-homeless bumper sticker on his truck that read, *Welcome to Ocean Beach Don't Feed the Bums.* He got it in a headshop near the pier."

"Jesus," Vernadeane responded.

"One day, Davey asked his grandpa what the sticker meant, and Russell went on a tirade about homeless people in Ocean Beach. He told my son shit like: *How'd you like it if your grandma was mugged by one of those bums with a knife? What would you think if one of them trolls pissed on the rose bushes in your mother's front yard? Do you think it's okay to beg strangers for money instead of working at an honest job?*"

Vernadeane looked at Senior's face, twisted in grief and rage. "I'm so sorry," she finally eked out.

"And that isn't the worst of it. One day, he took Davey along on one of his protests. The scene crawled with cops. Protesters objecting to the sale of the bumper stickers formed a picket line outside the headshop. Counter-protesters yelled slurs against the homeless population. Chants *'Arrest the trolls'* rang from the whole pier area. The media and hundreds of onlookers only added to the chaos. Luckily, the whole mess didn't turn into a full-blown riot, but the pushing and screaming scared the crap out of my five-year-old son. When I picked Davey up after work, he was crying and shaking. And this was four hours after Russell brought the kid home. For months, I'd hear him mumble *'Arrest the trolls'* when he woke up with nightmares."

Vernadeane was quiet as Senior finished his story and wiped the sweat and tears from his face. She'd heard a lot of stories in her work with homeless people, but none topped this one.

"Thanks, Mr. Lathrop, for sharing this story. I think it explains a lot."

"It does. After I told the therapist in Ann Arbor about Davey's experiences, he said the same thing. He emphasized that they didn't cause my son's difficulties, yet they certainly impacted Davey's fragile mind."

"I hear you. What's next for Davey, now that he's been ruled NCR?"

"He's just been moved to Woodland Center Correctional Facility in Whitmore Lake for treatment. While it's still a maximum-security prison, its one-story building resembles a school more than a prison. Inmates live in small units of ten prisoners each and have opportunities for art and music therapy. Right now, Davey's in their Rehabilitative Treatment program, which involves partial hospitalization for the first six months, sometimes longer. I don't know whether he'll become one of the fifty or so permanent residents there or if he'll eventually find his way to a less restrictive environment, but at least he's getting proper care now."

"Yes, I've heard good things about Woodland. It used to be the former Maxey Boys Training School. I understand it's been retrofitted as a therapeutic environment. And what about you, sir? What's your next step?"

Lathrop sighed before answering. "This has been an awful experience not only for the families who lost loved ones but for Davey and me also. The guilt over sending him here to live with Susan during the pandemic has been overwhelming. I knew she wasn't much into mothering when I got custody of him after the divorce. What made me think she'd do any better now?"

"I hope you can make peace with your decision, Mr. Lathrop. You sent Davey to Michigan as a way to escape the pandemic, which was raging on the West Coast. You were only looking out for his best interests. You need to remember that. Have you and Susan been able to support each other through this ordeal?"

"No. We've had little to no contact. I've started seeing a therapist myself in Ann Arbor to work through the guilt and some other issues, too. I've rented an apartment there so I can watch over Davey's care and visit him as often as I'm allowed. I'm currently on family leave from my job, and I've been assured by my employer that I can work remotely once that ends. To be honest, I'm not sure what my next steps are beyond taking things day-by-day."

Chapter 58: February 11

They'd been hearing dire weather forecasts all afternoon. Extreme cold, strong winds, heavy snow. Quinn gave the warnings short shrift, knowing reports had been overblown in the past. But when she came home from her workday, she decided to watch the news, something she'd stopped doing during last fall's contentious election campaigns. Quinn made a bowl of popcorn for dinner and turned on her new smart TV. Ruby sat on the ottoman, hoping to snag an occasional stray kernel. As Quinn dipped her hand into the bowl, she noticed her arm was sore after getting her first coronavirus vaccine that morning. Healthcare workers and first responders were given priority due to their work with the public. Tomorrow, they'd start vaccinating senior citizens at the Hagerty Center.

The newscast started with the weather, something usually saved for midway through the half-hour report. Joe Charlevoix began talking about something called the polar vortex.

"The polar vortex is a large region of low pressure, cold, rotating air. It always exists at the poles, but in the winter months, it expands, sending cold air and the jet stream south."

"Hmmm. Why haven't I ever heard of this before?" Quinn muttered, making Ruby shift her focus from the popcorn to Quinn's eyes.

"The polar vortex is not something new or related to climate change. It was responsible for the historic winter storms of 1977, 1982, 1985, and 1989. We just didn't have a name for it then."

"Oh, yeah," Quinn said, remembering the storm that'd hit during her freshman year at Western. Classes canceled for a week because no one could navigate the roads. Snows up to the first-floor dorm windows. Playing bridge and euchre versus catching up on assignments.

"So, what should you expect over the next few days?" Joe asked, interrupting Quinn's reverie. "The vortex will bring tundra-like temperatures beginning tonight. Our normal highs are twenty-nine degrees, with lows around fifteen. Expect temperatures to be thirty degrees below that, with highs around zero and lows about ten to fifteen degrees below. Winds will pick up around midnight, bringing heavy snow. Accumulations will be high due to frigid air masses moving over the still-warm Lake Michigan. Expect 12-18" inches of lake effect snow over the next 24-36 hours."

"Meh," Quinn said. "Looks like our unseasonably warm weather is coming to a close, Rube." She clicked her new smart remote, changing from the news to Netflix. She'd started a new French mystery series called *Lupin* last night and decided to escape for the rest of the evening. After watching two more episodes, she let Ruby out for last call and headed to bed. Heavy snow had already begun to fall, and howling winds made it challenging to fall asleep.

At 4 a.m., Quinn awakened suddenly, her phone blowing up with texts. Blizzard warnings chimed from her three weather apps. Texts from the Sheriff's Department and FC2 calling all responders to report to work immediately. But the most ominous message came from the Homeless Alliance and read CODE BLUE.

Quinn immediately knew she'd put her priorities with the CODE BLUE, which was used to advocate for homeless people when there were blizzard conditions or temperatures dipped below ten degrees. This morning, both had happened. Even though the mission was open, a minority of homeless people still preferred living in the Pines during the winter. She remembered Mack sleeping under the Cass Street bridge during a storm last year and ramped up her speed. Quinn showered, shoveled a spot for Ruby to pee, and got them both an ample breakfast, not knowing when she'd be back home. Quinn headed through her garage to check the driveway, grateful to see it had already been plowed. Her condo complex was aware she was a police officer and gave her preferential treatment in making sure she could always get out.

FC2 was only a five-minute drive from Quinn's condo, but today, it took her three times that in the blowing, deep snow on Garfield. She trudged into the building, quickly checked her email and voicemail, and posted a message she'd be working on the Code Blue today. Heading back into the elements, Quinn made her way to the NoBo district and Middle Coast Mission, thankful her Outback could plow through just about any depth of snow. Vernadeane was already there and greeted her at the entrance.

"We're already over capacity and can't squeeze in another person. Currently, the few volunteers who could make it in are dealing with a COVID outbreak."

"Seriously? I thought they'd been testing regularly."

"They have, but with the dire weather reports of the last few days, homeless people living in their cars or outdoors have flocked here. The director just couldn't turn them away."

"Do you have numbers for the infection levels?"

"Yes, eleven of the new people have tested positive. Two have already been taken to the hospital, and we're trying to find hotels for the rest so we can isolate them, but most accommodations are already filled with travelers seeking shelter from the storm."

"What about the Pines? Has anyone been there yet?"

"No, but that's where you and I are headed. They're opening Greenspire School as an emergency shelter, and hopefully, whoever is left will be willing to go. No one can survive blizzard conditions and ten below temperatures in a tent."

Quinn and Vernadeane left MCM and jumped into the van. They brought along snowshoes and poles, knowing that would probably be the only way to navigate the Pines. The county had sent one of its smaller snowplows to clear the path into the homeless community. Once they arrived and donned their snowshoes, they began to push themselves through the deep snow. Hollering that help was here, their voices were barely audible above the howling winds. They went from tent to tent, looking inside for individuals who'd stayed behind. They found nobody. A few times, they stumbled over tents that had collapsed under the weight of the snow, but they discovered no one inside. With conditions worsening and the women hoarse from yelling, Quinn and Vernadeane left the Pines to return to MCM. Both were disheartened at not finding a single person to help. Neither voiced what they feared they'd find once the snow melted.

Chapter 59: February 27

Quinn had dropped Ruby off at the groomer and met Patrick at Rounds for a leisurely breakfast. At first, they chatted about work issues, Quinn sharing the latest on the David Lathrop case and Patrick telling her about the final results of the fall deer harvest. They'd both upgraded their telephoto lenses since their last meeting, so each assessed their recent purchases. It was the most fun they'd had together in a long time. With the election over and COVID no longer hijacking every conversation, they'd relaxed back into the easy friendship they'd developed from their camera club days.

Finally, Quinn's phone bugled, she answered and listened. "Ruby's done, and I have to pick her up."

As they walked to their cars, Patrick said, "I had fun this morning. Just like old times."

"Me too," Quinn agreed, moving closer for a hug.

"Hey, um, I'm sorry about the homeless people who died in the blizzard."

"Thank you," Quinn said, tearing up. "Even though Vernadeane and I searched the Pines at the height of the storm, we didn't find anyone. It wasn't until volunteers went back a few days later that they found three bodies buried in tents that'd collapsed from the weight of the snow."

"I'm so sorry," he said again. "I bet it brought back memories of Mack."

Quinn just nodded, thinking how great it was that Patrick's empathy had returned. He was right about it bringing back memories of Mack, but it also renewed her resolve to fight the Russian mafia and Pavel Pilecki. Vengeance for the beating she'd taken during the counterfeit pesticide case. The pledge she'd made when Mack died to stop the trafficking of illegal drugs. And now the wild falcon smuggling she'd learned about from Badr.

Quinn left Patrick and picked up Ruby. They were headed home when she passed a car pulled off on the side of the road. A well-dressed, swarthy-skinned man with a ponytail was bent over. It appeared he was changing the front tire on his Beemer. She drove past him and then thought better of it. Something didn't feel right. Quinn did a U-turn in the middle of Garfield Road and pulled her Outback in behind him. She pulled a portable red and blue police beacon from her glove box and planted it on the vehicle's roof. She grabbed her badge, identification, and lapel mic and affixed them to her jacket front. She exited the car, twisted her Glock holster around so that it was visible, and moved toward the man.

"Detective Quinn Macarthy. You having car trouble?"

"Yeah, officer. My low tire pressure light came on, and I was about to change my tire."

Quinn looked down at the tire and noticed it didn't appear flat. Her scar tingled. She'd left her car window down, and Ruby was whining, watching on high alert. Typically, her dog went to sleep when she stepped away.

"May I take a look at your license and registration, please?"

The man reached into his back pocket, pulled out his wallet, and handed Quinn the requested documents. She took them and read *Santiago Flores. 4375 Trawood Drive. El Paso, Texas.* She started back towards her car to run his identification and license plates when Ruby jumped through the open window and ran towards them.

"What the fuck's wrong with your dog?"

Ruby circled the Beemer, sniffed at its wheels, and sat just behind the trunk.

"She's a drug detection canine. Please open your vehicle's trunk, sir."

Flores started towards her, thinking he could overpower her because of their size difference, but Quinn was quicker. She drew her Glock and yelled 10-33 into her lapel mic, using police code for an emergency.

"Stop right there, Flores. You move any closer, and I'll shoot."

He continued towards her, and Quinn pulled the trigger, sending a bullet an inch from his ear.

"The next one will take out your cojones," Quinn yelled "Back the fuck up and open your goddamned trunk. Now!"

Flores retreated and opened the trunk of his vehicle. As it popped, Quinn could see boxes of bubbled-wrapped pills, several automatic weapons, and some bank pouches. She heard sirens approaching and was surprised when Gilda and Flint pulled beside the Beemer, effectively blocking it from leaving and keeping other traffic away. Both pulled their weapons and moved towards Quinn to help.

Quinn ordered, "Turn around and put your hands on the car roof, Flores."

She waited while Flint patted him down and found a Walther PDP tucked in the back of his belt. He pulled out the magazine and threw it on the ground. Gilda came forward, handcuffed Flores, and pushed him into the back of the squad car.

"How'd you guys get here so fast."

"We'd just finished with an accident over on Hammond and were heading back to Woodmere when your 10-33 came through."

"Sweet Jesus," Quinn said. "I had my hands full."

Quinn put Ruby back in her car, and all three went to examine the trunk's contents. Donning nitrile gloves, Flint pawed through the boxes, finding 5,000 bubble-wrapped little blue pills of illicit fentanyl. Another eight long boxes contained Soviet TKB-415 Bulkin Rifles. Flint's eyes met Quinn's in understanding.

"What about the money bags?" Gilda asked.

Flint gathered up the five pouches from the El Paso Commerce Bank, opened each, and counted. "Uffda. Looks to be $500,000 in each."

"Let's call this into the DEA," Gilda said.

Chapter 60: March 19

It was her first day back at work after taking a week off to drive downstate to celebrate St. Patrick's Day with her parents and brothers. It'd been a tradition they'd followed her whole life. Early mass at Most Holy Trinity, the Corktown parade, and a traditional Irish dinner prepared by their mom. But this year's observance was different, minimal even, due to their mother's failing health. She'd gone from using a walker last June when her parents rented a cabin near the Platte River to being completely wheelchair-bound because of her rheumatoid arthritis. They'd moved a hospital bed and commode into their living room because she could no longer manage the stairs to the second-floor bedrooms and baths. Finally, and reluctantly, her parents decided to sell the home they'd lived in for over forty years and purchase a one-floor, two-bedroom, two-bath, handicapped-accessible condo in a senior living community with various levels of care. Quinn's Detroit brothers Tully and Colin and their wives had facilitated the real estate process and packing while Rowan, Neil, and Quinn had come in to oversee the actual move.

Quinn began going through backed-up paperwork, sending much of it through the shredder. When she came to an official-looking envelope from the DEA, she tore it open and skimmed the contents. The report concluded the drug bust she and Ruby had made in February was tied to the Russian mafia and Sovietniks Vissarion Volkov and Iosif Zaitsev, the same two names Badr had ticked off on the list she'd given him at their last visit. Relief washed over her that they were closer to nailing those responsible for the drugs used in Mack's overdose. Quinn immediately picked up her phone and dialed Ian to give him the news.

"Hey, you're back," Ian answered, recognizing her number. "How'd it go in Detroit?"

"Difficult for everybody. Sorting, donating, and packing forty years of stuff was physically and emotionally draining. It was also hard to leave them and come home when I knew they had a lot of adjusting to do. I still think this was the right move, and I'm sure they know it too. They're just dazed from the enormity of change they've gone through."

"Give them a month or so to settle in, and they'll be fine. I think your dad, especially, will appreciate having help with your mom and people his age to interact with. Having a dining room where they can eat their meals takes a big load off them, too. So, did you call just to say hi?"

"No, I got a letter from the Drug Enforcement Administration. They traced the fentanyl that Ruby and I seized in the drug bust to the Russian mafia and the Sovietniks on the list you emailed me."

"Great news! At least we've been working the right angle. Now, if we could just complete the link between them and Pilecki."

Just then, there was a soft knock at her doorway. Quinn swiveled her chair to see her old grad school chum and FBI agent, Zoey Rogers, standing there. Motioning her into the office, she said to Ian, "Gotta go. The FBI is here."

"Huh?" Ian said, staring at his phone after she suddenly clicked off.

"Zoey, so good to see you. It's been a while," Quinn said as she hugged her friend. "What brings you here? You have an investigation going on with one of our detectives?"

"Yeah, we do. We've been following your detective work with your newspaper friend Ian Doyle into the Sovietniks Volkov and Zaitsev."

"What? You've tapped my phone or email?"

"No, no. Nothing that official. Not yet. We've had some people concerned about your safety since you've been poking your nose more deeply into Pavel Pilecki's people."

"Who? Not my brother Rowan?"

"For one. He's worried that you're in over your head when it comes to the Russians."

Quinn thought about who else could've snitched, then exclaimed, "Not Sheik Badr-Uddin, too? I thought he had my back."

"He does, and so does Rowan, which is why they called me in to talk to you. To give you an official cease and desist order to immediately stop investigating Pavel Pilecki and the Sovietniks." Zoey then threw an official-looking document onto Quinn's desk.

She looked over the letter warning her to end her inquiries into the Russians and what would happen if she didn't, which included losing her law enforcement licenses. Quinn looked up and said, "I don't believe this, Zoey. Don't you think you're taking this too far?"

"Your work is putting you and Ian in grave danger, Quinn. Leave it to the professionals."

"Huh. I thought that's what I was."

Chapter 61: April 8

Quinn was headed to Crystal Lake to meet Ian at his home office. He'd come across something big related to their case he wanted to share. The Doyles also invited her to stay for dinner as Hannah had made another batch of Irish stew, probably her last until fall.

Ian came out of the lakeside sliders and greeted her with hugs. As they went back inside and settled into his home office, Hannah came in with a welcome of her own, plus some oatmeal cherry cookies and tea.

"Ian, you emailed that you found out something new about our case," Quinn said after Hannah left the office. "Aren't we supposed to be off this case? I've been specifically warned I could lose my licenses if we continue investigating the Russian mobsters."

"I'm aware, Quinn. But I found out something that might bring Pilecki here to the States."

"I doubt that. According to the sheik, he rarely leaves the safety of his country or the Gulf."

"Here, read this article and tell me what you think?"

Ian handed her a printout from the newspaper *Al-Bayan*, one of the Arabic language papers out of the United Arab Emirates. The article was entitled *World's Most Expensive Falcon Sold in Dubai Auction for $465,000*. Quinn looked up, met Ian's eyes, and looked back down to read the content. A new world record had been set for the most expensive falcon when a white gyrfalcon from the U.S. was sold for $465,000 at an auction held in Dubai by the International Falcon Breeders Association.

"The gyr was from here?"

"Yes. Keep reading, Quinn. Don't get lost in your questions."

The falcon was a Gyr Qarmousha Falcon. An ultra white gyrfalcon, under one year old, bred from one of best international breeding farms, *Evergreen Falconry,* in the American Pacific Northwest.

Quinn looked up again but was silent, trying to place where she'd heard that name before.

According to the account, the falcon measured 16.5 inches long and weighed 980 grams. The report went on to talk about the auction, which had been broadcast on television and live-streamed on social media. The bidding for the bird had been fierce, but when the price increased to an earlier benchmark of $66,676, only five stayed in the competition for the gyr. The auction had been held in an auditorium where bidders sat every other seat due to the pandemic. Pictures showed most wearing white robes and red-checkered keffiyehs, but a few were in business suits. All wore COVID masks. When the bidding reached the previous record of $272,257, only two remained in the hunt for the pure white gyr, an Arab, and a suit. The bidding finally ended at the new world record of $465,000 when the suit threw down his bidding paddle and stomped out of the auditorium. The auction winner was identified as Prince Farouk Al-Kirdar Haboori. His competitor remained unidentified.

"You think the suit was Pilecki?" Quinn said.

"Or one of the Sovietniks acting in his stead."

"As I read the article, something niggled at me. The name of the breeding facility in the Pacific Northwest. *Evergreen Falconry.*"

"You've heard of it before?"

"I wasn't sure at first, but now I remember where it came from. The sheik told me about a breeding center in Washington State with the same name."

"Huh."

"He said the owners of *Evergreen Falconry* had contacted him about entering their gyrs in his festival's beauty pageant and falcon auction in May."

"A beauty pageant for falcons?"

"Don't even go there."

"Could you talk to the sheik about what we've uncovered about this record gyr sale at the Dubai auction?"

"He probably already knows, as well as he keeps up on falconry news worldwide. Plus, I'm still not clear how this article relates to our case. Can you connect the dots for me?"

"This might be a real chance to nab Pilecki?"

"How so? I'm still not getting it."

"Think about it, Quinn. If Pilecki left the Dubai auction angry because he didn't win the bidding on this rare, pure white falcon, the sheik's event might give Pilecki a second chance to acquire a gyr from *Evergreen Falconry*. It sounds like they are one of the top falcon breeders worldwide. The auction might provide the lure we've been looking for to bring the Russians to the States."

Chapter 62: April 19

Quinn was on her way to Badr's training center, even though it was a workday. He'd left her a message inviting her to see the finished compound before the weeklong festival began the first Saturday in May. He sounded especially excited to show her the Hospitality Center with vendors in place. He also wanted to discuss the final security details for the event.

As she reached the entrance, Quinn noticed the new landscaping. Sod, flowers, and ornamental grasses had been planted around the entrance, which now bore a permanent sign that read *Peregrine Falcon Breeding and Training Center*. As Quinn walked, she wondered what the sheik was thinking, putting plants in the ground when it was only mid-April.

The most striking addition to the center's exterior was the twenty-foot tall statue of a peregrine falcon, its wings outstretched in flight, and a houbara bustard grasped in its talons. The three-dimensional object was made from gray fabricated metal, and the detail was amazing. The bird's eyes, beak, and talons were inset with gold. Parts of the head were made of darker metal to indicate the peregrine's signature black hood and sideburns. While the body and head were solid metal, the extended wings had openings to simulate its barred flight feathers.

As Quinn took in the statue, the sheik came up behind her and asked, "You like it?"

"I don't have words to describe it, Badr. Incredible is the best I can do."

"I'm pleased with how it turned out. Let's go inside the Hospitality Center so I can show you the completed souks."

They walked past the breeding and training centers toward the building closest to the racetrack. As they entered the Hospitality Center, Quinn noticed the place bustling with activity. Some dressed in Arab garb and others in Up North casual crisscrossed the floor carrying last-minute goods to the various bazaar stalls. They wandered through the souks, Quinn taking in the smells from the food booths and admiring the goods that now filled the retail stores.

"Let's grab some falafel and shawarma and head to my office. I wanted to show you the completed souk before we talked."

They entered Badr's office at the back of the hospitality building and settled into the white chairs arranged in a conversation area.

"Mmmm. This is tasty. What's in this dipping sauce for the falafel?"

"Mostly tahini, yogurt, lemon juice, and a few spices. Can we talk about security for the festival? I have a few questions."

"Sure, go ahead."

"We've already sold out for each of the eight days of the event. We allotted a hundred fifty tickets per day. Attendees had to purchase them online, and we've sent all names and credit card information to the FBI for checking. No red flags thus far."

"You're nervous about your safety?"

"Not really, but it's always better to err on the side of caution."

"Were there any foreigners among the attendees who registered, especially from the Gulf?"

"None. The only people who're coming from outside the United States are from Canada."

"Will the FBI be present during the festival?"

"Some. Zoey Rogers and her partner Garrison Perry will be in and out, I guess. They're not very happy I'm hosting this event. They think it goes against the plan to keep me safely stowed away in the Northwoods."

"Hmmm."

"I have another fifteen security people who will be dressed in the center's uniforms and discreetly armed."

"No M4 carbines or AK-47s?"

Badr laughed. "We'll have them within reach, but no one will be carrying them. Do you think we need a local police presence at the event? In a uniform that people recognize. I'm a little concerned people might be nervous with all the 'Arabs' running around in white robes," he added, raising his fingers to make quotation marks as he said the word Arabs.

"Probably a good idea. I can provide five more uniformed law enforcement officers each day. A mix from the Sheriff's Department and TCPD. How would that be?"

"Perfect. Thank you."

"From your description of the prior ticket sales, it sounds like there'll be no walk-ins allowed at the festival. Is that right?"

"Yes, mostly. On the last day of the festival, we'll hold the auction. There may be a few bidders who didn't pre-register for the whole week, but it shouldn't be a problem. One or two at the most."

Just then, there was a soft knock at the door, and the vendor where they'd bought the falafel entered. He brought in some kofta kebabs and manakeesh for them to sample. As they ate the new snacks, Quinn thought about how to approach the topic she and Ian had been researching.

"I want to talk more about the auction. Last time we met, you told me about the conflict you were having with *Evergreen Falconry* about whether they would participate in your beauty pageant and auction with their gyrs. Did that get resolved?"

"Oh yes. Naomi and Daryl Duncan are wonderful folks and very easy to deal with. They are bringing two pure white gyrfalcons, plus three of their new peregrine-gyrfalcon crosses."

"You mean hybrids? Didn't know they did that with falcons."

"They've been doing crossbreeding in the Middle East for a while, but it's just getting underway here in the States. The Duncans are one of the first."

Quinn knew something about hybrids because Ruby was a cross between a miniature poodle and a golden retriever. Hybridization typically brought hybrid vigor, referring to the improved biological qualities in the offspring from mixing the genetic contributions of the parents.

"What are they learning about the peregrine-gyrfalcon cross?"

"It results in a larger, faster bird that is more disease resistant and better able to cope with environmental stresses."

"Interesting," Quinn said, finally taking the leap and handing Badr the article Ian had found. "Have you heard about this auction in Dubai where a gyrfalcon went for nearly half a million dollars? Your former partner Prince Farouk was the buyer."

Badr read the article, his brow furrowing as he did. Finally, he looked up and said he didn't know about the auction or the sale of the gyr to Farouk.

"Why'd you want me to read this, Quinn?"

"Ian and I thought the losing bidder might be Pavel Pilecki or one of his Russian Sovietniks. Then I remembered *Evergreen Falconry* was going to be one of your auction vendors. We wondered whether their birds might lure the mobsters here so we could arrest them for the crimes they've committed. Especially the murder of George Watkins but also those related to drug trafficking, counterfeit pesticides, and wild falcon poaching."

"Utter nonsense, Quinn. Neither Pilecki nor his Sovietniks will ever set foot on American soil. It's too dangerous with Interpol and the FBI tracking their every move. And you, Miss Quinn, have got to stop this craziness. You're putting yourself at risk. Maybe me, too. Don't forget you have a cease-and-desist order from the FBI. One phone call to them could end your career."

Chapter 63: April 30

The last day of April was always difficult for Quinn and Vernadeane because Middle Coast Mission closed for the season, pushing its residents back to the Pines with only a tent, tarp, and sleeping bag. The two officers were angry there wasn't a year-round solution, especially for the seventyish chronically unhoused people who had no other options. For Quinn, the day was especially hard because it brought back raw memories of Mack's troubles and demise. She thought about how she must keep working to capture that bastard, Pilecki. It was the only way to honor Mack's memory and resolve her own assault.

Today, Vernadeane and Quinn, along with a band of volunteers, were helping the MCM guests move themselves and their few belongings out of the shelter to wherever they were going. Some carried their personal effects in backpacks. Others pushed their possessions in some kind of cart. An extra set of clothing from Goodwill. A warm coat and boots. A few toiletries: toothpaste, toothbrushes, hand sanitizer, menstrual supplies. Unfortunately, the Pines didn't yet have bathrooms or running water to use these items, although the city was talking about it.

A church that served breakfast to the homeless handed each displaced resident a small, refrigerated bag containing sandwiches, fruit, and snacks, enough to get each person through their first day without shelter. They also gave each guest literature on how to receive medical assistance from the mobile Street Medicine unit, a list of free-meal sites, contact information for crisis assistance, and a free bus pass for transportation. Another group of volunteers lined up to offer rides to the residents wherever they were going.

"Where you headed, Lester?" Vernadeane asked.

"The Pines, I guess. Is there another option? Perhaps a motel voucher?"

"I'm sorry. We only have a few of those for people who are ill."

"Figures. I guess I'm gonna have to work harder at getting sick."

Another guest, Rochelle, a woman in her late sixties who walked with a cane, pulled Quinn aside and talked to her animatedly. "Do you think someone could give me a ride to the Arbutus Lake State Forest Campground? I'll have to pay $20 a night to camp there, but it'll be safer than the Pines, I think."

"If you can wait half an hour, I'd be happy to drop you off."

"Oh, thank you. It'll be nice to have running water and outhouses. You can also build fires there to cook food and keep warm."

"Will you have enough left to live on after paying twenty dollars a night? That adds up pretty quickly. $600 a month."

"I think so. My social security pension is $866 a month. I think I can make some extra money from canning, too, with all the big garbage bins at the campground. I'll find a way to make it work because the Pines ain't safe, especially for women."

Rochelle's mention of canning reminded Quinn of Mack again. How he also earned extra money by going through trash barrels for soda cans then redeeming them at grocery stores for their deposits. Not a very dignified way to supplement an income, she thought.

Lonny Taylor was the last resident to leave MCM. One of the lucky ones. He was the first person to move into an apartment at the newly renovated Beachcomber Motel. The East Bay Township facility had been purchased with grants and tax credits to provide permanent supportive housing for the homeless community. Lonny had recently completed a month-long program at the local behavioral health facility for depression and methamphetamine addiction. They'd also helped him secure work at the car wash near his apartment.

Lonny came out of the building with Ozzie McKay, the executive director of MCM. Earlier in the week, they'd shopped thrift stores for minimal furnishings for the apartment. Furniture for the living room and bedroom, dishes and silverware, pots and pans, and some lamps. They'd even purchased new sheets, towels, and a comforter at Bed Bath & Beyond. With those items packed into a small U-Haul, Ozzie was ready to drive Lonny to his new apartment and help him get settled.

"You ready for the big move?" Vernadeane asked, giving him a warm hug.

"I'm excited but also a little nervous. When you've lived on the streets as long as I have, well, this is a huge step. Truthfully, I didn't think I'd ever be housed again."

"We'll be here for you, Lonny, every step of the way. You'll always have us as your support system."

"Thank you, Vernadeane. Thank you, Quinn. I want to make a difference in this community, so I'll be looking for ways to help those who've helped me. We're all neighbors now."

Chapter 64: May 1

They'd gotten an early start for Old Mission on this sunny yet chilly morning. Quinn thought the temperatures just under fifty would be perfect for the falcons on the opening day of Badr's festival. The ten-day forecast on AccuWeather reported these conditions would continue for the next five days before a slight warming trend arrived. Gilda, Flint, and Patrick were riding in Quinn's Outback. TCPD Chief Hank Yeager and Detective Buzz Broderick followed in a squad car. At the last minute, the Michigan State Police decided to join the security contingent by bringing in K-9 Troopers Nick Wagner and Avery Hollister, who'd been Ruby's handler during her drug detection testing. The two sniffer dogs, Grit and Ruby, quietly panted in the back end of the Chevrolet Blazer.

It was just before 7 a.m. when they arrived at the center, but the parking lot was already half filled with cars three hours before the event opened. Quinn also counted sixteen motorhomes, each easily thirty feet long, hooked up to connections in a separate area.

"Geeze, Louise," Flint said, following Quinn's gaze to the rigs. "Pretty swanky camping."

"Truly. It may be the best way to transport falcons to festivals, though."

As the rest of the security contingent disembarked from their cars, Quinn went over to Avery, who'd just leashed Ruby, and lifted her from the back of the K-9 vehicle. The dog wagged her tail when she saw Quinn approach but kept her composure, knowing she was working.

"I can't thank you enough for keeping Ruby this week. It would've been dreadful for her with me being gone so much."

"Not a problem. She's such a delight anyway. Grit loves having a playmate, and Nick loves Ruby as if she were our dog," Avery said, referring to the other handler, who was also her husband. "Besides, this type of activity will be good training for Ruby."

Quinn restrained herself from petting her dog, grateful she had people in her life to share her beloved pet with. Checking her emotions, she moved over to the center's entrance, where tables were set up outside the fence for check-in. Alphabetically-labeled boxes contained credentials for the registered guests. A line of golf carts waited to transport the security team, with Abdul Salaam driving the first cart carrying the sheik. Badr was dressed in a light-weight khaki suit, the first time she'd ever seen him without his white robe and keffiyeh. His hair and beard were conservatively trimmed. She didn't know whether to comment or keep quiet.

"Welcome, officers. Thank you so much for your help this week. I'm hopeful we won't need you for anything beyond crowd control, but I'm grateful you're here," Badr said, bowing and shaking everyone's hands. "Ah, this must be Ruby," he said when he came to the end of the line. She's as adorable as I thought she'd be," stooping to pet her.

Avery stepped back, Ruby moving with her. "Sorry, sir, but Ruby is working now."

"Of course. I apologize," Badr said.

Just then, Ian and Hannah Doyle hurried across the parking lot to join them. Ian was covering the event as TC Bureau Chief for his downstate newspaper, *The Chronicle*. He planned to write daily features about the festival events, running them jointly in his paper and the *Record-Eagle*. Hannah had come along for the ride to help wherever she was needed. With everyone present, workers dressed in smart garnet-colored uniforms gave credentials to the officers and guided each to a golf cart, where they were also supplied with walkie-talkies for communication. From there, drivers took the officers on a tour of the festival site. The two buildings for propagation and training, the Hospitality Center, the racing and spectator grounds, and back through the lots where vehicles and motorhomes were parked. When ten o'clock arrived, people thronged the entrance to obtain their security cards and programs. The festival was underway.

As Quinn and Patrick drove their golf cart towards the stands, where the participants had been directed to go after check-in, Quinn noticed the large number of assistants dressed in the garnet uniforms versus in white robes and head cloths. Maybe the workers from Dearborn were more assimilated to American culture than she'd thought. Perhaps even the sheik. While she hadn't seen Zoey Rogers yet, Quinn easily spotted other FBI agents by their white shirts, business attire, and shined laced-up shoes. She watched from a distance as Avery guided Ruby through the crowds, sniffing the ground and air the whole time. They reached the spectator grounds just as Badr mounted a platform and turned on his lapel mic.

"Welcome, everyone, to the grand opening festival of the *Peregrine Falcon Propagation and Training Center*. My name is Badr Uddin, and I'm the director of the center. The purpose of our project here in Northwestern Lower Michigan is to breed peregrine falcons and release them into the wild. Peregrines have been an endangered species, and we're working to change that through our repopulation project. We're also hoping to educate people on falconry, both its traditions and its sports. I encourage you to check your programs for activities you can avail yourselves of throughout the day, including tours of the breeding, training, and hospitality centers and workshops on various aspects of falconry and hawking. The Hospitality Center also contains booths for shopping and eating, as well as a museum giving the history of falconry."

At the mention of activities available that day, spectators thumbed through their programs to decide what they wanted to attend. Badr paused for a few moments before continuing.

"You'll want to return to the stadium at 5 p.m., where I will demonstrate how traditional falconry uses falcons to hunt. Finally, I want to welcome the three falconry clubs who've joined us this week. The Michigan Hawking Club. The Great Lakes Falconers' Association from Illinois. And the Ohio Falconry Club. They've brought along their birds and will participate in many of our activities. One last note, if anyone has questions or difficulties, you can ask our guides, who are wearing deep red uniforms, or one of the uniformed police officers who are with us this week. Have a great day, everyone."

As the sheik finished his welcome, the crowd began to disperse, and the law enforcement contingent drove their golf carts throughout the grounds, looking for anyone needing help or anything that seemed out of place or suspicious. Everything seemed to be going smoothly until Quinn's walkie-talkie went off. She answered and found it was Badr.

"We appear to have a press difficulty at the entrance," he said. "I'm tied up with something at the Hospitality Center, can you handle it? See if you can get your newspaperman to come along with you."

When Quinn and Ian arrived at the tables just outside the secure entrance, they saw three men in suits conversing with one of the garnet uniforms. One of the three carried a fancy camera, and the other two had iPads, possibly for notetaking. All wore N95 COVID masks obscuring most of their facial features except for their eyes. The photographer had dark, coarse hair, deeply bronzed skin, and large downturned brown eyes. The two tablet holders were taller and had fair skin, blond hair, and blue eyes. They all spoke excellent English except for a twinge of an accent she couldn't place.

Quinn stepped forward and asked, "Do we have a problem here?"

"These men are from a downstate newspaper. They say they only learned of the festival a day ago and didn't have time to pre-register. They seem to have legitimate press credentials," the garnet uniform said, handing the paperwork to Quinn, who looked it over and then passed it to Ian.

While Ian was familiar with the Detroit press corps, he'd been Up North long enough not to know the new hires at either *The Chronicle* or the other downtown paper. He looked over the paperwork, shrugged, and said, "Looks legitimate to me."

"Okay, go ahead and issue them each a security card and other press credentials," Quinn said, absently brushing her hand against her jawline and wishing Badr were here to make the decision. While the garnet uniform put together three press kits, Quinn photographed their credentials and pictures, deciding to pass them on to the FBI to be safe.

But the rest of the day had kept her busy. Helping families find bathrooms. Reuniting lost items with their owners. Giving directions to three 4-H youths looking for the booths where they would exhibit their pet raptors. Several times, she noticed Avery and Ruby busy at work and felt regret she wasn't handling her dog. She also spotted the three newspapermen mixing with the crowd during the workshops and tours. They were easy to pick out, being the only people wearing COVID masks to the outdoor activities. When five o'clock came around, the crowd descended on the stadium to watch Badr and Abdul Salaam, both in traditional robes and keffiyehs, wow the spectators as peregrines Taufan and Thamina hunted pigeons and woodcocks, dropping from high in the sky at speeds up to two hundred miles an hour to make their kills. As Quinn and her colleagues left the festival near midnight for the drive home to Traverse City, they were all enthralled and chatty about the opening day's success. In her excitement and fatigue, she never gave another thought to the masked threesome whose credentials with pictures remained on her phone.

Chapter 65: May 2

The second day of the festival started differently for Quinn and Patrick. They met at the Cherry Capital Airport, where Badr and Abdul Salaam had already arrived in borrowed wine touring buses to pick up the honored guests arriving on overnight flights. Daryl and Naomi Duncan from *Evergreen Falconry* in Washington State were bringing five falcons to the festival: Three pure white gyrfalcons, who'd be favorites at the beauty pageant, and two gyr-Shaheens, who were crosses between gyrfalcons and peregrines. Also flying in were brothers Cliff and Kent Wyatt, who'd been running the Lac Seul Bird Farm for thirty years in Northwestern Ontario. They'd brought gyrs, too, plus four gyrfalcon-saker hybrids. Sakers were nearly as fast as peregrines but were an endangered species. The Wyatts were working to repopulate them in Canada, similar to what Badr was doing with peregrines in Michigan. The final breeder coming to the festival was Leonard Sprout, a Nevada breeder who was just getting started in falcon racing. He'd come to learn more than compete.

Transporting falcons by airplanes was commonplace in the Gulf States, where Qatar and Emirates Airlines had regular accommodations for these revered guests. But in the United States, flying falcons on planes was rare, and the breeders had gone to great expense to have their birds fly with them in the cabin. They knew the new breeder in Northwest Lower Michigan was already gaining a reputation for excellence in breeding, training, and sport, so they wanted to attend, regardless of the cost involved. As the planes landed and the regular passengers disembarked, Badr, Abdul Salaam, Patrick, and Quinn boarded to help the visitors and their birds.

"What's the sheik doing?" Patrick asked.

"He's checking the falcons' passports against his records to make sure they're in order."

"Falcons have passports?"

"Yeah. It started in the Middle East where most festivals and sales are conducted, but it's now a requirement for all avian companions."

"I don't see how they can identify these birds with them wearing the eye-covering helmets on their heads."

"Each falcon is fitted with a leg ring inscribed with an identity number that ends up on the passport. It guards against bird smuggling by separating legitimate falconers from those operating illegally."

When the sheik finished his paperwork, he, Abdul Salaam, and the falcon owners began lifting the hooded birds from their seats, which had been outfitted with perches. Quinn and Patrick followed with the portable stands and attached them to the wine-touring bus seats.

"What unusual-looking falcons," Quinn exclaimed as the Nevadan Leonard Sprout stowed his last two falcons onto their perches.

"They are Aplomado falcons," he said. "They're quite rare in the States, mostly coming from southern Mexico and Peru."

"They're really beautiful," Quinn said, admiring one bird's white mustache-striped face and its slate-gray upperparts and wings. "Are there two kinds?" Quinn asked, noticing one bird had a cinnamon-brown face and underparts."

"The one with orangey coloring is a juvenile."

"Huh, makes sense. What do you train them for?"

"I'm mostly breeding them for repopulation, but we've also started using them with farmers for depredation abatement."

With all the birds stowed in the buses, they headed to Old Mission for the festival. Badr was anxious to get going on the second day's main event, the new face of falconry, racing. By the time they arrived and all the new falcons were settled into their accommodations at the center, it was late afternoon before Badr again took the platform for today's demonstration.

"My friends, welcome to the second day of our grand opening festival. Yesterday, you saw the traditional sport of falconry, using birds to hunt prey. But falconry of the past has taken a toll on both the birds and their prey, greatly reducing their populations. Since the sport is in the blood of most Middle Easterners, they have sought new ways to continue their sacred relationships with falcons. Captive-bred birds have mostly replaced wild-caught ones. And new sports have replaced hunting. Today, we're going to introduce you to Telwah, which is a classic line race. Falcons fly close to the ground over a distance of 400 meters to a catcher who twirls a fake prey. I want to draw your attention to the field where falconers will demonstrate the sport with three of my birds. Their times and speeds will be posted on the scoreboard. You can also watch on television inside the Hospitality Center if you prefer. Enjoy the races!"

Three falconers lined up at the racecourse entrance with their birds. The first racer was Maeveen. She was handled by Hamza, one of Badr's assistants, who was dressed in a traditional white robe and checkered headcloth. Maeveen was perched on a roll of green artificial turf on the assistant's gloved arm. Once Hamza took off the bird's hood, she looked around to orient herself and saw Abdul Salaam standing at the end of the 400-meter course, twirling a rope with a pigeon wing lure attached. The catcher also danced around and shouted in Arabic to attract the peregrine. Hamza released Maeveen without thrust, and she took off, barely skimming the course surface as she flew towards the catcher and his prey. She passed the end of the Microgate timing device, and it immediately threw her name and twenty-three seconds onto the scoreboard. The crowd roared, not really knowing whether the time was fast. Abdul Salaam immediately rewarded Maeveen with a pigeon heart and returned her on his arm to Hamza. Badr's three-year-old peregrines,

Taufan and Thamina, went next posting times of twenty and twenty-two seconds, respectively. Again, the spectators went crazy at their performances.

Badr took the stage again, delighted in the crowd's response. "I can see you've enjoyed our demonstration. Thank you," he said, bowing slightly towards the audience in appreciation. "While you probably haven't thought of falcons as athletes, think of them like the human sprinters who complete one lap on a 400-meter outdoor running track. Only peregrines are much faster. Twice as fast as South Africa's Wayde van Niekerk, who holds the world record of 43.03 seconds at that distance. And today, these falcons weren't even racing; they were just demonstrating our new sport. I can't wait for you to see what'll happen over the next few days as the real competition begins. And, who knows, if skateboarding and BMX freestyle cycling can become Olympic sports, who's to say falcon racing won't be next."

Chapter 66: May 7

The last four days of the festival had been busy with falcon demonstrations and racing competitions. Before the visiting falcons could participate, they spent half a day getting examined at the center's veterinary clinic. While all the birds had come with complete health records, it was standard procedure to double-check for bird flu, dehydration, and vitamin deficiency through lab tests. Once all the falcons passed their exams, the Telwah competitions began. Because the festival was small, the birds weren't separated by breeds. All competed equally for the fastest times. The winner of the race was a gyr-saker hybrid from Canada with a time of eighteen seconds flat. *Evergreen Falconry's* gyr-shaheen took second, and Taufan placed third with a time of just under nineteen seconds. Badr was disappointed in his peregrine's performance but was happy to be giving his bird some real competition.

The event wasn't all about racing and winning, though. The sheik wanted his grand opening to be about teaching and learning, too. The crowd had gotten into watching Leonard Sprout fly his adult Peruvian Aplomado, who was just beginning to race. They groaned when the bird flew off the track in its first two tries, then gave it a standing ovation when the falcon made it down the track successfully to grab the lure from the catcher.

But the real darling of the festival had been ten-year-old Lacey Greenway from the Ohio Falconry Club. She was just starting to train her young North American kestrel named Deke. Even though her father had trained his red-tailed hawk, he'd reached out to the sheik for help in getting them started right. Nine-month-old Deke had already become acclimated to his new home and red-tailed companion. He'd also become accustomed to going from his perch to Lacey's glove to feed. The family next wanted the sheik to help Deke take food from a lure.

So Badr and Lacey, both miked so spectators could hear their conversations, came onto the field. Lacey carried the small, hooded kestrel on her fist. A five-foot perch covered in artificial turf stood downfield. A rope with an attached leather lure lay on the ground nearby.

"Ladies and gentlemen, I'd like to introduce my fellow falconer Lacey Greenway," Badr said. "She's here with her family from Yellow Springs, Ohio. Why don't you tell us about yourself and your beautiful bird."

"My name is Lacey, and I'm in fifth grade at Riverside Middle School. This is Deke, my North American kestrel. He's not quite a year old."

"How did you end up choosing a falcon for a pet?"

"My dad has a red-tailed hawk, and when we were out hunting with him and our yellow lab Benny, we found Deke on the ground. He was barely breathing. We don't know what happened to him, but Dad thinks he fell out of a nearby nest. We took him to the bird sanctuary near our town, and they nursed him for about six weeks. When it was time to release Deke back into the wild, I asked my dad if I could keep him, and he said yes."

"Do you enjoy him like you do your dog?"

"Well, I love Deke almost as much as I do Benny. I think he's smarter than our lab, but he's not as cuddly."

The spectators laughed, and Badr began the teaching demonstration. Lacey unhooded Deke and fed him small bits of quail while he was still on her fist. Then she walked over to the perch and gently placed him on the turf, giving him more meat.

"I'm nervous he'll fly away, Mr. Badr."

"I've been watching you and Deke most of the week, Lacey. I can see you two have already developed a bond. While it's always possible a falcon will return to the wild, I think Deke will stick with you."

Hesitantly, Lacey left Deke on his perch and walked with Badr to the lure and rope lying on the ground. They knelt and attached meat to the lure. Badr picked up the rope and gently tossed it low to the ground towards Deke. He immediately swooped down, grabbed the lure, and began eating, extending his wings over the prey.

"Why is Deke hiding the meat with his wings?" Lacey asked.

"It's called mantling. It's how he protects his food from someone stealing it, a human or another predator."

"So he doesn't trust that I won't take his meat."

"Actually, by letting Deke alone while he eats, you are building that trust."

They watched the kestrel finish his meal and relax his wings. Badr nodded to Lacey, who took another piece of meat in her hand and smacked her lips. Deke immediately flew onto her fist. Lacey beamed.

"Are you ready for one last lesson today?" Badr asked.

"Yeah, it's so fun."

Lacey returned Deke to the perch, then attached another piece of meat to the leather lure. This time, instead of throwing the lure onto the ground, she twirled it low in the air, as Badr had previously shown her. Deke immediately flew towards the meat and pushed the lure to the ground. He again began eating, but this time, he mantled the prey less than he'd done earlier. Once Deke was finished, he returned to Lacey's fist, and she hooded him. The spectators rose and applauded both the young falconer and her mentor.

As Badr and Lacey walked Deke back to the mews, they made plans for one more lesson before the festival ended. Badr was as excited as Lacey with the progress they'd made. It was a part of falconry he enjoyed, introducing young people to the sport. He was especially delighted to be doing it with Lacey because girls didn't get these opportunities often in his native land. With his teaching completed, Badr rushed to the Hospitality Center for the day's main attraction. The falcon beauty pageant was about to begin.

Chapter 67: That Afternoon

The Hospitality Center was packed with people ready to watch the beauty pageant. Falcon stands lined the middle of the huge room. In a ceremonial entrance, the falconers strode in one by one, their hooded falcons on their fists. Badr led the way with his eleven-year-old gyrfalcon Zohra, followed by Lacey with her kestrel so the sheik could help in her first pageant. Abdul Salaam came next with Badr's peregrine Maeveen. The Duncans from *Evergreen Falconry* walked behind the bodyguard with their pure white falcons, followed by the Wyatts from Canada, also with gyrs, just not pure white ones. They'd also entered one of their gyr-saker hybrids. The Nevadan Leonard Sprout came next with his juvenile aplomado. Bringing up the rear of the procession were several hawkers and their pets, two red-tailed hawks, a cooper, and a northern goshawk. As the falconers reached their assigned stands, they placed their birds on the perches and stood behind them, waiting for the judging to begin.

"Would you look at those hooded caps," Patrick said to Quinn, who'd both been assigned to the pageant's security. "Not the simple leather hoods we've seen so far."

"No kidding. I can't believe the craftsmanship involved in the decorative needlework, beads, and feathers."

"The plumage on top of that pure white gyr from *Evergreen* looks heavy enough to topple the poor bird."

"Yeah, and what about that hybrid with the single peacock feather?"

Because Badr had entered his own birds in the pageant, he'd designated the presidents of the three amateur falconry clubs as judges. They decided on three categories: gyrfalcons, peregrines, and others, which would include the hybrids and other visiting birds. They'd also decided on less stringent criteria for the judging than was typically used at international events. They'd be judging on overall appearance, feathers, head, beak, and talons according to a ten-point scale. The falcon with the highest score would win the category. Because there weren't a large number of entrants in the pageant, Badr had decided to award only one winner in each category. He'd also added a People's Choice award, allowing the attendees to vote on their favorite.

As the assessments got underway, the judges went from stand to stand to evaluate each bird. The owner would remove the bird's hood and then stand back to allow the judging to occur without impeding the process. The judges started at the opposite end from where Badr stood, which allowed him to act on what he'd been thinking about the whole festival.

The sheik went over to Daryl Duncan from *Evergreen Falconry,* who stood with his pure-white, year-old female gyrfalcon.

"She may be the most beautiful falcon I've ever seen," Badr said. "What's her name?"

"Nova. Like a brilliant explosion of light."

"How fitting. Will you be entering her in the auction tomorrow?"

"Of course. While I came to support your new enterprise, I also came to make money."

"Would you consider selling her before the auction?"

"You have an interest? Are you aware of what this gyr would go for?"

"Yes. Your last pure white falcon went for $466,667 at the Saudi Arabian auction."

"Hmm. You're keeping up on the international circuit."

"You don't think you'll get that kind of money here at my little festival, do you?"

"If not here, somewhere else."

"I'm interested in purchasing Nova, and I'm prepared to offer whatever it takes to get her. Would you take $550,000?"

"Hmm. Will you be breeding her?"

"Yes. I'm looking for a gyr younger than Zohra, who is now eleven. I hope to develop a cross-breed with one of my peregrines. Looking for a little more size along with the speed. More importantly, I hope to develop a gyr hybrid that's better suited to this climate."

"Because you'll be breeding her, my price is $600,000."

"Sold. If you bring Nova to my office at the end of the pageant, I'll pay you then. I'm assuming I can take possession without you entering her in tomorrow's auction."

"Correct. She will be your bird once I've received payment."

By the time the negotiations were over, the judges had reached Badr, Lacey, and Daryl. They took the hoods off the birds and allowed the judges to look over their falcons. Then, with the judging done, the threesome retired to the computer terminals to enter the scores and determine the winners. While everyone awaited the results, the spectators milled around the contestants, praising the birds' beauty and asking questions. Suddenly, Quinn gasped, noticing the same three downstate newspapermen she and Ian had encountered the first day of the festival. The ones who appeared to have legitimate press credentials but hadn't pre-registered. Quinn eventually issued them security cards and press packets. Today, they again wore business suits and N-95 masks. She noticed they were hanging around the *Evergreen Falconry* stand, talking animatedly with Daryl Duncan about his beautiful white gyr. Quinn wondered why she hadn't seen them since the first day of the festival.

"What's wrong?" Patrick asked. "You just gasped, and you're white as a sheet."

"Oh, nothing. I just forgot to do something," Quinn said as she fumbled with her phone to send the pictures she'd taken last Saturday of the elusive threesome to Zoey Rogers, her friend in the FBI.

Just then, Badr took the stage in the Hospitality Center to announce the winners of the beauty pageant. Not surprisingly, Daryl Duncan's pure white gyrfalcon Nova won the award for most beautiful gyr. Maeveen, handled by Abdul Salaam, won the peregrine prize, and Leonard Sprout's juvenile aplomado won the other category. But the biggest applause was saved for the last category, The People Choice Award, won in a landslide by Lacey's pet kestrel Deke. With the day's event concluded, Badr headed to his office with Daryl and Nova to complete the transaction they'd negotiated during the pageant.

Chapter 68: May 8

Unable to sleep due to the excitement of the festival's last day, Badr rose before dawn and walked the beach at his home. Before leaving for the Hospitality Center, where the falcon auction would be held, he visited Zohra in her mew and moved her indoors for the day. Nova was already lodged inside his home under more security than usual. The sheik had no worries about anyone trying to steal his new falcon, but he felt better adding protection for his $600,000 investment until the festival was over.

When Abdul Salaam transported them to the Hospitality Center, Badr could see the auctioneers had the room already set up for the main event. Owners were arriving with their falcons and setting up their hooded birds on perches. *Evergreen Falconry* was offering its two remaining pure white gyrs, plus their two gyr-shaheen hybrids. Cliff and Kent Wyatt from the Canadian Lac Seul Bird Farm had the largest number of falcons entered, three dark variant gyrs and their four gyr-saker hybrids. As a courtesy, the auctioneer had also allowed several hawkers from the amateur clubs to display their falcons for possible sale or barter. The Nevadan had decided not to offer either of his aplomado falcons in the auction. The auction would be small yet potentially profitable.

Spectators had begun entering the large hall to look over the birds for sale. Each was given a printed prospectus listing the bidding rules and describing all the falcons entered. Numbered paddles sat on the seats for the bidders to use in tendering their offers. On this last day of the festival, Badr also relaxed the rules to allow non-registered potential buyers to attend. He'd upped the security detail, too, knowing the amount of money that might be exchanged.

Just as the auction was getting underway, Quinn and Patrick heard loud shouting near the display of birds from *Evergreen Falconry*. They rushed over to see what was going on.

"Where is your #1 white gyrfalcon? The one you call Nova?" The man yelling at Daryl Duncan was one of the three suited men in N-95 masks.

"Hey, what's going on?" Patrick asked.

"This man listed his bird in the prospectus, and now it's not here," the mask said.

"The prospectus clearly states an owner can withdraw a bird from the auction at any time. I'm not the only one who has done that," Daryl Duncan said.

"But we've come a great distance to bid on this bird," the mask yelled. "I will not be denied this purchase."

"Sir, I think it's clear what Mr. Duncan has done is appropriate according to the rules. It's time for you to calm down or leave," Patrick ordered.

His eyes pierced Daryl's, then Patrick's, and finally Quinn's. Her jawline scar burned at the anger she saw in his look. Finally, the threesome turned abruptly and stomped out of the center. Quinn was again puzzled by these men and wondered what it was that bothered her. Was it their slight accent? It wasn't Middle Eastern like Badr's, but she'd heard it before. She was sure of it. With the commotion resolved, the auction went off without a hitch, and all except two birds had been sold for extraordinary prices.

As the afternoon event came to an end, the bazaar owners from the souks in the Hospitality Center laid out a huge feast on the racing grounds for the spectators to enjoy. Not only did they feature foods from their native countries, but they also included American favorites like hamburgers, hot dogs, French fries, and an assortment of fruits and pies for dessert. The picnic dinner was both a thank you to the festival goers from the sheik and a preview to the night's closing event, the U.S. opening of the documentary *Wild Allies*. The film explored falconry in Saudi Arabia by following 1000 falconers from around the world as they participated in the annual King

Abdulaziz Falconry Festival. So, as the picnic ended and night fell, they watched *Wild Allies* on the massive outdoor screen they'd borrowed from a film festival. Some watched from the stands, others had brought lawn chairs, and a few stretched out on blankets on the ground. When the movie concluded and the applause finally ended, festival participants filed through security for the last time. Badr stood at the gate, shaking their hands and thanking them for coming. For a few, like Lacey Greenway with her pet kestrel, he shared goodbye hugs, promising to stay in touch.

With the festival grounds nearly empty except for vendors closing down their souks, waste collectors clearing the grounds, and security teams making final checks of the buildings, Badr said to Quinn, "Let's take a walk. I need to burn up some energy before heading home." He'd already changed from the business suit he'd worn much of the festival back into his comfortable native robe and head cloth.

"I hear you," Quinn replied as they began walking the outside perimeter of the grounds. While the golf cart was nearly silent, they knew Abdul Salaam trailed behind them. The temperature was crisp, probably in the mid-forties. Night songs serenaded them as they passed the security fence. Owls hoo-hooing from distant trees. Spring peepers whistling from a nearby pond. "You must be very happy at the turnout and how well the festival went, Badr."

"I am. It's hard to put into words. I wasn't sure I could pull it off up here in the Northwoods. Not only the festival but the whole center. I think we have a bright future."

"Well, you did. Think you'll do it again next year?"

"Not next year. It's too much for an annual event. But I will do it again someday."

As they neared the parking lots where only a few cop cars and one motorhome remained, Badr shouted, "Quinn, look! There's a fire inside that RV!"

Both took off running towards the coach while Abdul Salaam drove next to them, yelling, "*Udkhil, udkhil*. Get in, get in."

But Quinn and Badr were more intent on reaching whatever was burning inside the RV than their safety or following Abdul's commands. Just as they reached the vehicle, rifle fire pierced the night.

Chapter 69: May 9

It was just after midnight, and law enforcement teams had finished securing all the buildings. They were ready to head home, but no one seemed to know where Quinn, Badr, and his bodyguard had gone. They hadn't seen them since the last visitor left, and the gates were closed. Patrick and Gilda had texted Quinn, but neither had received a reply.

"I think the sheik has a home somewhere near the center. Maybe that's where they are," Patrick said.

"We've already been over the grounds, so I'm confident they're not within the fencing," Gilda added.

"Maybe we should check the parking lot to see if her car's still here," Flint suggested.

"Quinn wouldn't have left without us," Patrick argued. "We all rode together."

"Let's check anyway," Gilda said. "Be on the lookout too for the golf cart the sheik's beefcake usually drives."

They left the gates and walked towards the parking lot, switching on their iPhone flashlights. As they neared the site, Flint's light caught the reflector at the back of the golf cart.

"There it is," he yelled.

They broke into a dead run, and when they reached the cart, they found Abdul Salaam slumped over the steering wheel, bleeding.

"He's been shot," Gilda said. As she touched his neck, she could feel a faint pulse. "He's alive. Call an ambulance."

While she attended to the bodyguard, Patrick looked beyond the golf cart and saw a tin of Jiffy Popcorn burning on the ground. A red-checkered keffiyeh and a cell phone lay nearby. He rushed to grab the phone, recognizing Quinn's emerald-green cover.

"Wait, Patrick!" Gilda yelled as she looked up. "This is probably a crime scene. You're gonna contaminate it."

"Too late. It's Quinn's phone, and there's a red emergency alert on the lock screen," he replied as he turned it over.

"You probably can't get in without her passcode," Flint said.

"I've got some guesses," Patrick said, trying *Ruby* without success. Next, he plugged in *crane,* and the screen opened. "Quinn Macarthy, you are too predictable," he muttered.

Patrick and Flint hunched over the phone's screen and began reading the emergency alert.

"Guys, read it out loud. I'm a little tied up here trying to keep this man alive," Gilda shouted. In the distance, she could hear sirens. Too soon for an ambulance. Probably EMS from Peninsula Fire #3, she thought as she pressed harder on Abdul's bleeding abdominal wound.

"It's from FBI agent Zoey Rogers," Patrick said. "This is what she wrote: *I've been trying to call you. Why haven't you answered? Didn't recognize the masked men in your pix but sent them on to Interpol. Just heard back their facial recognition software identified them as three Russians. Sovietniks Vissarion Volkov and Iosif Zaitsev. Mafia kingpin Pavel Pilecki. Do not engage. Armed and dangerous. Sending help.*"

"What pictures is she talking about?" Flint asked.

"I wasn't there, but it seems that Ian and Quinn were called to the security gate when three downstate newspapermen tried to check in without pre-registering. Their press credentials looked valid, so she issued them security passes. To be safe, she took pictures of their paperwork and planned to send them to the FBI but forgot until yesterday. You might've seen them at the festival, walking around in N95 masks."

"Geez, Louise. I hope we're not too late."

Just then, the parking lot erupted with activity. EMS, accompanied by a red fire engine, pulled in first, and Flint directed them to the golf cart. Zoey Rogers and her partner Garrison Perry arrived next in their marked FBI Chevy Suburban. They were followed by TCPD Police Chief Hank Yeager and Detective Buzz Broderick. Then State Troopers Nick Wagner and Avery Hollister entered the lot with detection dogs Grit and Ruby. Like the TCPD officers, they'd been on their way home from the festival's closing events, heard it on their scanners, and turned around, sirens and light bars blazing. The ambulance came in next, and medics rushed to treat Abdul Salaam. Last to the scene was CSI, which dispatch had alerted after the call for an ambulance and extra hands. With dawn still hours away, Gil wished they'd brought portable light stands so they could get a better look at the scene. Finally, trying to organize the sudden chaos, Gilda, Hank, and Zoey huddled to decide their next steps.

Chapter 70: That Morning

The rest of the night had been insane, but at least with sunrise imminent, the scene had lost some of the malevolence of the night. Abdul Salaam had died shortly after the EMS arrived. Medical Examiner Ted Roberts pronounced him dead due to abdominal gunshot trauma. He said the penetrating injury had most likely pierced the stomach, lung, and a major artery. He wouldn't know for sure until after an autopsy. Usually the jokester of the group, Roberts remained somber that morning, fearing the danger Quinn and the sheik faced.

Ian and Hannah Doyle had arrived with a bag of McMuffin sandwiches and coffees from the Front Street McDonalds, knowing there was no fast food on Old Mission. They'd bugged out of the festival last night during the closing credits of *Wild Allies*, exhausted from their weeklong duties and realizing they had a long drive back to their Crystal Lake home. Ian usually turned on his police scanner before going to bed, but he'd passed on that ritual last night, turned off his phone, and quickly fell asleep. In the morning, Hannah had flicked on the early news and caught rudimentary details about some incident at the falconry center. She woke Ian, and they headed back to the peninsula to see how they could help.

"Oh, thank you," Patrick said, passing around the food bag. "We've been pooling energy bars since midnight."

"So, what's going on?" Ian asked. "The morning news is only saying there's been an incident here. The police scanner also mentioned a death."

Gilda began explaining, "After we secured the festival site and were ready to leave, we couldn't find Quinn."

"The sheik and his bodyguard were missing, too," Patrick added.

"We decided to check out the parking lot and found the bodyguard shot in his golf cart. He didn't make it," Flint said.

"Quinn's phone, the sheik's head thing, and a burning tin of Jiffy Pop were on the ground," Patrick continued.

"Are Quinn and Badr okay?" Ian asked.

"We don't know. They're missing."

As everyone ate their sandwiches and drank their coffees, Chief Yeager filled the Doyles in on the FBI alert on Quinn's phone. The one identifying the threesome as two Sovietniks and their mafia boss, Pavel Pilecki.

"Oh, shit!" Ian exclaimed. "Not the guys with N95 masks who tried to enter the festival without proper registration?"

"Yeah, thems the ones," Gilda said.

"Quinn and I checked the newspapermen in and photographed their credentials. They had a slight foreign accent we couldn't identify," Ian added. "Did you see them hanging around the festival throughout the week?"

"Not until the last couple of days," Patrick answered. "Quinn and I saw them talking to the guy from *Evergreen Falconry* at the beauty pageant. The one who won with his pure white gyrfalcon. We saw them talking to him again, but this time at the auction, and they were very angry. They were arguing about why the winning gyr wasn't entered in the auction. Apparently, they'd been interested in bidding on it. Quinn and I broke up the argument, and the N95s stomped off. We haven't seen them since."

"Damn. You think this is about buying a bird?" Gilda asked.

"I know it is," Ian said. "A few months ago, Quinn and I were looking into Pavel Pilecki."

"What! You supported her lone rangering about a mafia godfather?" Patrick yelled.

"Hey, Patrick. Hang on," Yeager said. "I know everyone's scared about Quinn's whereabouts, but it sounds like Ian might have some helpful information. Go ahead."

"I got involved to keep Quinn from investigating on her own. She couldn't get Pilecki out of her brain. The unsolved counterfeit pesticide case and murder of George Watkins from two years ago. Mack's death from illegal fentanyl imported from Russia, at least in her mind. Falcon smuggling originating from a Russian peninsula. Russia, Russia, Russia was all she thought about."

"So what did you discover that can help us, Ian?" Gilda asked.

"I came across a newspaper article about a pure white gyrfalcon that sold for half a million bucks at an auction in the Middle East. Prince Farouk happened to be the buyer. Through our research, we learned Farouk was Pavel Pilecki's buddy. They partied together at social events. The Prince even dated Pilecki's sister, Mika. Quinn identified her through pictures in the press as the nurse who administered the fatal dose of heart stimulant to George Watkins. When the Prince outbid Pilecki for the gyrfalcon, it ended their friendship. The Russian wasn't used to losing. He's probably still angry about not getting the gyr, and maybe he came here for a second chance at the rare bird. Not the same one, but equally beautiful."

"Christ Almighty, Ian," Gilda said. "You kept this from law enforcement?"

"They didn't," Zoey Rogers answered. "The FBI was in on it."

"Uffda," Flint said. "So, you're thinking whatever's happened to the sheik and Quinn is related to the gyrfalcon who won the beauty pageant?"

Nobody answered, everyone too stunned about what Ian had shared. One of the CSI techs came over to show them the casts he'd made from tire tracks in the parking lot.

"We're lucky it wasn't paved," he said. "I got excellent impressions."

"So what're our next steps, folks?" Zoey said, taking charge. "I'm going to check with Interpol and the Border Patrol to see if they have more on the Russians' entry into the country."

Patrick added, "Now that it's morning, I think we should grab a few golf carts and traverse the area outside the fence to see what else is here. I'm curious where the sheik lived."

"I also want to contact the guy from *Evergreen Falconry*," Patrick said. "Maybe he'll be able to fill in some details about the argument."

"I'm gonna run these casts back to FC2," the CSI said. "The faster we identify the vehicle they were driving, the better chance we have of catching them."

"Why don't you take the sheik's head cloth and Quinn's phone with you," Gil suggested. "We might come up with some prints."

"Good work, everyone," Zoey said. "Let's spread the crime scene tape to keep intruders out and get on with our tasks. Seems like we have a kidnapping."

Chapter 71: That Same Day

A false allurement to bring them to the motorhome. That's what the Jiffy Pop fire had been, Quinn thought. It was one of the oldest ruses in crime. Sexual predators had done it for years, luring children with the promise of candy or a new toy. Cutting power to someone's home to bring them outside. As a cop, she should've known better. She'd blindly followed Badr's shouts as he ran towards the motorhome fire. She'd even ignored Abdul Salaam's yelling to get in the golf cart. When they reached the RV just as shots rang out, they'd been ambushed. Tied up, black hoods put over their heads and pushed inside the coach to a bench at a dinette table they couldn't see. Told to keep quiet. Quinn knew Badr was next to her from the woody oud fragrance he wore. Someone else sat across from them, but she couldn't tell who. She wondered if it was Abdul Salaam.

Soon after they were seated, the motorhome started up, turned left out of the parking lot, and headed towards Center Road. But a series of ten-minute straightaways, followed by turns, curves, and more straightaways, made Quinn lose track of where they were going. After about thirty minutes of this, she gave up. It shouldn't be this hard, she thought. We're on a peninsula that's less than twenty miles long. Had they taken back roads to get off?

Then something changed. Drastically. The drive became more rugged. They'd left the pavement, Quinn realized. Dips and turns in the road sent them jostling against each other. She felt the motorhome wheels squiggle as they shifted into low gear when they hit a patch of sand. The road had narrowed, brush and tree limbs scraping the sides of the vehicle. The RV finally came to a halt.

"We can go no farther," Volkov said.

"We'll go the rest of the way on foot," Pilecki replied. "Remove their hoods so they can see where they're going, but keep their hands bound. Keep the gun on them, Zaitsev."

As their hoods were removed and they were nudged out of the motorhome by the muzzle of a rifle, Badr said, "Where is Abdul Salaam, my bodyguard?"

"We left him behind with a bullet in his gut. The same will happen to you if you don't shut up and keep moving," Pilecki said.

As they trudged along the road, Quinn's feet turned and squished through the sandy spots. The place looked somewhat familiar. Not surprising since there weren't many places in the county she hadn't explored with her camera and dog. Still, she felt oddly calm, certain the Russians were bluffing. They needed something from Badr, and they wouldn't shoot him until they got it. They walked on, making two turns onto equally rutty, sandy roads, but no road signs gave away their location. Quinn suddenly smelled something earthy, both fertile and rich. The roadway darkened as they entered woods of hemlock, white pine, and beech. She spotted a bald eagle nest atop a dead tree in an opening in the middle of the forest. I know where I am, Quinn screamed inside. Brinkman Bog Nature Preserve. Sanctuary for bald eagles. Somehow, knowing their location made her more confident. Even gave her a sense of peace. It also made her angry. The Russians had driven them in circles only to arrive at the back end of Badr's property. They were directly behind the festival grounds off Tompkins Road. No wonder it looked familiar. She and Patrick had hiked both Eagle Rise and Murray Road several times to reach the bog to photograph eagles. Those fuckers.

Their walk seemed to be changing, though, as the Russians pushed them into a field of winter wheat that reached just above their ankles. When Quinn saw a dilapidated shed on the far side of the meadow, her jawline scar tingled and itched furiously. Is that where we're going? Her body remembered the last time she was stuck in a shed with Meyer Garfield, the Clare mobster who'd been the middleman for Pavel Pilecki in the counterfeit pesticide case.

Garfield had chased her in circles through the woods surrounding the shack. Then came the assault. Garfield had pulled her hair so tightly that her scalp was sore for weeks. His fist had cracked her nose, blood spraying everywhere. He'd broken her hand when he kicked her Glock out of reach. Finally disabling her, Garfield had locked her inside the outbuilding with hands and feet bound. He'd taped her mouth shut, making it hard to breathe because her nose was clotted with blood. Choking back the sour bile of fear and pain, she'd been sure she was going to die.

A hidden dip in the ground brought Quinn back to the present. She stumbled, finding it hard to balance with her hands bound. Pilecki grabbed her before she fell. Pulling her up, he stared at her with his light blue, piercing eyes the shade of ice water. She shivered, knowing what this man was capable of, fearing it was happening all over again.

Chapter 72: May 10

The rest of Sunday, the law enforcement teams had jumped into action following leads, spurred on by knowing one of their own was missing. Zoey had learned from customs that the three Russians had flown into Detroit from Moscow on April 25th via Turkish Airlines. They'd taken a pre-booked Uber to an address in Bloomfield Hills, where they rented a 36' Ford Windsport motorhome. The passports used by the Russians were all counterfeit, bearing false names. They'd only been identified after the fact by Interpol, who'd matched the eyes on Quinn's pictures to eyes on international flight passengers using automated facial recognition software. Once the Russians boarded their rental RV, the authorities lost their whereabouts.

The CSI team had worked late, too, confirming the motorhome's identity as a Ford Windsport through its tire track castings. They were waiting for the Bloomfield Hills dealership to open Monday morning to learn more about the vehicle, especially its telematic system. They'd struck out, though, on finding any new prints on Badr's keffiyeh or Quinn's phone.

But it was Patrick who'd worked the latest, not reaching *Evergreen Falconry* in Washington State until nearly midnight Michigan time. Both the three-hour time change between the two states and the Duncans' long cross-country return flight had caused the delay.

"*Evergreen Falconry*," Naomi Duncan answered.

"This is Michigan Conservation Officer Patrick Elliott calling from Traverse City. We've had an incident at the falconry training center I'd like to talk to you about."

"Let me get my husband and put us on speakerphone." Minutes later, Daryl arrived and said, "What's this about?"

"Sheik Badr-Uddin and Detective Quinn Macarthy were abducted right after the festival ended on Saturday night. We think the three masked gentlemen who argued with you at the auction were involved. What can you tell me about that argument?"

"Jesus Christ, how awful," Daryl said. "I didn't know the men, but they seemed particularly interested in my pure white gyr Nova, the one who won the beauty pageant. They talked with me about her yet gave no indication they were interested in bidding on her. When they appeared at the auction after I'd withdrawn her due to a pre-auction sale, they got very angry. Seemed set on that particular bird even though I had others offered."

"Were they aware that Badr had purchased Nova and was responsible for her not being in the auction?"

"No, at least not from me. Well, maybe. They'd hung around the beauty pageant and fawned over my gyr. A lot of people were too. Perhaps they overheard Badr and me talking about Nova and negotiating her sale. We were careful to make our discussion as private as possible, but we were still in a public place."

"Have you had any prior experiences with these three men? They're actually mob operatives from Russia."

"You're kidding me. I'd never seen them before until the beauty pageant."

"You sure? We think they might've pursued the white gyr you sold at the Dubai auction held by the International Falcon Breeders Association. The one that sold for a record price of nearly half a million."

"Hmmm. They still weren't familiar to me. In most international auctions, especially in the Middle East, all sales are transacted by agents due to language and money exchange differences. Security is huge there, too, with the demand for high-quality captive-bred falcons being so steep. Most of the time, I never see who buys my birds."

Patrick had thanked them, given them contact information in case they remembered something new, and fell into his bed well past midnight.

The one thing the law enforcement teams hadn't accomplished on Sunday was surveying Badr's property in golf carts. Not only had they run out of time, but the keys had been removed from the fleet and were likely locked somewhere inside the security fence. So when the local E-Z-GO golf cart dealership finally arrived Monday morning with spare keys, they set off in groups to see what they could find on the grounds surrounding Badr's festival site. The TCPD officers took the route to the south while Gilda, Flint, Patrick, and Ian took the land north of the site, closer to Grand Traverse Bay. Hannah had stayed behind with Vernadeane to handle any communications that came through.

They'd made several passes back and forth through the meadow beyond the festival security fence until they came to woods, where they found several footpaths leading through trees. They got out and inspected the paths, seeing some had been made by golf carts or another kind of ATV. They proceeded to the one appearing to have the most wear. As the trees thinned and they came to an opening, Patrick stopped the golf cart.

"Geez, Louise," Flint said, staring at the scene spread out before them. The expanse of northern Grand Traverse Bay. A large boathouse and slips constituted a small marina along the shoreline. The pergola on the beautiful beach. A modern home full of windows nestled up a hill among low dunes. Several nearby outbuildings. Even a helipad and small helicopter hangar.

"I think we've found where Badr lives," Patrick said, restarting the golf cart. Not seeing any signs of activity, he headed up the path towards the home. As the pathway turned into a paved driveway to the residence, he turned off the cart. The four of them disembarked and started walking towards the spacious abode. They didn't get far, though. Two steps from the cart, the four of them were immediately accosted by six white-robed, head-scarved, gun-toting men pointing M4 carbines at their chests.

Chapter 73: That Afternoon

Quinn, Badr, and the Russians had finally traversed the meadow to reach the shed. It wasn't a communications building like the one she'd been confined to near Clare. This one was just a shed. Weathered wood with missing panels that let the light through. The slanted roof sagged at one end. A single window near the top. It seemed out of place, though, as the only building in sight. Shouldn't there've been a barn or farmhouse? Pilecki said something to Zaitsev in Russian. He went inside, briefly looked around, and returned, nodding to Pilecki.

"Let's go," he said, nudging Quinn inside first.

The interior was empty except for an old wooden table and six chairs. At one end of the table were piles of power bars, prepackaged cheese and crackers, and bottled water.

"What the fuck," she muttered as she saw the stash. Does this guy have a string of layover spots across the Northwoods? While she entertained the idea, she didn't have time to decide as Volkov unclipped the zip ties binding their wrists and motioned them toward the chairs.

"We have fifteen minutes for rest," Pilecki said. "We still have a long walk ahead, so take in some food and water before we set out again."

Quinn said, "I have to use the bathroom. Is there one nearby?"

"Zaitsev will take you to the woods. The only bathroom we have."

With his weapon pointed straight at her, he motioned towards the tree stand a few yards beyond the meadow. She thought about making a move to escape but remembered what happened the last time she'd tried that with Garfield. She went into the woods, relieved herself, and returned to the shed without incident. She and Badr ate some food and drank some water before Pilecki rebound their hands and started them out again.

They came to the end of the meadow and picked up a faintly-worn path that climbed gently through the woods. Quinn wondered if it was a deer trail. She could tell they were traveling along a ridge and occasionally caught sight of the bay. Delicate trillium carpeted the forest floor, and she felt sad she wasn't here taking pictures. Or maybe she was angry. She wasn't sure, with her emotions all jumbled up. Maybe they'll still be here when this is over, she thought, trying to plant hope into her psyche.

They finally came to an opening in the trees at the edge of a paved road. Pilecki put out his arms to hold them back while Volkov stepped into the road to check for traffic. He looked in both directions and nodded to Pilecki. No cars in sight.

"Cross now," he ordered, pointing to a narrow seasonal dirt road running perpendicular to the paved one.

Quinn gasped as she crossed the pavement that was part of the ridge they'd been traversing. For as far as she could see, blooming cherry trees filled the landscape. She drank in the scene, wanting its beauty to sustain her for whatever came next. As they walked alongside the orchards, Quinn watched bees swarm above the pollinator boxes and into the blossoms. She prayed some cherry farmer would see them and call for help. Wouldn't it raise suspicions if someone saw this motley crew, she thought? A Middle Easterner in a white robe, a female uniformed detective, and three men in suits following with rifles.

Quinn looked over at Badr as he trudged along silently at a measured pace. She was concerned because he hadn't uttered a single word since they'd been captured in the parking lot. For someone who loved to talk, his behavior was highly unusual. Why hadn't he yelled or fought back in protest? Maybe he was deep in thought planning their escape. Perhaps he knew something about the Russians that she didn't. Badr had begun to limp, too, perhaps a sign that the knee he'd injured last fall had begun to bother him.

"We've arrived," Pilecki said, pointing to an old home situated on a slight rise. Surrounded by overgrown golden grasses, the building was sided in white clapboard. Two large front windows on the lower level were boarded over. Dormers broke through the newish patterned roof, their windows uncovered. A single electrical wire hung from a foliage-enveloped post to a nearby telephone pole.

They followed Pilecki around to the back. A burgundy Buick Enclave sat just outside the door. Quinn looked down at the license plate: GVR 4924. Standard white plate with blue lettering surrounded by a Hertz plate holder. They entered the home, their eyes adjusting to the dark. Quinn saw four men sitting around a Formica table playing cards. A half-empty bottle of vodka sat at one end. Shot glasses sat next to the ashtrays at each man's spot. When Pilecki entered, they all rose.

"*Rat teebya veedet*," one said directly to Pilecki. I'm happy to see you.

"*Spasiba*," Pilecki replied. Thank you.

Puzzled by this unexpected influx of Russians, Quinn stole a glance at Badr. Staring at the Russian who'd spoken to Pilecki, his face was beaded in sweat.

Chapter 74: May 11

The six security men who'd accosted Patrick, Ian, Flint, and Gilda when they reached Badr's property nudged them up the driveway with their guns. Separating them from each other, they patted them down, removing their weapons and tossing them aside.

Patrick said, "WAIT. WE ARE PO-LICE OFF-I-CERS," pronouncing each syllable plainly so the robed bodyguards would understand him.

"Then what are you doing here?" one asked in perfect English.

Embarrassed about the assumption he'd made, Patrick explained, "Badr-Uddin and Quinn Macarthy are missing. We wondered whether they might be here."

Gilda added, "Actually, we're all but certain they've been abducted because the sheik purchased a white falcon that a trio of Russians wanted and are willing to kill for."

The security detail quickly apologized, returned the weapons to the officers, and beckoned them inside Badr's home.

"The sheik and Miss Quinn are not here. We've been worried since we haven't seen them or Abdul Salaam since the festival ended Saturday night. Badr-Uddin gave us strict orders to guard his new gyrfalcon Nova until he returned, so we've been doing that."

Another guard added, "We've been discussing what to do next, but it's not customary to disobey the sheik's orders."

"I'm afraid we have bad news," Gilda said. "Abdul Salaam was shot and killed during the sheik's abduction. We are very sorry."

Ian's phone rang, and he stepped away from the grieving bodyguards who'd begun to pray. He nodded several times before he hung up and returned to the group.

"That was Hannah," he said. "They've located the motorhome."

"How'd they manage that?" Gilda asked.

"Ford Motor Company used their telematics to ping the GPS in the vehicle, which gave them the motorhome's location on Eagle Rise Road."

"That's not far from here. But what are these telematics?" one of the bodyguards asked.

"Oh, sorry," Ian replied. "Telematics use the computers inside the motorhome's head unit. You know that box that's at the top of your windshield just behind the rearview mirror? Most vehicles have them now. OnStar and STARLINK are the two names you hear most. It pings a satellite to find your location."

"It's how GPS is being used to fight crime," Patrick explained.

"Let's head over to the motorhome," Gilda said to her colleagues. "Keep in touch if you hear anything new," she added, handing her business card to one of the guards."

Gilda, Patrick, Flint, and Ian rode the golf cart back through the woods to the parking lot, where they found the rest of the team in a huddle around Zoey, who was holding out her phone so everyone could listen.

"What's happening?" Gilda asked.

"I just got another alert from Interpol," Zoey said. "Turns out Pilecki, Volkov, and Zaitsev weren't the only mobsters on that plane from Moscow. Four more have been identified too, including Melor Golubev."

"Is that name supposed to mean something to us?" Patrick asked.

"He's known in Russian circles as *Muchitel,* which means The Torturer. From what I just learned, he's the most brutal of them all. According to Interpol, the foursome rented a Buick Enclave at the airport. They don't know whether the two groups are working together, but it's too much of a coincidence to think otherwise."

"Uffda," Flint said. "Let's get over to Eagle Rise Road to see if we can stop them before the electric shocks begin."

The security guard from Badr's house had been correct about the road's proximity. Chief Yeager, Buzz, and patrol officers Darlene Hamilton and Mike Louks piled into the TCPD's white SUV while Zoey, Garrison, Gilda, Flint, and Patrick got in the FBI's Chevy Suburban. Using the vehicle's GPS to guide them, they reached Eagle Rise Road in less than ten minutes. The seasonal dirt road ran off M-37, about two miles south of Old Mission Light. They started up the hilly road, bumping along the ruts and squishing their way through the sand swirls.

"Stop," Gilda said. "I see the motorhome ahead. I wonder if it's stuck."

"Or whether it's too large to get through. It appears wedged between the trees."

Both cars stopped, and everyone pulled their weapons as they left their vehicles and crept forward.

"FBI," Zoey yelled. "Exit the motorhome now."

After repeating their warning with no one answering, they continued. Garrison and Zoey motioned for everyone to stay put while the two agents continued until they reached the RV. The front door was wide open, and no one was inside. They checked the grounds surrounding the coach and found a myriad of footprints. The agents backed away from the scene and returned to the others.

"It appears the motorhome wasn't able to traverse the road any farther, and they've gone the rest of the way on foot. Let's get CSI out here to see if there's any evidence Quinn and the sheik are with them."

"I think it's time we call in the dogs," Chief Yeager added.

Chapter 75: Late Afternoon

The four Russians had gone upstairs with Pilecki. Quinn didn't know what was up there or why they'd left. Maybe to discuss their next steps in private. She and Badr were left in the main room guarded by Volkov and Zaitsev, who sat on a nearby couch. No one was talking, and the Russians appeared drowsy. It wouldn't matter if they fell asleep, though, because Quinn and Badr were bound to their chairs with no chance of escape.

Quinn could hardly believe the mess she'd gotten herself into. Locked up by mobsters again, only this time there were seven instead of one. It felt like déjà vu. While she was definitely on police business, Quinn knew personal issues had driven her deeper and deeper into the Russian mafia. Part of it was avenging Mack's death by stopping the flow of illicitly-made fentanyl. At a deeper level, though, it was about getting Pilecki. Finishing the counterfeit pesticide case she'd worked on two years ago. Retaliation for the vicious assault she'd undergone. Oh, yeah, the middlemen responsible were either dead or in jail, but the kingpin hadn't been captured to pay his dues. Now that he was within reach, Quinn wasn't going to let this opportunity pass to finally close the case.

"Psst," Badr said so softly she almost didn't hear.

She looked at him as he nodded at the two Russians asleep on the couch.

"You're not thinking escape, are you?" Quinn whispered.

"No way, but at least we can talk. I'm so sorry I got you into this predicament. I never thought Pilecki would ever leave Russia for a bird."

"Well, he has, and now we have to get him."

"We're pretty outnumbered. Listen, Quinn, the new Russians that arrived today are far worse than Pilecki and the Sovietniks."

"I didn't think it could get any worse."

"The one who addressed Pilecki when they came in is Melor Golubev. He's known as The Torturer."

"I saw that you broke out in a sweat when he entered. Was he the one who did all those horrible things to you? The scars and missing fingertip?"

Before Badr could reply, the Russians returned from upstairs, and the Sovietniks on the couch sat up at attention. Pilecki and Golubev sat down at the table across from Badr and Quinn with the armed guards behind them.

"Untie them," Pilecki said to Volkov. "Put your hands on the table where we can see them," he commanded Quinn and Badr.

They complied. She noticed the sheik's face was again drenched in sweat.

"It's good to see you again, Badr-Uddin," Golubev said, throwing his head back and laughing.

The laugh sent shivers through Quinn's body, reminding her of the character Jack Torrance's haunting evil laugh in *The Shining*. She went for her jawline scar but remembered Pilecki's order to keep their hands on the table and resisted.

"We are not here to hurt you," Pilecki said. "We only want one thing. The bird. Give that up quickly, and you'll be set free."

"I don't know what you're talking about," Badr said.

More quickly than Quinn could believe, Golubev pulled a hammer from underneath the table and smashed its face on top of the sheik's hand, crushing bones as he did. Both Quinn and Badr screamed. He fell off his chair, and the Sovietniks quickly uprighted him. Tears streamed down his face, and his mouth moved silently.

"I will ask again, Pavel Pilecki. Where is the white gyrfalcon Nova?" Pilecki said. "Why are you making it so hard on yourself? We only want the bird."

The sheik didn't reply and continued to move his mouth in prayer. He appeared vacant, almost catatonic. He didn't observe

Pilecki and Golubev look at each other, and Pilecki nod. He didn't notice the Sovietniks come forward and hold Quinn to her chair. He didn't see Golubev bring out his denailing pliers and rip Quinn's pinky fingernail from its bed. It wasn't until Quinn's scream pierced the air that Badr returned to reality. He also heard the sound of barking dogs approaching from a distance. The Russians had heard them, too, and Badr watched the seven rush out the back door and drive off in their Buick Enclave. It'd never crossed Badr's mind that the mobsters were getting away. He was more concerned about Quinn and rushed to her side. Curled up on the floor, her body shook as she sobbed from pain and trauma.

Chapter 76: That Evening

Ruby and Grit burst through the screen door the Russians had left open when they escaped in their Buick. Grit quickly regained his composure and lay down, sensing his wild behavior might get him in trouble. Ruby, Quinn's scream still ringing through her dog brain, rushed to her owner curled up on the floor. Quinn's sobs subsided as Ruby licked her tear-stained face. She drew her dog closer, immediately comforted.

Minutes later, handlers Nick Wagner and Avery Hollister carefully entered the home and took in the scene. Badr bent over, limply holding his mashed hand. Quinn hugging her whimpering dog, a bloody pinky finger bent and extended. Both victims grimacing and moaning in pain.

"What the fuck happened here?" Nick whispered as Avery knelt at Quinn's side, assessing her injuries as the detective writhed on the floor.

Avery immediately pulled out her phone and called 9-1-1, asking for immediate medical assistance. She didn't know their exact location because they'd been tracking cross-country, but dispatch quickly identified the GPS coordinates from her iPhone. Help was on the way.

"They're getting away," Badr said. "Seven Russians in a burgundy Buick Enclave."

From the floor, Quinn mumbled, "License plate GVR 4924. Hertz rental."

Nick fumbled with his portable police radio to call Gilda. "We've found the sheik and Quinn, both injured but alive. Seven Russians left the scene in a burgundy Buick Enclave Hertz rental about 15 minutes ago. GVR 4924. Copy that?"

"Understood. We're still at their abandoned motorhome on Eagle Rise Road. I'm gonna call for extra help. Get some roadblocks set up."

Gilda hung up and immediately realized the problem she faced with their remote location and lack of a nearby police force. Then she remembered the Peninsula Township Fire Department station, just minutes away on M-37. She called, and they were eager to assist.

But Gilda worried time was fleeting for capturing the Russians. They already had a lead of at least twenty minutes. It would take another ten or fifteen minutes to get roadblocks in place. They could be off the peninsula and slipping into Traverse City by then.

Gilda called Nick again for more details, then pulled together her team to brief them. They'd stayed near the empty motorhome watching the sheriff's every move, waiting to hear more. All nine of them: Hank, Buzz, Zoey, Garrison, Gilda, Flint, Patrick, and patrol officers Darlene Hamilton and Mike Louks.

"I don't know what you've picked up from my radio conversations, but Grit and Ruby tracked Quinn and the sheik to an abandoned home on Swaney Road. Both had been tortured by Russians who were holed up there. Quinn and Badr are currently en route to the hospital by ambulance and are going to survive, although both suffered significant trauma. Seven Russians, including Pavel Pilecki and his two Sovietniks, escaped in a Buick SUV a half hour ago. The fire department is setting roadblocks up, hoping to stop them before they leave the peninsula. We need to decide our next steps."

Before they could make plans, the officers heard a vehicle shifting into low gear as it lumbered up the sandy hill near where they were gathered. Everyone momentarily froze as they watched a large dark red SUV come into view, the Buick's prominent three-shield logo announcing the Russian's arrival.

"Jesus," Patrick croaked. "It's them."

"Take cover," Zoey yelled as she and Garrison moved behind the FBI Suburban. "They're armed and dangerous." Hank, Buzz, and their two patrol officers went behind the TCPD's white SUV. Flint, Patrick, and Gilda concealed themselves behind the massive motorhome.

Both sides waited to see what the other would do. Finally, the Russian who was driving threw the Enclave in reverse and rolled backward down the hill.

Wee-oh, wee-oh, wee-oh, a fire engine siren wailed as it roared up M-37 and screeched to a halt at the entrance to Eagle Rise Road. The large pumper could go no farther, but at least it effectively hemmed in the Enclave from getting away. Two firefighters holding rifles jumped down from the sides of the engine and tentatively approached the stranded SUV. Suddenly, all six doors of the Enclave opened, and the Russians poured out of their vehicle.

One of the firefighters yelled, "They're on the run!"

He'd barely gotten the words out when a Sovietnik turned and fired, bringing the firefighter down. The second returned fire and hit the Russian, as the remaining six scattered in the woods. At the sound of gunfire down the road, Gilda and the others moved out of their hiding places and ran towards the hilltop. They got a wide-angle view of what was happening. Pavel Pilecki and his remaining Sovietnik had the largest lead and were heading southeast into the woods towards Murray Road. Torturer Melor Golubev and one of the Russians had gone northeast in the direction of Old Mission Point. The last two Russians crossed Center Road and fled down an embankment to Grand Traverse Bay.

Zoey immediately took charge and barked orders, "Hank, Buzz, and Mike, follow Golubev and his man. Flint, Patrick, and Darlene chase the two Russians running the shoreline. Garrison and Gilda, let's go after Pilecki and his goon."

Hank, Buzz, and patrolman Mike Louks took off after Golubev and his associate as they fled through the woods northeast towards the water. The two Russians were dressed in black, so it was difficult to see them in the dark forest. The TCPD officers heard something crack, followed by a loud groan, and they saw Golubev go down. He'd not seen the large tree branch blocking his pathway. His associate knelt to help Golubev, giving Hank, Buzz, and Mike time to catch up.

"Stop right there," Hank said, gun pointed at the torturer's chest. "Give up your weapons."

But Golubev wasn't about to surrender. He twisted his body as he rose and awkwardly aimed his Makarov directly at Hank and pulled the trigger. But Mike was faster and expertly shot Golubev in the head. As he went down, Buzz raced to the associate and knocked him over. They wrestled on the ground, throwing punches, but the effort was useless, with Mike and Hank standing over the Russian with weapons poised to shoot. Finally, Buzz rolled away, and Mike cuffed the associate and walked him back to the patrol car. Hank went along to arrange for the ME to retrieve Golubev's body.

While the TCPD officers were apprehending Golubev and his associate, Flint, Patrick, and Darlene crossed Center Road and started down the rocky embankment towards the bay. Patrick noticed the beautiful golden hour had settled across the still water. Daylight's not gonna last much longer, he thought. Suddenly, a shot from the shoreline rang out, and Flint toppled onto the rocks. Darlene returned fire and immediately felled the Russian shooter. Blood from both victims spread from the shoreline into the water. The second Russian held up his hands and yelled, "*Ya podchinyayus! Ya podchinyayus!*" I surrender. I surrender. Patrick quickly moved towards the Russian, disarming and handcuffing him as he pushed him towards his partner lying on the shoreline. He bent and felt for a pulse. Finding none, he moved towards Darlene, who was tending to Flint.

"How're you doing, buddy?" Patrick asked.

"Uffda. Think I'm okay. Bleeding a lot, and it hurts like hell, but I think the bullet went through the muscle in my upper arm," Flint said as Darlene applied a tourniquet to stem the bleeding.

Patrick pulled out his phone and dialed 9-1-1. As soon as dispatch answered, he said, "We've got an officer wounded, a dead Russian, and another in custody. We need an ambulance, a squad car, the ME, and a CSI team, a-sap. Tell them to bring lights too, as it's getting dark."

"Roger that. Text your location coordinates. Lots going down out there right now, and we want to make sure we find the right spot."

Patrick complied by reporting his GPS numbers. He cuffed the Russian to a *No Dogs on the Beach* sign, checked with Darlene and Flint, and took off running.

Chapter 77: During the Night

Zoey, Garrison, and Gilda hadn't been as lucky apprehending Pilecki and the last Sovietnik. A combination of the Russians' head start and night setting in made them lose the trail. They decided to postpone further searching until morning when they'd call on Nick and Grit to track the remaining mobsters. Firefighters had brought the officers food and blankets so they could bunk in the motorhome overnight.

Meanwhile, Patrick had continued running along Center Road until he reached the falconry center. Except for the darkness, it had been an easy jog of less than two miles. The run gave him time to process how this Russian craziness could happen in a small town like Traverse City. Maybe TC no longer qualified as a small town, he thought. He'd heard the city's population had swollen during the pandemic as folks came North to escape COVID in the big cities. Some were seasonal residents who already had summer homes here. Others were buying property in what they considered a safer area to live. The increasing numbers had driven up home prices. Quinn had told him the median home price in TC was $400,000. He would've been priced out of the market if he hadn't purchased his East Bay Township ranch ten years ago for $175,000. The added population also stressed the city's infrastructure. Patrick remembered the bumper-to-bumper traffic clogging Airport Road and other east-west thoroughfares last summer. He guessed the growth was bringing more complicated problems. He didn't have to like it, though.

When Patrick arrived at the sheik's center, he found Fire Chief Theodore Tompert had set up a communications hub in the parking lot. Tompert, a second firefighter, and Ian Doyle were sitting under a portable light stand snacking on chicken wings a volunteer had brought. As Patrick emerged from the dark, Theo jumped up and pulled a concealed gun from his holster.

"Wait!" Ian yelled, throwing his arm out to stop Theo from shooting. "It's Patrick Elliott. DNR Conservation Officer who works with the Sheriff's Department."

"Holy shit," Patrick exclaimed. "I hadn't expected this kind of reception."

"Sorry, man," Theo said. "With the Russians on the run, we've been on high alert. Even though it's legal for a fire chief to carry a weapon, I've never done it until today. It wasn't loaded, either. We're not used to this kind of drama up here."

"Where's everyone else?" Patrick asked, eyeing the chicken wings.

The second firefighter noticed and said, "Here, sit down and help yourself to some chow."

"Vernadeane and Hannah went to town to be with Quinn and Flint," Ian answered. "Everyone else is out in the field."

Patrick dug into the food, nodding as he ate. He hadn't had anything to eat since morning, so he was starving. As he finished, he asked, "So, what's the plan?"

"Uh, we don't exactly have one," Theo said. "We've just set up as a central place where people can check in with new leads. Did you have something in mind?"

"Has anyone been back to Badr's property since we visited there two days ago?"

"Not that I know of," Ian replied.

"Okay, that'll be the plan," Patrick said. "Let's get a golf cart and head over there."

"Shouldn't we wait till morning?" the chief asked. "It's dark now, and we'll have to go through woods, won't we?"

"We'll find it," Patrick answered. "Anyway, carts have lights."

The four of them piled into the E-Z-Go with Patrick at the wheel and Ian next to him. He headed around the fenced propagation center towards the sheik's home. They drove back and forth several times until they located the worn path through the dense, pitch-black forest. When they came out of the woods, they couldn't make out the water, marina, or helicopter hanger due to the night's inky darkness, but the sheik's house was lit up like a glowstick. They raced up his driveway, expecting another encounter with the Arabs who'd accosted them before.

"It's too quiet," Patrick said.

"I agree. Where are the sheik's buddies?" Ian asked. "They rushed us immediately the last time we were here."

"Maybe they're asleep like normal people," Theo added.

"I doubt it," Patrick said. "Not with every light in the house on. Let's go check it out."

Patrick led the way, pulling his weapon as they walked up the driveway. They reached the door only to find it ajar. He quietly pushed it open and listened. Nothing. He stepped inside and listened again. Still nothing. He silently wished Quinn was here.

Finally, Patrick yelled out, "Anyone here?"

Suddenly, someone on the other side of the kitchen began pounding on a door and making indistinct sounds. Patrick rushed towards the sound and opened the door, which led to a lower level. One of the sheik's Arabs stood on the top step, his hands and feet bound with rope and his mouth taped shut. Five more stood at the base of the stairs, wiggling and murmuring through their closed mouths. Patrick, Ian, and the two firefighters quickly freed them. It looked like two of them had taken a beating.

"What happened here?" Patrick asked.

"Three Russians burst in on us just before dark. They wanted to know where the rare gyrfalcon was hidden. We knew better than to tell them," one replied.

"But when they started beating Hashir and Sufian, we were forced to lead them to the mews where Sheik Badr-Udden had hidden Nova. Otherwise, they would've killed our friends," another continued.

"So they took the bird and fled?" Patrick asked.

"Yes. They ran with Nova down to the boathouse and drove off in the sheik's Chris-Craft."

"If you were tied up, how'd you see all this going down?"

"The sheik's lower level is a walk-out. We watched the whole thing through sliders."

"Did you get a sense where they might be headed?"

"No, they spoke mostly Russian," an Arab replied.

"I think I heard the word 'Canada' once or twice, but I could be wrong," said another.

"Son of a bitch," Patrick cursed.

They all stood around processing the details of the situation. Finally, the fire chief said, "I think we need to call in the marine division from the Sheriff's department. They have a variety of boats they use on the Great Lakes."

They were quiet again as they thought about Theo's suggestion.

Patrick said, "I think the job's too big for local law enforcement, especially since these turds already have a huge head start on us."

"I agree," Ian added. "Searching for a 25'foot pleasure craft in the middle of Lake Michigan is beyond the sheriff's capabilities. Plus, this situation has become an international affair with the U.S., Russia, and maybe even Canada involved."

"I think it's time we contact the Coast Guard."

Chapter 78: The Next Morning

Nick and Grit returned to Eagle Rise Road before daybreak, just as the sky was pinking and the birds began their morning song. Avery and Ruby had followed the ambulance carrying Quinn into Traverse City and were unavailable for further tracking. Zoey, Garrison, and Gilda had spent a restless night in the motorhome and were more than ready to resume the hunt.

With it light enough to begin work, Nick said, "We need something Pilecki or the Sovietniks wore so Grit can get a scent."

They found several items left in the Enclave. A COVID mask on the dashboard. A lightweight sweater in the middle row. A Detroit Tigers baseball cap on the floor in the back. In truth, they had no idea whether any of the items belonged to Pilecki's group or the other four Russians.

Nick grabbed the mask and passed it in front of the dog's nose. "Go find, Grit."

The Belgian Malinois ran in circles around the Enclave and then headed west across Center Road to the site where Flint was wounded, and the first Russian died. CSI had finished processing the scene and was just packing their equipment to leave. Nick knew they'd chosen the wrong scent item, but he allowed Grit to finish the job and rewarded him with his favorite treats before they returned to the Enclave to try another scent item.

"What's your vote?" Nick asked. "Sweater or baseball cap?"

"Try the sweater," Zoey said. "I have a feeling the four Russians picked up the Tigers hat when they arrived in Detroit."

Nick grabbed the sweater, allowed the dog to scent it, and watched Grit take off southeast through the woods toward Murray Road. Zoey, Garrison, and Gilda gave a collective cheer and followed the dog through woods, meadows, and bogs until they came to the back end of the sheik's falconry center. A firefighter left behind at the communications hub told them everyone was at the sheik's home awaiting the Coast Guard's arrival. He gave them the low-down on what'd happened, and the officers took off through the woods towards the Lake.

Just after Gilda, Zoey, and Garrison arrived and joined Patrick and the others, they heard the thick vibrations of rotor blades before they saw them. Three distinctive orange and white Coast Guard Jayhawk helicopters appeared over the low dunes next to Badr-Uddin's compound. One landed on the 40-foot circular helipad while the other two hovered in the airspace above. Immediately, the commanding officer exited the open door and ducked beneath the still-rotating blades.

"Who's in charge here?" he barked as he strode towards the two groups of people waiting nearby. Patrick, Ian, the fire chief, and six Arabs. Gilda, Zoey, and Garrison, who'd just arrived.

Patrick looked at the others, and when no one answered, he finally said, "I guess I am, sir. Patrick Elliot, conservation officer for the DNR."

"Tell me what's going on here. This better not be some fucking wild goose chase."

Patrick pieced together the story, with others contributing occasional details. Sheik Badr-Uddin's grand opening festival for the falconry training center. Pilecki, the Sovietniks, and four other Russians' arrival to purchase a rare white gyrfalcon, which'd already been sold to the sheik. The capture and torture of Quinn and Badr to find out where the bird was hidden. The barking tracker dogs that sent the Russians on the run. The shootouts with the Russians as Pilecki and a remaining Sovietniks went in the wind. Pilecki's arrival at the sheik's home, taking the Arabs hostage, and escaping with the gyrfalcon in Badr's Chris-Craft, presumably headed for Canada.

"Holy Christ," the CO said. "A full-blown clusterfuck."

"Yes, sir. I agree," Patrick mumbled.

"After you called us last night, I contacted Station Frankfort, and they've deployed two response boats," the CO said. "They're currently around Cathead Bay, near the tip of the Leelanau Peninsula. We're unsure whether the Russians are still in Grand Traverse Bay or are further up the coast. I've gotta get back in the air so we can locate their boat."

"Good luck, sir," Patrick said as the CO walked towards his chopper.

Once the CO's helicopter was back in the air with the other two Jayhawks, they followed a search grid pattern from their radar screens. The turquoise blue waters of Lake Michigan were nearly empty this early in the season. Each time they came across a potential cabin cruiser, a chopper would swoop low for a closer look. It felt like searching for a specific grain of sand in the middle of the Sleeping Bear Dunes.

But they kept hunting. Finally, the CO spotted a wooden twenty-five-foot boat and went down again for a better look. Machine gun fire immediately erupted from the pleasure craft's deck, nearly blowing the Jayhawk out of the sky.

"We found them," the CO said to his mate as he quickly opened the chopper's power to send them into a climb out of the Russians' reach. "You see anything when you were down there?"

"Not much. Just the gunner and another person."

"Anything else?"

"There were a lot of red gas cans sitting on the deck."

"Hmmm. They must be planning a long ride."

The CO radioed the other two Jayhawks for backup. Besides the CO, a co-pilot, and a mechanic, Coast Guard aircrews often included an airborne marksman. The choppers and their sharpshooters were deployed to run down fast-moving, drug-smuggling boats. If a suspected boat failed to stop when ordered, the marksman fired warning shots or took out its engines.

The commanding officer also contacted the two Coast Guard response boats to give them location coordinates for the escaping Chris-Craft, currently in open waters halfway between the Leelanau State Park and Norwood. Response Boat-Medium was a 45-foot utility boat used mostly for search and rescue but also for coastal security and defense missions, sometimes associated with Homeland Security. The RBM's speed ranged from 30 to 42 knots, and it was armed with two M240B general-purpose machine guns, similar to what the Jayhawks carried. The second Coast Guard boat was a Response Boat-Small, similar to the RBM, but smaller at 28 feet. Both boats were armored with ballistic panels to give their crews protection.

The three Jayhawks and two boats converged just out of machine gun range of the Russians, who hadn't slowed their pace toward their suspected Canadian destination. The Coast Guard decided to try another communication before disabling the craft. First, they attempted the VHF marine radio to reach the Russians but got no response. Either they didn't know how to operate the equipment, or they were ignoring the order.

Finally, as the CO lowered the chopper within 300 feet of the Chris-Craft, the co-pilot used a high-powered megaphone to shout, "This is the United States Coast Guard. All hands on deck. Immediately lay down your arms and surrender."

When the Russians failed to comply, he repeated the order, getting the same result. No one waved from the boat or acknowledged the military presence. Pilecki and the remaining Sovietnik appeared to be huddled inside the boat's tiny cabin.

"Disable the craft," the CO ordered the marksman. The chopper swiveled so the sharpshooter had a clear view of the Chris-Craft's twin engines. After three expert shots, the boat slowed and bobbed in the calm sea.

With the pleasure boat disabled, the CO vectored the other Jayhawks into place and yelled, "Prepare to board."

Since the Chris-Craft was too small to use as a landing platform, three gloved Jayhawk co-pilots jumped out the chopper sixty feet above the wooden boat and began thick-roping down two-and-half-inch braided nylon ropes.

Suddenly, when one co-pilot was just ten feet above the craft, he began yanking on the rope and screaming, "Pull up, pull up! There's gasoline all over the deck. Pull up now!!"

The chopper moved out of range as quickly and gently as it could while the thick-ropers swayed in the rotor wash, hanging on for dear life. Finally, the co-pilots were able to shimmy up the ropes enough so the mechanics and marksmen could haul them back inside the aircraft.

Just as the co-pilots reached safety, Sheik Badr-Uddin's vintage wooden Chris-Craft exploded, sending high flames and black smoke into the air. Both the Jayhawk and response boat crews watched as the heat of the fire consumed much of the wooden craft. Only parts of the cabin remained, floating on the water's surface. The RBM pulled close and waited for the cabin to cool enough to see if there was any sign of the Russians.

"Will you look at that!" one of the crew members yelled, pointing to the sky.

They all turned to watch a soot-covered white bird gracefully rise from what was left of the cabin, circle the floating wreckage, and then fly off into the mid-day sky.

Chapter 79: May 14

The shootout between a group of Russians, the FBI, and local police had occupied breaking news locally and nationally for the past two days. It'd also fueled the rumor mill into a frenzy about a possible Russian invasion. There'd even been suggestions that Pilecki and his band were advance scouts ahead of an attack. Sheriff Gilda Hansen and Police Chief Hank Yeager quickly held a press conference at Fire Station #1 on Old Mission Peninsula to quash gossip and calm nerves. They revealed details that the bizarre incident was really about the Russians trying to steal a rare gyrfalcon from Sheik Badr-Uddin versus an assault on the country. Once the sheriff and chief had finished their prepared statements, they opened up the conference to questions.

"Are you releasing the names of the dead and the injured?" a local journalist asked.

"The Russian mafioso who died included Pavel Pilecki, noted kingpin who oversaw the counterfeit pesticide case here two years ago, Melor Golubev, Iosif Zaitsev, Vissarion Volkov, and one more whom we've not yet identified," Chief Yeager said. "The officers who are hospitalized include Flint Thompson from the Sheriff's Department and Detective Quinn Macarthy from the Five-County Forensic Center. Sheik Badr-Uddin was also wounded and is hospitalized. A firefighter was grazed by a bullet early in the conflict but didn't require hospitalization."

"I just heard the Coast Guard was involved in the final phase of the takedown. Can you elaborate on that?" a reporter from WWTV asked.

Sheriff Hansen stepped to the microphone and said, "Yes, that's true. The details are still being released, but we know that Pavel Pilecki and one Sovietnik escaped the tracking dogs, returned to the falconry center, stole the white falcon, and absconded with it by water in Sheik Badr-Uddin's pleasure boat. We called in Coast Guard helicopters and response boats, which located the craft and attempted to board. As they did, the Russians spread and ignited gasoline on the deck, blowing up the boat in the process. None of the Coast Guard personnel were injured, but both Russians died in the fire. That's all we have for now."

With the press conference over, Chief Yeager headed back to the jail where FBI agents were interviewing the two Russians under arrest. Gilda picked up Patrick and went to the hospital to check on their wounded colleagues.

Flint had sustained a through-and-through wound to his upper arm. Luckily, no bones or ligaments had been involved. His wound had been cleaned and sewn shut, but he'd been kept overnight to manage pain and shock. Gilda and Patrick would drive him home after visiting the other two patients.

They came to Badr's room next. Gilda gasped when she saw the contraption that held his hand in the air. He remained unconscious following intricate surgery to repair the crushed metacarpal bones in his right hand. The surgeon had restored them to normal alignment and then used metal implants to hold them in place. The whole hand was now externally fixated by pins and screws that projected out of Badr's skin and attached to elevated metal bars, which would be removed once his bones sufficiently healed.

When they came to Quinn's room, they found her red-eyed and somber. Vernadeane had been staying with her for support.

"Hey, how're you doing, girl?" Gilda asked, touching Quinn's shoulder gently. Patrick stood at the foot of the bed, his hand lightly massaging her foot.

"So, so," Quinn replied with a short nod.

"What's your doctor say?" Patrick asked.

Quinn shrugged her shoulders. She seemed distant like she was somewhere else.

Vernadeane answered for her. "The doctor said denailing is one of the most painful types of torture because human fingertips contain a ridiculous amount of nerve endings. They're one of the most sensitive parts of the body. The trauma will require both physical and emotional healing."

Gilda and Patrick looked over at Quinn, whose face was wet with tears.

"Does your finger hurt?" Patrick asked.

Quinn shook her head.

Vernadeane again answered, "The doctor was just here and gave her an injection in her finger to manage the pain. He said that when she goes home, Tylenol should be enough to control any lingering discomfort."

"Will your nail grow back normally?" Patrick asked.

"Jesus, Patrick. Stop with the third degree," Gilda scolded.

"No, that's okay," Quinn said, not answering the question.

Once more, Vernadeane stepped in. "The doctor said the results from Quinn's denailing are unpredictable at this time. Her nail matrix was mostly intact, so her nail might grow back quite normally over the next several months. Only time will tell how she heals."

Chapter 80: June 22

They'd not been far from each other's sight the last six weeks while Quinn was on medical leave. When Quinn went to the kitchen to make a meal, Ruby followed. When Quinn went to the bathroom, Ruby went in also. Tonight, as she settled into her chair to watch the Tigers play the Cardinals, her dog squeezed in tight beside her. Quinn knew Ruby's barking had saved her life by sending the Russians on the run, and she welcomed the closeness.

Besides hanging with Ruby, Quinn had been watching a lot of Detroit Tigers baseball, for good reason, too. Following the sudden retirement of manager Ron Gardenhire last fall, the Tigers had hired A.J. Hinch as their new skipper. They'd been lucky to snap up a manager who'd been a post-season staple and had won the 2017 World Series. Then, early in June, Major League Baseball allowed teams to operate their stadiums at capacity for the first time since COVID struck in 2019. At least one thing in her life seemed normal.

Quinn's denailed pinky was healing even though she wore a covered splint and had to see her hand surgeon every two weeks to inspect the nail bed and matrix. He still hedged when she asked if her nail would grow back normally. At least her recovery wasn't as serious as Badr's. He'd spent a month in the hospital hooked up to a space-age contraption to keep his surgically repaired hand immobilized so it could heal. He'd returned to his home on Old Mission ten days ago, but his hand was in a soft cast. They'd talked on the phone a few times, but both had been off in their own separate mind spaces. Badr mourning the death of his long-time bodyguard, Abdul Salaam, and Quinn numb with melancholy. She was going to visit him in a few days and could better assess how he was doing after seeing him in person. He'd even said she could bring Ruby if she wanted.

Suddenly, electrified cheers from the Comerica Park fans on her television brought Quinn out of her reverie.

"Badddooo!" Quinn squealed as rookie Akil Baddoo crossed home plate after the Cardinal's pitcher made a throwing error.

Ruby twirled on the ottoman.

"Keep it going," Quinn whooped as Nomar Mazara reached after grounding into a fielder's choice. Both Willi Castro and Harold Castro walked next.

"Yes!" she yelped as catcher Jake Rogers hit a double, scoring both men on base.

"3-0 Detroit! And the inning's not even over!"

Ruby grabbed her orange and blue Chuckit ball and dropped it next to the ottoman. Quinn threw it down the hallway towards her bedroom, and Ruby gave chase just as Jonathan Schoop homered, scoring Castro, Rogers, and himself.

"6-0 Detroit!" Quinn shouted as if she were at the ballpark. "Damn! Why's Hinch making a pitching change when we're doing so well?" Ruby cocked her head.

The break in the game brought Quinn back to her musings. Truth be told, she wondered whether she needed a change too. She'd been involved in police work for twenty-nine years now and had been hospitalized three times for injuries sustained in the line of duty. None of them had been life-threatening, but they'd taken their toll. Quinn was surprised she didn't feel better with Pilecki dead and out of the trafficking picture. Instead, she felt worse. Sometimes, it felt like she had the flu. A couple of times, she even tested for COVID, thinking that might be the cause of her malaise. However, after a complete physical, her doctor determined her symptoms were from stress and anxiety related to untreated trauma.

Quinn had tried pushing the disturbing scenes from her mind. The fall from the barn loft in pursuit of bicyclist killer Xander Tobin. The assault at the hands of Meyer Garfield before being bound and gagged in the communications shed. Watching Golubev smash Badr's hand with a hammer. And, of course, her own denailing experience. But the images had returned through nightmares and flashbacks. They made her edgy all the time. Her doctor suggested she might benefit from a few therapy sessions, but Quinn fought the idea, arguing she'd already done that when she'd seen a counselor for critical incident debriefing after each violent occurrence. She insisted it hadn't helped, so her doctor didn't push.

Ruby jumped onto the ottoman at the sound of cheering on the television. Lost in her thoughts again, Quinn had missed the last innings with the final score Tigers 8 – Cardinals 2.

"Another great game," Quinn said, buoyed by the win. "We're gonna get to .500 yet."

Deciding she wasn't ready for bed, Quinn filled her popcorn bowl and headed to her study. She turned on the computer and pulled some paperwork onto the screen. She knew with July rapidly approaching, she had a decision to make.

On continued follow-up visits to her family doctor, Quinn had begun to share details about each of the traumas. She'd confided she was also having misgivings about whether a career in police work was right for her.

"Sometimes I feel like I've followed my family's footsteps blindly," Quinn told her. "I played ice hockey because my brothers did. We all went into law enforcement because that's what dad did. It's in our blood."

Her doctor nodded and smiled, encouraging her to continue.

"I think working on these last two cases has probably sent me over the edge. I started to get out of whack when I obsessed about finding George Watkin's killer. I was certain it was Pavel Pilecki. Arresting him would close the counterfeit pesticide case. It would also pay back Pilecki for his minion's assault on me."

"Makes sense, Quinn," the doctor said.

"Things began going sideways after Mack died, and I blamed Pilecki for trafficking the fentanyl that killed him. Then, I started holding Pilecki responsible for smuggling rare falcons. While all of that was probably true, I can see how I might've gone out in left field."

"And don't forget the other stresses you've been under. Solving the murders of homeless people. A raging pandemic none of us knew how to navigate," the doctor reminded her.

"Whew!" Quinn exclaimed. "Looking back, it was a lot. I've also wondered whether I'm having some kind of midlife crisis."

They both laughed, but the comment started them considering some new directions. The doctor's kind, nonjudgmental attitude had coaxed Quinn into trying a low dose of medication to help with anxiety and sleep. They'd also talked about how a break from police work might be beneficial. Her doctor even hinted that Quinn might apply for short-term disability leave from her current job to rest, heal from the trauma, and figure out her next steps. Maybe even taking off the next six months.

As Quinn began thinking about the possibility of a leave, the more sense it made. She wasn't ready to give up her career, but this seemed like a good interim move. Give her some time to think about next steps. Or how to approach police work differently than she had been.

But taking six months off from her job by hanging around her condo didn't feel like much of a break. Too close to FC2, Centre Ice, The Pines, and Middle Coast Mission. Maybe she needed to get out of Dodge altogether. Thinking where she'd most like to spend the rest of the year was a no-brainer. Sleeping Bear. And so, she'd begun to look. She'd thought she was probably too late in the season to find anything, but with travel still not at pre-COVID levels, she'd lucked out. She'd found a cute A-frame rental cabin in Glen Haven, a short walk from the beach. Fortunately, it had internet, cable TV, and allowed dogs. She'd already filled out the online rental agreement. She took another look at the short-term disability paperwork on her computer. They were both ready. All she had to do was hit send.

Chapter 81: June 27

As soon as she arrived at the *Peregrine Falcon Propagation and Training Center*, Quinn felt the difference. Through the slatted windows, she could see activity going on in the breeding building, but the rest of the site was largely quiet. Most of all, Abdul Salaam didn't greet her in his golf cart. In fact, the sheik hadn't sent anyone to drive her to his residence. He probably just forgot, she thought. Or maybe pain medication had fogged his brain.

So Quinn and Ruby headed on foot to Badr's home. It was a nice walk through the woods, and she was always awed by the beauty when she reached the low dunes. She leashed Ruby as they walked up the driveway and expected Badr to throw open his sliders and welcome her. But he didn't. As she peered inside the windows, she saw him sleeping in a chair, his injured hand propped on pillows, a book fallen from his lap. She tapped softly on the window, and Badr started. Zohra, his old white gyrfalcon, screamed, *"Kack-kack-kack"* from her perch. Ruby slunk back and lay down behind Quinn.

She watched Badr wince as he rose from the chair and walked towards her. She was amazed at the change in his appearance since the torture. He wasn't wearing his head scarf, and his white, lightweight robe hung on his body. His face was gaunt. He'd lost twenty pounds at least.

"Quinn, good to see you," Badr said as he bent down to pet Ruby with his good hand. Zohra continued to squawk from inside the house. "I think both our pets will be happier if we sit outside under the pergola."

"You've lost a lot of weight, Badr," Quinn commented as they walked to the beach.

"Have I?" he said, seeming unaware of the changes. "I understand you've decided to take a leave of absence from your police work," he continued.

"Where'd you hear that?"

"From Zoey. She's stopped by a couple of times to bring news of the investigation."

"Huh. I thought that was all wrapped up."

"It is, except for a few new details that emerged after the medical examiner did autopsies on what remained of Pilecki and his Sovietnik after the fire at sea."

"Care to share?"

Before Badr could reply, Ruby brought Quinn a long stick of firewood and dropped it at her feet. She flung it into Lake Michigan, and Ruby bounded through the waves to retrieve it. Badr laughed at the dog's antics, and for a moment, he seemed like himself.

"I don't know how much will be released to the public. Even though the two bodies were nearly destroyed by the fire, the ME found significant evidence that the Russians died from single gunshots to the head. Both had bullets lodged in their skulls."

"Jesus, Mary, and Joseph," Quinn whispered. "Some kind of murder-suicide pact?"

"Looks that way. A quick death versus being burned alive."

Quinn was about to ask Badr how he was doing with Abdul Salaam's death when something in the sky caught his eye. He stood up, and Quinn followed his gaze. They watched as a grayish-black bird circled high in the sky, watching a rock pigeon flying below. Suddenly, the bird went into a long stoop and nabbed the prey in its talons, smashing it to the ground ten feet from where they stood. They watched as the bird tore apart the pigeon and hungrily consumed the meal.

When the bird finished eating, Badr smacked his lips, and the bird immediately hopped onto the sheik's extended arm.

"You are home, Nova," he said, petting his soot-covered gyrfalcon. "We need to get this grime cleaned off your feathers."

"Nova? I assumed she died in the fire, too."

"That was the second thing Zoey stopped by to tell me. The Coast Guard had seen a white bird escape skyward from the burning boat."

Quinn's eyes widened at the story, and she was just about to say something about Nova being like a phoenix rising from the ashes but decided it sounded too cliche. Instead, she said, "I'm happy for you, Badr. And Nova, too."

He'd already started walking across the sand towards his home with Nova perched on his arm. He seemed to forget that Quinn and Ruby were still there. But he hadn't. He turned and replied, "*Mashallah*." As God has willed.

Acknowledgments

Thank you for reading *The Lure*, the second book in my Northwoods Mystery series. As in the first book, *Calling*, *The Lure* features Forensic Detective Quinn Macarthy, Sheriff Gilda Hansen, Conservation Officer Patrick Elliot, and newspaperman Ian Doyle as they work to solve crimes around Traverse City, Michigan.

My monthly writing group was instrumental in the book's development. They helped improve my writing by giving suggestions, proofreading for errors, and lending support. Thank you, friends: Alison Arthur, Diana Stover Burton, Julie Eakin, and Karen Mulvahill.

Another thank you goes to my brother, Mark Casebeer, for designing a cover that fits the book's storyline so well. The original photograph was taken from iStock Photo.

A final thank you to Draft2Digital, the company that publishes the Northwoods Mystery series. Their user-friendly platform and customer support have simplified the publishing process for indie authors like me.

My interest in falconry started young when I read *My Side of the Mountain* by Jean George. The book is about twelve-year-old Sam Gribley, who runs away to his grandfather's abandoned farm to live in the wilderness with his pets, Frightful, a peregrine falcon, and a weasel, The Baron. As a young educator, I also taught the book to seventh graders. I also have enjoyed the recurring character Nate Romanowski in C.J. Box's Joe Pickett novels. Nate is a falconer who runs a bird abatement business. I've read many nonfiction books on raptors to aid my photography hobby, too. Sy Montgomery's *The Hawk's Way: Encounter with Fierce Beauty* is a favorite.

While *The Lure* is a work of fiction, much research informed my writing.

Several online articles helped my understanding of the history of falconry and the new sport of falcon racing. Those especially valuable included the following articles: "Peregrine Falcon Reproduction in Southeast Michigan" in *State of the Strait*; "Behind the Scenes at the World's Largest Falcon Race" in *National Geographic* (2021); "Appeal of Falconry Remains Strong" in the *New York Times* (1984); "Arabian Flights: Inside the Lucrative World of Middle Eastern Falconry" by Jonathan Wells in *Gentleman's Journal*; "Kings of the Sky" by John C. Silcox; and "Falconry: Ancient Past and Sustainable Future" in *National Geographic* (2021). I also learned about the history and sport of falconry in the Middle East from the 2021 highly acclaimed documentary *Wild Allies*.

Homelessness in Traverse City has made many headlines in recent years. News and feature stories about the Pines encampment have been especially prominent. While the murders, homeless situations, and organizations supporting the unhoused in *The Lure* are fictitious, the information and statistics are rooted in real stories I've followed through the outstanding reportage in both *The Traverse City Record-Eagle* and *The Ticker*. The following articles were especially helpful: "Goodwill, City Team-Up on Housing Plan" in the *Record-Eagle* (2024); "What are the Biggest Misconceptions about Local Homelessness" by Craig Manning in *The Ticker* (2024); "Homeless People Are Becoming Writers in Traverse City" on *Interlochen Public Radio* (2014); "Rising Numbers, Incidents at Library Spur New Conversations about Local Homelessness" in *The Ticker* (2021); "It Feels Near Impossible to Climb Back Up: Homelessness Takes Disproportionate Toll" in the *Record-Eagle* (2022); "City Officials Try to Balance Security, Safety at Pines Encampment" in *The Ticker* (2023); "Life in the Pines" in the *Record-Eagle* (2023); "Homeless in Traverse City" in the *Record-Eagle* (2023); "Mobile Homeless: A View from Living at the 'Walmart Hotel'" in the *Record-Eagle* (2024); "A Silent W" in the *Record-Eagle* (2023); "Shelters Open, Even as Social Supports Vanish for Northwest Michigan's Homeless" in the *Record-Eagle*

(2021); "How Far Can Cities Go to Clear Homeless Camps? The U.S. Supreme Court Will Decide" on *National Public Radio* (2024); "A Life without a Home" by Lori Teresa Yearwood in the *New York Times* (2024); "Homelessness and addiction: Surviving the Opioid Crisis" in *Housing Matters* (2023); "People are staying homeless for longer than ever before in Clark County – experts say fentanyl is a factor" in *The Columbian* (2024); "A Rising Tally of Lonely Deaths on the Streets" in the *New York Times* (2022); and "Why Do People Hate the Homeless" by Doug Porter in *San Diego Free Press* (August 2016).

The character Keegan Cammack/Mack is a composite of several professional athletes who became homeless following their playing careers. Articles contributing to this topic included: "Former NHL Star Joe Murphy Homeless and Battling Mental Illness" in the *Toronto Sun* (2018); "All and Nothing" by Ryan Dixon in *sportsnet.ca*; "Homeless Athletes Special Report" in *Sports Illustrated* (2014, 2020); and "What Former Athletes Becoming Homeless Says about Housing" in *Invisible People* (2022).

Falcon trafficking is a real crime being played out on the black market. Russian President Vladimir Putin has been extensively involved in falconry projects in his country, some of which are suspected of fueling this black market trade. The following research informed this topic in my book: "Russia Is Turning into Hunting Ground for Rich Sheikhs" by Michael Romanov in *raptors.ru* (2022); "World's Most Expensive Falcon Sold in Saudi Auction for over $465,000" in *Al Arabiya, English* (2021); "Kremlin-backed Falcon Project Sparks Smuggling Fears" in *Express Tribune* (2024); "Falcon Trafficking Soars in Middle East, Fueled by Conflict and Poverty" by Lyse Mauvais in *Mongabay* (2023); and, "The First Russian Centre for Conservation of Rare Species of Birds of Prey Was Created in Kamchatka" in *Ecotourism Expert* (2022).

Articles that helped me understand the justice system as it relates to homeless and mentally ill populations included: the outstanding "Healing Justice" series by Karen Bouffard in *The Detroit News* (2019); "Officials address growing concerns inside Grand Traverse Jail in the *Record-Eagle* (March 2018); "Jail Report Flags Concerns with Mental Health" in *The Ticker* (2020); and "Changes in Mental, Medical Healthcare Coming to County Jail" in *The Ticker* (2022).

Finally, although COVID is still active with its continual mutations, it is no longer at pandemic levels. I learned of the virus's beginnings and early progress through the following: "COVID-19 Timeline" from the *CDC Museum*; "First Local Cases of COVID-19 Identified in Traverse City, Gaylord" in the *Record-Eagle* (2020); "Homeless Outreach Continues in Traverse City Under 'Stay-at-Home' Order" on *Interlochen Public Radio* (2020); "First Ever COVID Winter Threatens to Leave Millions Homeless" in *Invisible People* (2020); "The Second COVID Wave Has Hit Munson" in The Ticker (2020); and "COVID-19 Pandemic in Michigan" in *Wikipedia*.

About the Author

Karen grew up in southwestern Michigan and graduated from Western Michigan University, where she studied writing with Ken Macrorie. She taught secondary school English and Latin for twenty-five years in Portage, Michigan. After retiring from teaching, Karen returned to WMU to obtain a doctorate in Counselor Education and Counseling Psychology. She practiced as a licensed psychologist in Kalamazoo for fourteen years. After moving up north in 2006, she taught social science at Davenport University. She currently is retired and devotes her time to writing and photography.

About her writing, Karen states: "Writing has always played an important role in my life: keeping a journal, writing professional articles, helping students become authentic writers, and writing college papers and a dissertation. Writing a novel didn't start until I moved to Northwestern Lower Michigan. There, my love of the Northwoods, crime fiction, and psychology came together with my first e-book mysteries, Culpable and Spinning. It wasn't until my newest novel, Calling, published in both e-book and paperback formats that I feel I've found my stride as a writer."